MARVEL

SPIDER-MAN

HOSTILE
TAKEOVER

Novels of the Marvel Universe by Titan Books:

MARVEL

SPIDER-MAN
HOSTILE TAKEOVER

DAVID LISS

TITAN BOOKS

MARVEL'S SPIDER-MAN: Hostile Takeover
Print edition ISBN: 9781785659751
E-book edition ISBN: 9781785659768

Published by Titan Books
A division of Titan Publishing Group Ltd
144 Southwark Street, London SE1 0UP
www.titanbooks.com

First edition: August 2018
10 9 8 7 6 5 4 3 2 1

FOR MARVEL PUBLISHING
Jeff Youngquist, VP Production and Special Projects
Caitlin O'Connell, Assistant Editor, Special Projects
Jeff Reingold, Manager, Licensed Publishing
Sven Larsen, Director, Licensed Publishing
David Gabriel, SVP of Sales & Marketing, Publishing
C.B. Cebulski, Editor in Chief
Joe Quesada, Chief Creative Officer
Dan Buckley, President, Marvel Entertainment

FOR MARVEL GAMES
Isabel Hsu, Assistant Creative Manager
Mike Jones, Executive Producer & VP
Becka McIntosh, Senior Operations Manager
Haluk Mentes, Executive Director, Business Development & Product Strategy
Eric Monacelli, Senior Producer & Project Lead
Jay Ong, Senior Vice President, Games & Innovation
Bill Rosemann, Executive Creative Director
Chuck Roquemore, Operations Manager
Tim Tsang, Art Director

Cover art by Alexander Lozano

Spider-Man created by Stan Lee and Steve Ditko

Marvel's Spider-Man developed by Insomniac Games

This book is a work of fiction. Any references to historical events, real people, or real places are used fictitiously. Other names, characters, places, and events are products of the author's imagination, and any resemblance to actual events or places or persons, living or dead, is entirely coincidental.

A CIP catalogue record for this title is available from the British Library.
Printed and bound in the United States.

For Claudia, my long-suffering wife.
She had no idea what she was getting into.

ONE

NEW York City had *everything*, and that was usually a plus, but not so much when that something was a snake store.

Or was it *still* a plus? Maybe the weird, gross, and possibly dangerous implications of a shop dedicated to limbless reptiles embodied everything he loved about this city, Spider-Man mused as he swung through an open second-story window.

He'd planned to land on the floor, but it was already occupied. So at the last moment he performed an in-air flip and clung to the ceiling, staring down at the dozens of hissing, slithering creatures.

He'd set up his computer to monitor emergency channels, and then alert him when they picked up anything where he might make a difference—fires, robberies, and the all-too-frequent appearances of villains doing super-bad things. He'd also played with the coding to catch anything that might be, well… amusing.

It was Saturday night, and his girlfriend Mary Jane was off doing something she didn't want to tell him about, and he'd wanted to be diverted… so snakes. He'd chosen snakes, and he'd gotten snakes. There was a lesson in there somewhere, he thought. Maybe that when life gave you options, it was best to choose more carefully.

In perfect New York style, Steve's Serpent Storehouse wasn't just a small curbside shop he could scan with a single glance. It was located in an old, narrow, multi-floored brownstone, with each of its many rooms dedicated to a different variety of reptile. Venomous, non-venomous, constricting—all your slithery needs in a single location. A true convenience for the busy snake shopper.

And for the busy snake thief, if that was what he was dealing with here. He was beginning to wonder. All of the cages had been smashed, and while some of the animals might have been collected, he couldn't tell for sure. To add to the confusion, he was starting to get a headache from the smell.

Who knew that snakes even had a smell?

Then he saw it. A shadow in the hallway outside the room. A person crouched low, holding something in his hand. Maybe a sack—which, under the circumstances, would likely be a sack full of snakes. The figure moved just enough that Spider-Man could get a better view in the light from outside the window.

The shadow's head jerked around, and then he dashed into the hall. Spider-Man pushed himself off the ceiling and clung to the doorjamb. There was no way he was touching the floor. He peered into the hallway and saw the snake thief—running upstairs!

Who tries to get away by going up? Someone with a well-thought-out plan or someone with no plan at all. Spider-Man grinned under his mask.

The chase was on.

HIS real name was Peter Parker, and eight years ago he'd been bitten by a radioactive spider. Only in New York, right? The encounter left Peter with abilities—*spider* abilities. He could leap incredible distances, cling to almost any surface, and sense when something threatened him, allowing him to leap, dodge, roll, or twist his way out of dangers others might not notice.

While the spider bite had enhanced his body, giving him enhanced strength, stamina, and reflexes, Peter's mind had done the rest. He'd designed his now-iconic red-and-blue suit which offered anonymity, protection, and comfort—all while making him look cool, if he did say so himself. He'd designed web shooters which helped to propel him across the city and enabled him to snare victims.

Peter had always loved science, inventing and tinkering practically from the time he started crawling—in the traditional sense—and while it helped him chase shadows up a narrow and twisting stairway, life was more than the endless glamor of catching snake thieves.

In his "day job" he worked in a laboratory, which allowed him to focus his mental skills on challenging and important research that, in its own way, made a *difference*. Though exciting, it was way more than a forty-hour-a-week job.

So Peter had to find the time to be Spider-Man. More than a desire, it was a responsibility, and he dedicated every minute he could to helping his city any way he could. He stopped bank robbers and carjackers and muggers, rescued people trapped in collapsing buildings and rushed victims to the hospital.

He also seemed to be spending more of his time facing guys who wore suits and possessed their own unique abilities—criminals like the Rhino, the Scorpion, the Lizard, Shocker, Electro… the list went on and on. It seemed as if there were more of these "super villains" every day. They, like Peter, had been granted powers by chance, fate, or design, but unlike Peter they didn't choose to use those powers to help others. Someone had to keep them in check. That sometimes meant spectacular confrontations. Broken glass, brick, and concrete turned to powder, fire, electricity, explosions, and mayhem.

Somehow, he didn't think tackling the snake thief was going to be quite that dramatic. This was going to make for a funny story when he told MJ—the only person he'd trusted with his secret. No, this was shaping up to be a relatively uneventful night.

Shouldn't think that, he told himself as he leapt up another flight of stairs too fast for an ordinary eye to follow.

I might jinx myself.

o——————————o

SPIDER-MAN launched himself onto the fourth and topmost floor in time to see the thief dashing into a room at the end of the corridor.

The guy was fast. Not super-powers fast but definitely track-star fast. The ambient light was still bright up here, and he caught his first glimpse of the thief. Probably not even twenty. He had short hair dyed the color of a tennis ball and big brown eyes and the barest hint of a mustache. His face was round and babyish, though, and he might as well have been wearing a T-shirt that said, I HAVE NO IDEA WHAT I'M DOING.

As the Web-Slinger entered the room, the guy reached into an open tank and grabbed a snake, which he hurled at his pursuer.

The thief had a good throw. This was a big snake, too. As thick as his arm and twice as long. It had been balled up, probably comfortably sleeping and dreaming its snake dreams, when the thief grabbed it. Now it unspooled and twisted in serpentine alarm as it came hurtling toward Spider-Man.

It would've been easy to dodge, but it was a living creature, and even slithery things deserved soft landings. He was no snake expert, but Spider-Man seemed to recall that the big ones usually weren't poisonous. Anyhow, if he grabbed it the right way, it couldn't bite him. Propelling himself forward, he caught the reptile in midair, placing a hand just under its head. He landed, dropped the creature, and lurched backward while shaking off whatever the snake might have left on his glove. He knew the answer was nothing, but it was a snake and it was icky.

With the snake safe, Spider-Man turned in time to see the thief leap out the open window as if he could fly.

Seriously?

Sprinting to the window, he stuck his head out in time to see the snake thief land on an awning two stories down, bounce onto another, lower awning, and then stick the landing on the street. With his bag o' snakes clutched in one hand, he glanced up, spun, and raced in the direction of the river.

Shooting his webs onto the side of a building, Spider-Man hurled himself forward, then again, and then again. It was as close as he could get to flying, and it never got old. He had a mic and earpiece embedded in his mask, so while he propelled himself westward he toggled his phone to give MJ a call. There was no better way to begin a conversation with your girlfriend than, *"I'm chasing a guy holding a bag of snakes,"* but— once again—she didn't answer.

Briefly he lost track of his quarry, then he saw that the thief, who had a decent head start, was making his way toward the Manhattan Cruise Terminal. It seemed like a pretty stupid destination. He could hide out in any of the docked or decommissioned ships there, but there'd be no escape except the river. Besides, Spider-Man's aerial view would make it almost impossible for the thief to elude him.

He'd never been to the cruise terminal—or on a cruise ship, for that matter—so this would be a novelty. Sort of like the snake store, but without the icky part. He imagined an impossibly luxurious place that—during the daytime—would be filled with men in top hats and women who cooed while feeding treats to their tiny lapdogs.

The reality was more like a giant parking garage spotted with poorly maintained buildings that flaked paint like eczema. Docks that reminded him of hastily set bones jutted out into the river, some of them sporting dark ships that loomed as inert as felled trees.

The thief chose one of the docks and hurried toward what looked like a decommissioned ship that was speckled with massive patches of rust and algae. There was no way onto the ship, however, so it looked like the end of the line. Swinging forward, Spider-Man let loose with a blast of webbing that wrapped around both the thief and one of the dock's concrete posts.

Mission accomplished.

Sort of.

This was one of the things that made being Spider-Man frustrating. He'd caught this guy in the act and he'd apprehended him, still clutching his bag of stolen reptiles. He would now call the police, but chances were the thief would never be charged. He could argue that Spider-Man had abducted him and planted the evidence. It would be hard to prove otherwise. Yeah, the guy was just a snake thief, but people guilty of much bigger crimes had gotten away after he'd put everything he had into stopping them.

One criminal in particular had gotten away with far too much—something that never ceased to haunt him.

One problem at a time. Spider-Man took the bag

from the webbed-up thief and opened it. He expected to find a nauseating, slithering mass of scales and peering eyes and flicking tongues, but there was nothing alive in there at all. At first, he thought the snakes were dead, but then he realized they'd never been alive.

The thief had been running with a bag of rubber snakes.

"THE accumulated wisdom of my life experience tells me I really shouldn't ask," Spider-Man said, "but I'm going to ask anyhow. Why did you break into a snake store to steal a bag of rubber snakes?"

The webbing that coiled around his torso really didn't do much to make the thief look any less clueless. "Who *are* you?" he demanded.

"Really?" Spider-Man asked. "What am I paying my PR team for?"

"You're one of them super heroes!"

"So is the '*who are you*' more of a philosophical question?"

"Sorry," the thief said. "I just get nervous sometimes, you know?"

"Perfectly normal, given that you've been apprehended while committing a stupid felony," Spider-Man assured him. "Now, let's start by talking about why you would steal a bunch of rubber snakes."

"I didn't," the thief said.

Spider-Man sighed. "Okay, let's start over. I'm Spider-Man."

"I thought you were Daredevil."

"Do I look like Daredevil?"

"Kind of," the thief said. "But kind of not. Less horns and more… uh, webs."

Spider-Man went for the theatrical cough into his balled fist. "How about you tell me your name."

"Andy!" the guy said brightly. He looked pleased to know the answer.

"Okay, Andy, I caught you, after you broke into the snake store, and you ran away clutching a bag of rubber snakes. Walk me through this."

"I didn't get a chance to steal anything," Andy said. "You showed up and messed with the plan. So I didn't do anything wrong. The rubber snakes in there are mine. I paid for them."

Don't ask, Spider-Man told himself. *There is nothing to be gained by asking.* He asked anyway. "And you brought them with you why exactly?"

"So the snakes I put in the bag wouldn't get lonely."

The Web-Slinger made a deliberate decision to spare Andy's feelings and not face-palm in front of him.

"I had a list," Andy continued. "A guy was looking for particular snakes."

"No ordinary snake would do," Spider-Man prompted.

"Right, but you showed up, and then things went bad, so I didn't steal anything. So I'm not in any kind of trouble, right?"

"What, for breaking into a store and destroying

private property?" Spider-Man asked dryly. "Surely there's no law against that."

"Come on, S-Man," Andy protested. "No harm, no foul."

"Actually, there's plenty of harm and foul, not least of which is calling me 'S-Man.' You broke the law, and I'm going to call the police. You'll stay webbed up until they arrive."

"But I didn't do nothing." Andy's face was a mask of cartoonish terror.

"I think we've covered this already," Spider-Man said. "Maybe you want to review your notes."

"I knew I shouldn't have done it," Andy said. "It was my brother's idea. He said it would be easy money, but I guess I should have known he wasn't being straight. He just didn't want me around because he was off doing stuff for Scorpion."

"Wait a minute…" Spider-Man might have been letting his thoughts wander a little there, but now Andy had his full attention. "Scorpion. Like *the* Scorpion? Big guy? Anger problems? A tail?"

"That's him." Andy brightened. "You know him? Are you guys, like, friends?"

"No, we're not friends, because—and this may have escaped your notice—I'm a good guy, and he's a bad guy. Those sorts of dynamics don't usually promote lasting friendships. But you don't seem so much evil as… let's say, misguided. So how about you tell me everything you know about the Scorpion, and if it seems useful, I can let you go."

"I don't know nothing," Andy said plaintively, "except that he's using this construction site as a hideout or something. He's, like, stashing his equipment and plans and stuff there."

"That actually seems like a decent amount of knowledge."

Andy looked pleased. "My brother likes to brag when he's drinking," he replied, "and if he's breathing, he's drinking." It seemed like too much to hope for, but the kid knew exactly where the building was. His brother had shown it to him when—big surprise—he'd been drinking.

Figuring he'd gotten everything he was going to get out of Andy, Peter sprayed a dissolving agent on the webs.

"Okay, get out of here."

The kid looked over at his gym bag. "Can I go back to the store and get my snakes?"

"Andy…" Spider-Man said in a warning tone, like a parent talking to a toddler.

"Right." Andy nodded. "No more stealing."

Spider-Man let out another sigh. "Andy, what do you do all day, other than listen to your drunk brother?"

The kid shrugged. "I don't know. Come up with plans, I guess."

"Listen, you seem like a nice enough kid. I've got an idea that's a lot better than sticking you in a cell. There's a place in Little Tokyo," Spider-Man said. "It's called F.E.A.S.T., and it's where the homeless go for help. They could really use some volunteers, and you'd pick up some marketable skills working there. It's a win-win kind of thing. What do you say?"

Andy's face lit up again. "That would be great. I like being helpful."

"Okay then, you should skedaddle before the cops show up."

With that the Web-Slinger turned and shot out a strand, pulling himself into the air. This had been an amusing, and occasionally frustrating, little interlude, but now there was something really exciting in the works. Ruining the Scorpion's night seemed like a good way to make the night *very* eventful.

TWO

THE construction site was at 46th Street and Ninth Avenue, just where Andy said it would be. Spider-Man half-expected to find an empty lot or a supermarket, maybe even a giant hole in the ground. Instead there was the skeleton of a building that rose up twenty or so stories. So far, the kid's info was right on target.

He circled around it a few times to make sure there weren't sentries, or even just a bunch of guys with guns, but the place looked about as deserted as—what was the right metaphor?—a construction site after work hours. Yep, that sounded right. None of which meant Andy was wrong. It could still be a staging area, and if the opportunity to disrupt one of the Scorpion's operations presented itself, there was no way Spider-Man was going to pass it up.

Before heading in, he tried again to call MJ. He'd made an attempt after leaving the dock, but it had gone straight to voice mail. Same result.

"Me again," he said. "Just wanted to hear your voice before valiantly throwing myself into danger. But I know you're busy, so it's cool." He hoped his tone conveyed that he wasn't really serious, but also that he was a *little* serious.

Convincing himself that the construction site was empty, he landed in a central area on a lower floor, one that looked reasonably solid, and began to look around. First he checked the areas closest to the ground. Tools, piles of concrete blocks and rebar, equipment for pouring cement. No sign that it was being used for criminal purposes, but *every* sign that it was being used for construction—and recently, too. Why would Scorpion stash his gear in an active work site?

Maybe Andy had been wrong, after all.

Then he started getting a feeling. Not a Spider-Sense feeling, but a regular old *something's not right* feeling. It seemed reasonable that a thief might sell him a line, give him a bigger fish to go after as a way of getting off the hook. But Andy didn't seem like thinking on his feet was a particular strength, and the information about the building site, about Scorpion, had been pretty specific.

Webbing up to the next floor, he looked around for signs of any nefarious activity. Nothing he wouldn't expect to find at an ordinary, non-villainous building under construction. It looked like this was going to be a waste of time, but he still intended to check things out floor by floor. He had to be sure.

Climbing the girders, he moved to the next floor up, which he figured would be just as empty and non-evil as the last. Then he heard something. A clatter, like metal falling on metal, and it was coming from further up. *Way* further up. He also felt something, a faint prickling at the back of his neck—his Spider-

Sense was tingling. That meant he was getting closer to danger.

While danger wasn't a good thing, it did suggest that he hadn't been outsmarted by a criminal-in-training. That was something. Moving to the outside of the building, he began to climb, making almost no noise. As he approached the roof, his Spider-Sense began buzzing more aggressively. Just then his phone rang with a call from MJ.

After trying to reach her all night, he didn't want to ignore her. She'd understand if he did, of course. She was great that way. Mostly he just wanted to hear her voice.

"Hey," he said as he slowly pulled himself up onto the roof.

"That's your going-into-action voice," she said, doing what he thought was a pretty fair imitation of his going-into-action voice. "Everything okay?"

The tingling increased, telling him the bad guys probably knew he was there—which meant they were lying in ambush. It was still relatively low-level, so they probably weren't going to pose much of a problem. He could talk and fight at the same time.

Just to be safe he said, "Yeah, but I'm about to smack down a bunch of thugs, and chances are they're armed. If I stop talking, it's not something you said. Unless you say something totally insane and I have no response to it."

MJ laughed. Peter loved the sound of her laugh. Even after all this time.

"Well, I can call you back," she said wryly.

"No, this is going to be pretty routine," he said. "And I've been trying to reach you all night."

"The sixteen voice mails gave that away."

"Twelve tops. Where are you?"

MJ said something, but it was drowned out by the sound of gunfire. He was already up in the air, shooting out a web and contorting himself to avoid the bullets without thinking about what he was doing. His enhanced spider reflexes, plus eight years of experience at not getting shot, made it pure instinct. While spinning in the air, Peter took stock of the situation.

Four guys, each with firearms.

They jerked their heads left and right, as if he had vanished into thin air. These idiots didn't know to look up? It was almost too easy.

"You still there?" MJ asked.

"Yeah," he said. "The action's started."

"There's no reason we have to talk this second," she said. "I don't want you to get hurt just because—"

"Oh, please," he said, cutting her off. "It's not a problem." He pointed his web shooter at one of the gunmen, whose wrist was then attached to the wall behind him. The gun fell harmlessly to the ground. "That's one down." He landed behind another guy and shot out with both web shooters, pressing him face-first against a wall, his features all squished. "You should see these guys. It's hilarious." Using the suit's built-in camera, he snapped a picture. "I'll show you later."

"Something to look forward to," she replied

sarcastically. As she did, another assailant came around the corner and raised his gun. A quick web, and the guy was hoisted into the air, attached to an overhang.

"The cops might have a hard time getting that one down."

"Well, I'm glad you're having fun," MJ said, "and don't take this the wrong way, but listening to you narrate your exploits isn't what I need to be doing right now."

"But I'm using new tech!" he protested. "Girlfriends are supposed to love it when their guys show off their new gadgets," he added. "Aren't they?"

MJ laughed. "Call me back when you're done playing."

"Hold on—I'm just getting the last one now. He's creeping around in the dark, like being low means I won't be able to find him. It's adorbs."

"I'm hanging up in thirty seconds."

"I only need ten," the Web-Slinger said. Then he shot out webbing and incapacitated the last of the quartet.

"I'll call you back," he said abruptly, and he cut the connection.

His Spider-Sense went off like a tingly explosion. It wasn't exactly an eleven on a ten scale, but it was easily an eight. These guys weren't the threat, they were the bait, and Spider-Man had just blundered into a trap.

THREE

THE Scorpion had never much impressed Spider-Man with the quality of his henchmen. In fact, he rarely even *used* henchmen. Clearly he needed to rethink his employment agency, or however these guys operated. Have a little chat with the people down in HR. But these four had been underwhelming, even by Scorpion's standards.

They'd been expendable.

That, it seemed, had been the point.

Whoever he faced next would be the real threat.

It wasn't Scorpion. That was for sure. This guy was about Spider-Man's own height, slim and wiry like him, dressed all in black, nothing fancy—sweatpants and a loose sweatshirt. Over his head he wore a black balaclava, so nothing of his face was visible.

Or her, he supposed. There was no reason to assume this bad guy wasn't a bad woman. Just a bad person, though the only evidence he had of that was the tingling sensation that told him he was in for a serious fight. He led with a few web-shooter bursts, thinking maybe he could end the conflict before it began.

The webs hit nothing but wall. The person in black was gone, tumbling through the air. For a second, Spider-Man thought that the moves looked familiar—like he'd know who this was, if he could just remember where he'd seen a fighting style like that before. Then it came to him.

He'd seen those moves on news coverage.

This guy moved like Spider-Man. Like *him*!

"Nice style," he said, springing up to a far wall, then another, then another. The three-spring fake-out. It never failed to fool the garden-variety thug. An enemy couldn't dodge something if he didn't know where it was coming from.

This guy dodged it.

Time to shut him down.

Bracing himself on a wall, Spider-Man lobbed out a barrage from his web shooters—where the guy was, where he was likely to be in the next fraction of a second, where he might leap unexpectedly. Blanket coverage like that used up a lot of web fluid, though, and it had been a busy night. He was a fussy driver who liked to fill the tank long before it was empty, and he was already running low. Of course, the typical fussy driver didn't have to worry about being shot, stabbed, crushed, trampled, electrocuted, stung, or bludgeoned if he cut things a little close.

None of the webs hit home, because his assailant leapt and bounced and lunged in a style that was all too familiar. A second barrage missed, too, and Spider-Man started to wonder why he was bothering with this guy. Other than trespassing—a crime Spider-Man had also committed, when he thought about it—the guy hadn't actually broken any laws.

Even if he was able to catch this person, more likely than not he'd walk.

On the other hand, Andy sent him to this place, where there just happened to be a bunch of decoy henchmen and a guy with some awfully familiar abilities.

"This isn't passing the smell test," Spider-Man said, "and I'm not talking about your body odor—though that doesn't pass the smell test, either."

He leapt in, letting his instincts take over. He was ready to dodge, shift, roll, and lunge—whatever it took to get this guy at a disadvantage. The fun had gone on long enough. It was time for his opponent to be webbed up and explain just what was going on here.

Spider-Man landed behind the Man in Black. At least that was the plan, but his opponent was already gone.

No wonder the guys I fight get so angry, he thought. *That's just annoying.* Then he was struck from behind. It was like getting slammed by a speeding truck. His foe hit hard and fast, sending Spider-Man skidding across the paved surface. Then the guy was on top of him. He moved like Spider-Man, but fought like a brawler. There were hands everywhere, slamming into his face, his chest, grappling without letting up.

"Hands off the merchandise," he grunted. He slammed his forehead forward, hopefully into his attacker's general nose area. At least that was the plan. The guy jerked back, avoiding the blow. The move allowed Spider-Man to break free and leap to the scaffolding. He turned and aimed with his wrist, but there was no one to hit.

He tensed, ready for a surprise attack from any angle, but then he realized his Spider-Sense was no longer thrumming. It had gone to sleep. He moved around the perimeter of the roof, fast and erratically, changing his trajectory and speed to make an ambush more difficult, but it became apparent that this was nothing more than an exercise in caution.

The Man in Black was gone.

"So, no Scorpion is what you're telling me," he said to himself. This whole thing had been a setup, but a *weird* setup. The Man in Black had moved like Spider-Man, yet fought like a biker, and held his own. The throbbing on Spider-Man's cheek suggested he'd done *more* than hold his own. He had, in fact, had a real shot at beating the crap out of the original.

So why had he taken off while he was winning the fight? There was a lot he didn't know, but the bits and pieces suggested a new and dangerous enemy with a completely unknown plan. In other words, trouble. He needed intel, and, at the moment, the guy who set him up and made him look like a chump seemed like a pretty good source.

So it was back to the cruise terminal. Andy would be long gone, but even though he'd pulled the wool over Spider-Man's eyes, he still wasn't God's gift to intelligence. With any luck, he'd left some kind of clue behind, like his wallet or the keys to his apartment. If he couldn't find anything there, he'd check the snake store afterward.

As he swung toward his destination, however, he felt his stomach drop. It didn't take spider-powers to tell. Flashing blue and red lights, a police perimeter, the squawk of radio chatter.

Something had gone horribly wrong.

○━━━━━━━━━━○

ANDY was dead.

Spider-Man perched in the shadows on an upper deck of one of the ships and looked down at the scene below. The body was surrounded by a dozen police officers. They hadn't even bothered to call EMTs—there was no reason to do so. There was a large pool of blood on the deck beneath him, and a big stain on the front of his shirt.

An hour ago, the kid had been alive...

A woman was circling the scene, systematically taking photos with her phone. A guy in plain clothes—probably from the coroner's office—was studying the body and taking notes on a tablet. A handful of uniformed officers combed the scene with flashlights, searching for clues. A mustached man, most likely a plainclothes detective, stood impassively, sipping coffee from a Greek-themed paper cup and staring into the distance. His tie flapped in the breeze.

There had to be someone behind this—some sort of mastermind. The kid had just been a pawn.

Even more alarming, whoever was working with the fake spider-person had been confident that the *real* Spider-Man would respond to the break-in at a snake store. That meant that someone had been tracking his movements, following where he'd gone that night, or what kinds of police calls were likely to grab his attention—or both. That suggested an alarming investment of time and energy.

Peter didn't like to let emotions cloud his thinking, but the fact was that Andy was lying dead down there. He'd been a person, and probably not a terrible person. He'd had the right to live and make mistakes and hopefully learn from them, and someone had taken that away. They'd done it in order to mess with Spider-Man.

That made it personal.

It also meant that Spider-Man had information the police needed. The trick was figuring out the best way to pass it along. The guy with the coffee and the flapping tie was probably in charge, so Spider-Man would need to get him alone. Unfortunately, the detective showed no signs of moving.

"Hold it right there!"

The voice startled him. Raising his arms in the air, he turned slowly to face a woman—holding a very nasty-looking weapon of the sort favored by the New York police officers. Despite the pistol she held, his Spider-Sense hadn't tingled, so she didn't present an immediate threat.

"You know the routine," she said. "Hands where I can see them."

"Oh, come on," Spider-Man said. "Is this really necessary?" He could think of plenty of answers, but wanted to hear what she had to say.

"It's necessary," the woman replied, "because you're suspect number one in a murder."

FOUR

SHE was a slender woman in her thirties, wearing jeans, a leather jacket, and a yellow button-down shirt. She looked like she meant business, though she didn't seem terribly eager to shoot him.

Spider-Man relaxed a little.

"What are you doing here?" she demanded of him.

"I didn't kill him," he answered. As soon as he did, it sounded lame.

"I know that," she snapped. "Unless you've figured out how to hide a pistol in that skintight suit of yours. It'd stick out like a tumor."

"Thanks?" he offered.

"Don't be funny. Tell me what you know."

"Any chance you could put that gun down?"

The woman glared at him, then sighed. "I don't suppose it would do much good against you, anyhow." She holstered her weapon. "You'd just grab it with those rope thingies of yours."

"They're actually webs," Spider-Man said. "Powered by science. Anyhow, let's do this the polite way. I'm Spider-Man. And you are?"

"Lt. Yuri Watanabe," she said in a clipped voice, "and I'm not looking for a new pal. You're a person of interest in a murder investigation, and while bringing you to the precinct for questioning would present some challenges, putting out an APB on you would probably mess up your week. So how about you stop wasting my time?"

No nonsense, tough as nails, and willing to work with Spider-Man. He liked that—and it made him think. For years he'd wondered how much more he could get done if he had a direct relationship with the police department. His mind raced with the possibilities. The trick would be to prove his worth to her. That would involve a much lower percentage of wisecracks per sentence than what came naturally, but he was pretty sure—if he focused—he could get it done.

"Tell me how I can help," he said.

"Why did your voice suddenly get so deep?"

"It didn't."

"It did, and it still is. Before you sounded like a kid—"

"Hey!"

"—and now you sound like a kid trying to fool someone over the phone."

"How about less criticism and more crime-solving?" he proposed. A wry little smile flickered across Lieutenant Watanabe's lips. Then she was back to business.

"You see that trailer down there?"

She pointed to a white metal rectangle about 200 feet past where the other plainclothes cop was still sipping his coffee. He was also looking at his phone, and from this distance Peter couldn't be sure, but it looked like he was playing some kind of jewel-matching game.

"That's the terminal's security office," she said. "The door is on the far side, so if you can meet me there without anyone seeing you, I'd like to show you something. Give me five minutes."

Then she was gone.

———o———————o———

GETTING to the entrance was no problem. A little creative swinging, and he was through the door. Lieutenant Watanabe was seated at a desk, running her fingers along a keyboard. It was gloomy, but a half-dozen video monitors illuminated her face, each showing a different section of the facility. The trailer smelled of old gym clothes.

Watanabe turned the moment he entered, and her hand moved toward her gun, not quite touching it. She might be willing to work with him—she might even trust him on principle—but she wasn't about to let her guard down. Peter didn't like her any less for it. It was common sense.

"I told everyone I needed to concentrate in here, so we have a few minutes," she began without any preamble. "But we don't have all the time in the world, so save your comments and questions for the end."

Her fingers danced across the keyboard. One of the monitors went dark, then began playing a recording. The first thing she showed him was a black-and-white clip revealing his first encounter with Andy. A time signature spun rapidly in the lower left corner. It was always weird watching footage of himself. There was a part of his mind that never quite got used to seeing himself from the outside.

"When I left he was fine," Spider-Man said. The footage backed him up.

"Quiet," she said, forwarding the footage for what looked like only a few minutes. It showed Andy walking away from the dock, trying to keep to the shadows, probably mindful of the security cameras. Then Spider-Man leapt in behind him, landing lightly on his feet—so lightly that Andy seemed not to notice.

Definitely not how things happened...

He knew that move. Knew how to land from thirty or forty feet up, without making a noise. He did it all the time to get a drop on the bad guys. It had taken him months to learn the trick back when he first started out. Now it was second nature.

The problem was, that wasn't him. Was it? The moves were right—so much so, he had to remind himself that it was impossible. He looked at the time signature. By that point he was well on his way to the construction site.

Holy crap! It has to be the guy. The imposter.

He was about to open his mouth to say something when the Spider-Man imposter raised his right hand. He held a gun. It looked absurd and strange and grotesque. Spider-Man never touched a gun, unless it was to get it away from some idiot who had one. Even then, he usually used his webs. Guns were big and loud and nasty. They were difficult to nuance and frequently deadly. They were everything he didn't want to be.

The imposter must have said something, because Andy jumped, his shoulders lurching upward and his legs wobbling in mid-stride. He turned, and then started to backpedal. There was the burst of muzzle flash, a violent eruption of light that obscured everything else in the dark frame. When the light cleared, Andy lay on the ground.

The imposter took a moment to examine the body, then he fired three more shots into the prone figure. He paused for another instant, and then shifted his gaze to look—at the security camera. At least, it seemed like he did. It was hard to tell with the mask. He then raised his left hand, a web shot out, and he propelled himself out of the camera's field of view.

○————————○

SPIDER-MAN needed time to gather his thoughts.

There were a hundred things he wanted to say, and he didn't even know yet what half of them might be. Ideas burst into his mind, only to be replaced by others. Outrage, pity, indignation—raw emotions had the advantage here, but there were other things. Observations of minor details that some distant, calmer part of his mind knew might be of use to the detective.

It was hard to stick to logic, though. Andy had

died facing an impersonator. He'd died believing that Spider-Man had gunned him down. It didn't make the crime any worse, but it made him all the more determined to do something about it.

"I didn't do that," he said. "I would never do anything like that."

"It's inconsistent with your past behavior," Watanabe replied in a clinical tone, "and it would be hard to prove that one person wearing a mask is the same as another person wearing the same mask. The perp moves a whole lot like you do, though, and that's harder to mimic. If you have an alibi, it would help us. Maybe there's another place you might be on camera at the same time? Though, again, we still have the mask and identity problem."

"First of all, that's not me." His thoughts began to shift into focus—at least some of them. "I don't use guns, and I absolutely don't go around assassinating people. Even the *Daily Bugle*, back when Jameson was calling for my head, never claimed I would do *that*."

"I believe you," Watanabe said, replaying the footage, "but my opinion doesn't count as evidence."

Spider-Man leaned in closer to the screen, peering at the costumed figure who appeared there. "Freeze it," he said. "There. The suit isn't quite right. It's close. It's a decent copy, definitely better than something you'd get from a costume shop, but the design is a little off. I can't say anything about the color, but the spider icon doesn't look exactly like mine, and the web lines are too close together."

"I noticed that, too," Lieutenant Watanabe said. "Here, look at the earlier footage." She brought it up on another screen. "You would've had to change your outfit into something nearly identical, and then come right back. It doesn't make sense, but whenever we're dealing with costumed vigilantes, 'making sense' doesn't always apply…" She let her voice trail off in a way that indicated she was playing devil's advocate, and not actually arguing a position she believed.

Spider-Man took a deep breath, organizing his thoughts. He needed to tell her everything that had happened, and had to figure out what would be most useful. She pulled out her cell phone and he began, describing his encounter with Andy, getting the tip about the construction site. He went through everything that happened there, as well.

"It sounds awfully convenient," she said tonelessly as she typed. "A guy who can copy your moves just *happens* to show up, the same night Spider-Man is filmed killing a kid." She shook her head. "Like I said, things with your crowd don't always make sense, but this feels like a setup. The disposable henchmen were there to slow you down while the real bad guy changed his clothes and hightailed it over there to face you."

It sounded plausible, but there were still a lot of unanswered questions.

"Why change his clothes at all?"

"Maybe because he wanted you to see this?" she said with a shrug. "Probably figured you'd catch it on the news, rather than here with a cop, but I think the shooter wanted this video to be a gut punch. Someone is calling you out. I'd ask if you have any enemies, but that's a stupid question."

"If the construction site has video cameras, and most of them do, then it will at least prove that part of my story."

"I'm thinking the same thing," she said. "You got an address?"

He told her about the building, and Lieutenant Watanabe's eyes went wide. She set down her phone and turned to look at him.

"Are you kidding me? You're sure that's the location?"

"Yeah," he said. "Why?"

She let out a long breath that hissed between clenched teeth. "It's hidden behind hundreds of pages of documents and a half-dozen shell companies, but that construction site is owned by Wilson Fisk." She worked her mouth as if she was trying to get rid of a bad taste. "The frigging Kingpin of Crime."

FIVE

FISK, he thought. The anger blossomed inside him, radiating outward until it was hard to remain still.

Fisk was in the news a lot. Back when he'd first started Spider-Manning, Peter had been convinced Fisk was—as the tabloids claimed—the Kingpin of Crime, the most ruthless criminal in the city. Sure, Peter was just a high-school kid back then, but he'd been driven to prove that he could use his powers responsibly.

He'd made a massive mistake, soon after he got his spider-powers—a frivolous decision not to act when he might have acted, *should* have acted, and that had led to the death of his Uncle Ben. He'd sworn never again to sit idly when there was something he could do. Something that would make a difference.

That something had been putting the Kingpin behind bars. Spider-Man had dedicated months of his life toward that one goal—disrupting Fisk's operations, keeping him off his game, and looking for hard evidence upon which even a bribed or blackmailed district attorney would have to act.

Spider-Man had dug up that proof. He'd collected files, laptops, photographs, and witnesses. He'd found enough hard evidence to put Fisk in a bespoke orange jumpsuit for life.

Back then, it felt like the triumph of a lifetime. He remembered sitting on the couch with Aunt May, shoving fists full of popcorn into his mouth while the local news showed Fisk perp-walking into the precinct.

"You know, Peter, there was a time when I wasn't sure how to feel about that Spider-Man," Aunt May had told him, "but it certainly looks as if he's done the city a real favor." Coming from her, it had felt really good. That cocktail of pride and satisfaction and contentment—the sensation of knowing he'd really accomplished something important—had been hard to beat.

Then life beat it. Life beat it right down, and smacked it upside its metaphorical head.

Fisk's lawyers went to work, and suddenly half the news outlets in the city were on Fisk's side. "It was a setup," they said. Spider-Man was a thug, a criminal himself, and he wanted honest businessmen like Wilson Fisk destroyed so the criminals could have free rein. Evidence went missing. Documents vanished or changed. Photos were altered. Computer records disappeared. Witnesses "forgot" things or remembered entirely new accounts that exonerated Fisk, made him look innocent, made him look like a hero, struggling to save his business while a lawless vandal in a costume tried to tear down everything an honest man had accomplished.

Fisk walked.

He'd gone right out of the courthouse, and then out of the country. He'd been gone for years, too, and maybe that was good enough, Spider-Man had told himself. Sure, it wasn't perfect. No one wanted a guy like Fisk being evil on someone else's turf, but at least Spider-Man had cleaned up his own backyard. If people everywhere did the same, the bad guys would have nowhere to hide.

It was weak, Spider-Man knew, but it was all he had.

Then, a year ago, Fisk appeared back on the scene, throwing money around, investing in prominent real estate deals, developing long-neglected parts of the city, creating jobs and goodwill. The newspapers were full of stories about the Fisk Foundation, a new charitable effort which was aimed at promoting opportunities for New Yorkers of all incomes. Wilson Fisk was a changed man, he told anyone who would listen, which included a number of journalists whose organizations were flush with Fisk money. He'd never been what the vigilantes had claimed, he told them, but he *had* been selfish and greedy, focused on nothing but his own bottom line.

Hardship had taught him the price of selfishness. Now he understood that he had to do good to do well, and that was why every project he invested in would make the city a little better, improve the lives of its citizens. He didn't want to profit unless others profited, too.

That was what he claimed, and that was what plenty of people seemed to believe. The truth was, Fisk was back in drugs and extortion and hijacking and money-laundering. All of his old tricks. If it was dirty and violent and profitable, he had his hands in it. Spider-Man knew it, and he was *sure* he could prove it, but he didn't know if proving it would change a thing. It hadn't last time.

"I know you've got your own history with that piece of garbage," Watanabe said. "That's one of the reasons I'm giving you the benefit of the doubt. I've been trying to build a case against Fisk since he came back on the scene, but I've had to do it on the sly. There are plenty of people above me who don't want Fisk investigated."

"Fisk always had cops on his payroll."

"*Allegedly*," Watanabe said, but her tone made it clear there was no doubt. "Those charges were dropped, remember. You played a pretty big part in his arrest that time. What was that—five years ago?"

"Seven," Spider-Man said.

"Right," she said. "I guess the question is, what is Fisk after now? Why go to all this trouble? What does setting you up get him?"

"Seems like it's better to focus on catching this impersonator," Spider-Man proposed. "Fisk is slippery, and we can worry about his motives later. This bogus Spider-Man—bogus *me*—might provide all of the answers. Can you ask for the video-camera feed from the construction site?"

"We can ask," she said, "but if they say no, we'll need a search warrant, and without any evidence of a crime but your word, I don't see that happening. Even if we *could* get a warrant, it'll take time. Fisk might have his people erase or alter the feed by then."

"Why would Fisk even have a secret construction site?" Spider-Man asked. "Everyone knows he's a real estate developer."

"This building is nothing but high-end luxury co-ops," Watanabe explained. "There's nothing noble about it—nothing that benefits the 'common man.' It's meant to make a ton of money, so he doesn't want it getting out, since it's not consistent with his new 'good-guy' con."

"None of this tells us what he wants."

"It looks like good old-fashioned revenge to me," Watanabe said. "You messed with him. Now he's messing with you. You really put the hurt on him back in the day. You gathered a ton of good evidence, but Fisk's lawyers were able to kick up plenty of reasonable doubt—especially with evidence gathered by a guy dressed like a spider."

"So there's no point in going after him again?"

"I didn't say that," she replied. "If you'd had someone on the inside helping you out, someone who could clean the evidence the way Fisk launders money, things might've turned out differently the first time. I know you costumed types are loners, but maybe we could help each other out."

This was what he had been waiting to hear. It was a terrific idea, but he didn't want to appear *too* anxious. So he leaned back and folded his arms.

"Maybe."

"I'm usually out of Chinatown, but Hell's Kitchen is shorthanded tonight," she said. "That clown out there playing some stupid game on his phone isn't my regular partner, either." She gestured with her head, looking disgusted. "In fact, I think he could be one of those guys in Fisk's pocket, which is why I'm happy to let him play games on his phone instead of helping me out. I caught this case, and that moron will be happy to be off the hook. All of which means I call the shots.

"I'm going to go on the offensive, argue that we suppress the Spider-Man angle. Say the evidence makes it clear—and it does—that this is an imposter looking to stir the pot, and we don't want to play his game. Sooner or later, the guy will have to strike again."

"And someone else gets killed."

"Maybe, maybe not." She shrugged. "There's no reason to think he'll play the same hand twice. There's also no reason to think he won't use violence again, no matter what we do. Our best option is to keep him playing *our* game, rather than having us play his. Meanwhile, you and me—we go after Fisk."

"Go after him how?"

"I don't know," she admitted. "I need to give this some thought, but you can go places I can't, and I know things that you don't. Your abilities should be able to land us evidence I'd never get my hands on otherwise, and I can turn it into something that will hold up in court." She paused, then added, "Let me chew on this a little while. If you don't like what I come up with, you can tell me to get lost—but I have a feeling you'd like to see Fisk go down as much as I would."

She held out her hand.

They shook, and maybe it was just the emotion of the moment, but it felt as if something momentous had just happened.

"Let's hope we don't make things worse," he said.

Watanabe grinned. "I can see you're going to be a whole lot of fun to work with."

IT wasn't even eleven o'clock yet.

It felt much later, like the sun should be coming up soon. Peter still hadn't processed everything that had happened. The setup, Andy being murdered, the imposter, and Fisk. It was a bubbling stew of horribleness. The only bright spot was Lieutenant Watanabe. If she was willing to work with him, and to figure out how they could pool their resources, it might be a chance to set things right.

Inside his East Village apartment, Peter navigated the piles of clothes, dirty dishes, stacks of books, and torturously assembled computer components. The place was cramped, badly maintained, and way too expensive. He was behind with last month's rent, and couldn't even bring himself to think about this month's. Living in a shoebox he couldn't afford was just part of the glamor of being a super hero.

While he pulled off his suit, he tried to focus his anger in the right direction. Fisk was famous for counter-punching, so it didn't surprise Peter that—even after all these years—he'd be looking to get back at Spider-Man. Fisk didn't know how to hurt the man, so he figured he could hurt the image. Peter couldn't worry about reputation, though. He had to focus on doing what he could to help as many people as possible.

Uncle Ben had said it himself.

"With great power there must also come—great responsibility."

It was something Peter hadn't considered, the night he decided not to stop a thief—the thief who later killed his uncle. They were the words Peter tried to live by now. He had a responsibility to use his abilities the best way he could. He also had a habit of examining everything he did, picking over every move, every decision, to see if he could have done better.

Were there better choices he might have made tonight—choices that might have saved Andy's life? Peter thought he'd done what seemed to be the right thing at the time, not knowing that he'd been set down onto the board of a bigger game. If Fisk was involved, though, he couldn't afford to let his guard down—not again. Fisk was as corrupt as they came, and Peter couldn't change that. He could, however, stop him, and that meant doing everything in his power to make it happen.

First things first, though.

What he needed more than anything else was to see MJ. She always talked him down, helped him feel better. She wasn't answering her phone again, though, so he figured he should go out and look for her.

Turning on the shower, he took a cautionary sniff at his suit. There was a tear, a souvenir of the fight with his opponent. He'd need to fix that. It was starting to get a little rank, too, but cleaning it was complicated and time-consuming. It'd have to wait. Fortunately the outer layers were scent-proof, which meant that—for now—he'd be the only one who would have to live with the funk. When he took it off, however, the sweat seemed to rise from his body in undulating waves.

I, he thought, *am gross.*

o————————o

EVEN if Peter had examined himself closely in a mirror, he wouldn't have seen the tiny patch, no bigger than a thumbnail, stuck to his lower back. From the moment his attacker had torn through his suit and attached it to his skin, it had begun to blend in, matching itself to its surroundings in color and texture.

It didn't come off in the shower, either. It had its limitations, though. It would dry up and peel off in a few days. In the meantime, it would transmit its data.

o————————o

IT was 11:37, and Peter still hadn't made contact with MJ. He knew it was foolish to worry, but he worried anyhow. That was part of the package, and MJ knew it. Peter had lost his parents when he was very young, and that had impressed upon him the fragility of the world. He'd lost his Uncle Ben because of his own foolish choices. That had only made the feelings more intense.

He did everything he could to keep his identity a secret. No matter what, he had to keep MJ, Aunt May, and *all* of his friends out of the crosshairs. The possibility haunted him every day, though. No matter how careful he was, *someone* might learn who he was, and use the people he cared about as leverage.

Or worse.

So of course he worried. More than that, he wanted to talk to the only person who knew his secret, telling her about the things that had happened that night.

MJ rented an apartment near Washington Square Park, and he had the key. He let himself in, but only to make sure that the legendary night owl hadn't surprised him by going to sleep early. No luck there, though, so he considered his options.

He might call their mutual friend Harry Osborn. The three of them had been a team for years, and sometimes MJ told Harry things she didn't tell Peter. She said it was because Peter tended to worry. Objectively he understood, yet it bothered him— mostly because he was a worrier. This, he knew, was a vicious cycle. Besides, if MJ was going to confide in anyone else, Peter wanted it to be Harry. He was smart, insightful, and an all-around good person.

He also had a lot more free time than Peter. Unlike some people, who, say, labored all day in a lab, and then swung around the city half the night as Spider-Man, Harry had the advantage of a rich father. It was an advantage, Peter knew, that Harry would have traded away in an instant.

Harry had long resisted working for Oscorp, his father's company. He'd briefly been willing to work on a pet project for his mother, but that hadn't satisfied Norman Osborn. Then again, he was never satisfied. Now Osborn was mayor of New York City, and *that* might have been a blessing. Running the city meant Norman didn't have as much time to harangue his son, pressing Harry to do something with his life. He'd become a part-time thorn in his son's side.

So growing up rich had to come with its own burdens—though Peter might've been willing to bear burdens like that. Still, he thought he understood. He'd always been hungry to achieve great things, to make his own way in the world. Often it felt like thrashing around in a storm-tossed sea, struggling just to survive. Yet, how did you motivate yourself when— no matter what happened—you knew you were going to be okay?

Again, problems Peter wouldn't mind sampling.

But he knew Harry's struggles were real.

His friend had scheduled an upcoming trip to Europe, and he hoped some time away would help him out. Harry "wanted to travel, to see the world, to consider his options," he said. He'd be touring some of the European Oscorp facilities, but that was to placate his father. What Harry really wanted was some distance from his father, and to get his head together.

———○————————○———

SURE enough, Harry was home. It just proved that he really had no idea what he wanted, or how to get it. Here he was, a good-looking 22-year-old heir to billions, alone in his apartment on a Saturday night—reading *medical* journals. Sure, he'd never really been a party boy, but this was dreary even by Harry's standards.

"You thinking about medical school?" Peter asked as he took a seat. Harry's apartment was four times the size of Peter's and furnished with things people bought in actual stores. Truth be told, though, Peter had a certain fondness for New York's curbside treasures. The thrill of the hunt and all. Harry shrugged as he poured Peter a glass of flavored seltzer.

"Just considering my options."

Peter took the glass as Harry sat down across from him. It had to be hard, in its own way. Much of Peter's life had been dictated by what he felt like he *had* to do—to use his abilities wisely, to learn as much as he could, to pay the rent, to avoid disappointing the people who cared about him. Perhaps it was paralyzing, having everything handed over on a silver platter.

"Maybe you could look at some med schools in Europe?"

"Maybe," Harry replied noncommittally. Then he laughed. "Listen, Pete, stop pretending—I know perfectly well why you're here," he said. "We've been friends a long time, so you're not going to hurt my feelings. You want to know where MJ is."

"She's not answering her phone," Peter admitted sheepishly. "And it's late."

"Maybe for an old lady like you."

"Says the guy who's reading medical journals on a Saturday night."

"*Touché*," Harry replied. "Then again, what have you been up to that's so interesting? Wherever MJ is, why aren't you with her?"

There it was. Peter hated it. He'd considered many times telling Harry the truth, but he'd never been able to bring himself to do it. It wasn't that he didn't trust Harry. He trusted him completely. It always came down to the fact that he didn't *have* to tell him. He could be friends with Harry and not tell him, and that kept both of them a little safer.

There was a part of him, as well, that worried that somehow if he told Harry, Norman Osborn might find out. Harry might let something slip, or talk in his sleep. Something. *Anything*. He might let out a fraction of the truth, and the relentlessly clever Norman Osborn would piece together the rest. It wasn't that Peter thought Norman was bad, but he wasn't exactly good, either. He liked power a little too much.

Why else would a guy at the helm of one of the most successful companies in the world decide he had to be mayor of one of the most important cities in the world? It was ego, Peter thought, pure and simple. If there was a prize out there, Norman Osborn couldn't resist grabbing it—doing whatever he could to be the best, the most important, the most influential.

"I've been, uh, working at the lab," Peter lied. "There were some time-sensitive experiments." It was a classic from his bag of excuses. Harry never seemed to suspect, in part because there *had* been plenty of times when Peter really had gotten wrapped up in time-sensitive experiments. As the son of a scientist and inventor, Harry understood all too well.

"Yeah, you're living the wild life," Harry said. "How can I compete?"

"Look, if you're teasing me this much, it means you know where MJ is and just want to make me suffer."

"Maybe a little bit," Harry admitted. "Plus I didn't want you to go all protective when you found out that she's in Hell's Kitchen."

"She's *what*?" Peter said. "By herself? At night?"

"Easy, Lancelot," Harry said, and he laughed. "She can take care of herself, and you know it."

He did. If Peter hadn't been augmented by spider-powers, MJ could have beaten him up while checking her email. She'd studied martial arts for years, and on a few harrowing occasions she'd proved she knew how to practice what she preached. Logically, Peter pitied the poor guy who tried to take her purse. Emotionally, he wanted to be there to keep it from happening.

"It's an audition piece for the *Bugle*," Harry said. "She's doing some kind of feature on people who work late-night shifts. I forget the specifics."

"That sounds interesting," Peter replied, trying to

play it cool. "Maybe I should pay her a visit, see if I can lend her a hand. Give her the benefit of my years of journalistic experience, you know."

"As a photographer." Harry smirked. "What sort of hand do you think you could lend her?"

Peter opened his mouth, but couldn't think of anything to say.

"Relax, dude." Harry laughed again. "She told me to let you know if you happened to drop by."

"Then why didn't she just tell me herself?"

"Because if she did, then she *knew* you'd have to check on her." He gave Peter a look. "Maybe she knew about your 'time-sensitive experiments,' and didn't want you to feel obligated."

Trying not to seem too eager, Peter got Harry to give him the address. They talked a little longer— as little as he could manage—and said good night, agreeing to get together soon. Then Peter left.

○——————○

HE wasn't wearing his suit, so Peter took a cab he couldn't afford, and found MJ right where Harry said she would be. It was an all-night grocery in Hell's Kitchen, where she was finishing up an interview with the owner, a shy and polite man named Danilo Ocampo.

Ocampo was an immigrant from the Philippines. He'd been working eighteen-hour days for the past ten years and, in spite of owning his own business, was still having a hard time making ends meet. Like the other people she'd been interviewing, he'd won a lottery that would let him live in a new Fisk apartment complex at affordable rates. The piece she was writing was about how Fisk's real estate ventures were going to change the lives of the ordinary New Yorkers.

"Fisk," Peter snapped. "Are you kidding me?"

These days Fisk's name was everywhere. The media loved his riches-to-rags-to-riches angle, though Peter suspected the Kingpin never lost his fortune— just did a good job of hiding it. Suddenly he was New York's most benevolent businessman, putting up huge buildings full of luxury apartments mixed with equally spacious subsidized units, paying his workers well above standard wages, developing projects designed to attract jobs to the city.

In truth, the Fisk way was theft on a grand scale, drug dealing, human trafficking, extortion, and money laundering for some of the most dangerous criminals in the world. The Fisk way was power and corruption and acquisition at any cost.

"How can you agree to do a puff piece on that guy?" Peter asked.

"I know what Fisk is," MJ whispered, "but this is a good story. It could get me the job at the *Bugle*, and then I'll stick with it, because if I cover Fisk—even if it's from a features perspective—I might dig up the proof that pokes a hole in his PR balloon."

Peter thought back to what he'd learned from Lieutenant Watanabe—that Fisk was still developing high-end real estate, only hiding it behind shell corporations. A story like that could expose the hypocrisy of the "new" Fisk, but it might also risk Watanabe's sources. Worse, it could put MJ in Fisk's crosshairs, and there was no way he was going to do that.

Taking MJ by the arm, he gently led her outside. What he had to say next might elicit a loud reaction, and he didn't want that to happen in front of the smiling Mr. Ocampo. They stepped off to one side, out of the pool of light that came from the grocery.

"You do *not* want to cross Fisk," Peter said. "You don't even want him to wonder if you might be *thinking* of crossing him. Best of all, you don't want him to know you exist. A guy like that won't hesitate to have a journalist killed."

She glared at him for a moment before responding.

"What, you can take all the risks you want, but I can't?" MJ asked. "Is this the way it works now? Because it's the first I've heard about it."

"I'm not saying that." He groaned. "I'm just saying you could focus on other kinds of stories for the moment. That's all."

"Like dog shows," she suggested, "and the latest app craze."

"Come on, MJ."

"No, *you* come on," she said, poking him in the chest. She was so intense that he felt a buzzing in the back of his head. "I'm applying for the features job because that's where there's an opening, but my goal—my *real* goal—is investigative reporting. Once they see what I can do, I'll have a shot at it. This is my calling, Peter. It's what I want to do. It's how I can make a difference. You, of all people, have to understand—and you can't seriously tell me not to follow my dream."

He sighed. "No, I can't. I wouldn't. I shan't!"

That seemed to do it. She took a step back and smiled at him.

"Look, I know you worry," she said. "I worry about you too, but I learned how to deal with it. Now you're going to have to learn to live with it, too."

Suddenly Peter realized that the buzzing hadn't stopped. There was a scrape of shoe against pavement.

"What a sweet couple of lovebirds."

They turned, and there was a man standing there. He looked like every other passerby—cotton shirt, jeans, a jacket… and a switchblade.

"Hand over your wallets," he said. "Jewelry, too."

"You don't want to do this," MJ said, smiling sweetly. "Just walk away, turn your life around."

"Don't tell me what I w—"

That was as far as he got, because MJ's knee had made contact with his groin. Though it was hardly necessary, as he fell to the sidewalk she added a kick. Then she leaned over him as he squirmed on the ground.

"Remember, crime doesn't pay," she told him as she scooped up his knife, closed it, and dropped it into her purse. Then she looked over at Peter. "Good thing you were here to save me."

Peter gave her a wry grin. "Point taken."

SIX

SHE had a game on her phone where the point was to tap the screen along with the rhythm of a music video. Maya couldn't hear the music, though. She had never heard *anything*, yet she always did well at the game—perhaps better than someone who could hear.

There were other cues. The rhythm of shapes and colors, the pulse of the vibrations. People who could hear had no need to pay attention, to be mindful of all the ways the world directs you without sound.

This fight was like that. It had a rhythm, a pulse, an anticipatory beat. There was a music that she couldn't hear, that she could never know, and its absence put her at a disadvantage. It also freed her from its distractions. Her opponents were lost in the music, but she followed the rhythm.

She wore a simple black tank top and compression shorts. Her shoulder-length black hair was pulled back into a tight ponytail. She sought to expose as much of her skin as possible without offending her sense of modesty. It was important to feel every movement, every change in the air. She'd learned all this when she studied dance. She did not need to hear the world to be in touch with it.

Her opponent—the one she couldn't see—

approached from behind. He knew she couldn't hear him, so he wasn't bothering to be subtle. She felt him, though, through the pulsing of his feet on the canvas beneath. She sensed the slight breeze as he raised his arm, preparing to bring down his cudgel. She'd seen his moves before, studied them, and memorized every detail. Whatever he did, she could anticipate it, and she could copy it.

Maya knew the arc of his swing. She knew how high he would reach and how he would stick out his right foot, pointed slightly outward. At the apogee he would pause for the tiniest fraction of a second.

The two men in front of her thought they could box her in, set her up for the ambush. She let them believe they had her trapped. That was how she would win.

Had this been out in the world, if it were a real assault, it would be over already. The three men would be on the ground, unconscious or in too much pain to put up a fight. Here in the gym she drew it out, because Mr. Fisk enjoyed the show. He liked watching her outsmart adversaries who ought to have every advantage. Even so, in his mind she was the poor little deaf girl he had saved.

Mr. Fisk had given her so much. It was true—he *had* saved her. There was no other way to put it. Rescued her from a misery so dark and terrible she rarely let herself remember. He hadn't made her strong—that she had done for herself—but he allowed her to find her strength. Enabled her to become what she was. So if he wanted a show, then a show was the least she could give him.

The two men in front moved closer. They had cudgels, too, while Maya held the Cheyenne spear that once belonged to her father, and to his father, and his father again. It had been made in the late eighteenth century, and had been lovingly preserved. Mr. Fisk had presented it to her, and now it was the only thing she had of her family. She was always careful with it, but not so careful that she wouldn't use it.

She had sparred with these men, and others like them, many times before, so they had nothing new to teach her. Lenny, on the left, wanted to be a mixed martial arts fighter. He had the strength and the discipline, but he was plagued with self-doubt. To her right was Amal, on the cusp of middle age but still in great shape. What the years may have taken in speed they had given in cunning.

Behind her was Netto. He was a nice guy who clearly had no wish to strike her, but Mr. Fisk had been explicit in his instructions. *Do not hold back.* Netto had three daughters, two of them almost ready for college. He wasn't about to do anything that could risk his job, risk his ability to provide for his family.

Maya needed to defeat them, because that's what Mr. Fisk wanted, yet she was determined not to hurt them. They were decent men, all of them, and if they were to hurt her by mistake—not that it was possible—they'd feel sincere regret. So she plotted the middle ground. Knock them down, disarm them, dominate them, but do it all without risking any real injury.

Amal faked a swing, and then another, and then moved in, raising his arm high. He'd done it before, and with the first feint Maya knew what was coming. Lenny had less patience with theatricals, and simply came in hard and fast. He was all bludgeon, no finesse.

She raised her spear and, as Netto struck from behind, swept Lenny's legs out from under him, side-stepping Amal. Having already moved out of the arc of Netto's swing, she jabbed him in the solar plexus with the butt of her spear. There was a rubber cap affixed there, which she told Mr. Fisk was to protect the aging wood. It was really intended to soften the blows she inflicted in these sessions.

Netto went down, dropping his cudgel. She kicked it out of his reach, then took a step back and did the same with Lenny's weapon. It flew out of the ring. Amal turned to face her, and so it was one-on-one. A six-four, 240-pound slab of experienced muscle against a 22-year-old woman over whom he towered and who was half his weight. She saw it in Amal's eyes, too. Now that it was just the two of them, he was resigned to whatever pain came his way.

○————————○

WILSON Fisk stood in the shadows, near the glass window that overlooked his city. Watching the girl work, he allowed himself a smile.

She was a tool, of course, like the rest. He would use her as best suited his purposes, yet he took a particular pleasure in Maya Lopez. She'd been nothing when he found her, a wild, brutal, undisciplined victim, lost in the city's useless system. He'd made her into not his most formidable weapon, but certainly his most interesting one.

It was the piano. That's what had convinced him. He'd ordered one of his men to keep an eye on her after her father died. She was 14 years old, sucked into the foster system where neglect, cruelty, and apathy brought out her most brutal and dangerous impulses. Though she was only a child, Fisk did not want to take any chances. Would she discover the truth? Would she seek revenge? He had to make sure she didn't become a problem.

His man had shown him the edited surveillance video. The girl fighting for scraps to eat, fending off the advances of her foster father, of her foster brothers, with near-lethal results. He'd also seen her tenderly speaking in sign language to another deaf girl, one less capable of defending herself from the bullies and predators all around them. There was something human still there, but those manic eyes suggested it could not survive long.

"She's dangerous," Fisk's man had said. *"Maybe the best thing to do would be to take her out."*

Then he'd seen her at the piano. It was a wreck, out of tune, some of the keys broken, but she'd played Chopin. The third piano sonata, a notoriously difficult piece, and—faults of the instrument aside— she played it flawlessly. More than that, there was beauty and passion in her playing. A girl who had been born deaf, who could play like a virtuoso.

"I'm her new foster parent," he'd told his man. "Make the arrangements."

It took less than a week.

Away from the constant torment and fear, and finally given the space to grieve for her father, Maya had blossomed. She was more amazing than he could have imagined. How had she learned to play the piano? She'd seen a musician on the television play. Once. That was all it took. She could mirror any movement she saw.

She was among his most treasured creations. He still had no idea how he would use her, but her potential, and her loyalty, were bottomless.

He watched as his three men picked themselves up. They were bruised but not seriously hurt. The girl showed reluctance to actually hurt anyone. That could be a problem. He'd have to find a way to encourage a more ruthless approach. Until she proved she was ready, he couldn't risk revealing to her the full scope of his business.

"Again," he told them. "Netto, I didn't see you holding back, did I?"

"No way, boss." The man shook his shaved head. "You said no holds barred, and that's how we're playing it."

Fisk doubted it. The men loved her. They treated her like a kid sister. It might be best to bring in people who didn't know her for these fights, but then he might lose quality. For now, it was enough to let them know he was watching. They might not want to hurt her, but they'd want to cross Fisk even less.

"You mustn't restrain yourself with them either," he told Maya, when he knew he had eye contact with her. "They know as well as you that in life there is no escape from a checkmate."

She nodded, and the next round began. Fisk was convinced Maya could have dropped the three of them in less than thirty seconds, yet she was taking about two minutes per fight. Part of it was because she liked to control the pace. He understood that. But it was also to spare them the humiliation, and so she set up her blows to avoid doing any serious harm.

So strong in some ways, yet still plagued by sentimental weakness.

Hoang, his third-shift secretary, entered the gym, striding purposefully as though he weren't terrified. Never a good sign. No one liked to deliver bad news to a boss—and to this boss in particular.

"What is it?" Fisk demanded.

Hoang took an instant to plant himself, and then delivered the news with his best business-school efficiency.

"Damn it!" Fisk roared. He raised his fist and cocked back. Then Hoang trembled before him. If he delivered the blow, it would kill the secretary—but Fisk was learning to control his temper. It was something he had to accomplish if he was going to convince the world that he was a different sort of man. For his plans to work, he could never slip up in public, and the first step to not slipping in public was to not slip in private. He needed to be strong enough to withhold his strength.

He lowered his arm. "I'll deal with it," he told Hoang, waving the man away. Did Hoang know how close he'd come? The old Fisk wouldn't have hesitated, but the new Fisk had a media image to maintain. Rumors of workplace brutality weren't going to do him any good. His place in the world had changed.

He returned his gaze to the sparring ring. Amal and Lenny were down, but Netto was still on his feet. He was standing directly behind Maya, who had watched the exchange with Hoang.

Instantly Fisk locked eyes with Netto, who knew what he'd done. Terror appeared in his eyes.

"Boss," he said. He backed up, holding his hands palms-out, as if that would help him.

"What did I tell you?" Fisk said, approaching like an angered bull. "You do *not* hold back." Netto continued to back away, stumbled, and fell on his ass.

"She got distracted," Netto protested. "I'm not going to hit a deaf—"

That was as far as he got. Fisk raised one of his enormous feet and brought it down on Netto's knee. The cracking sound reverberated across the gym, and then the screaming.

THAT'S who he is, Maya told herself, but he's getting

better. For a moment she thought Mr. Fisk would keep stomping, and maybe there was a time when he would have, but he had himself under control now. He was learning to be a better person. *So much anger, yet he does so many good things.*

Poor Netto. He would be out for weeks, maybe longer. He might never be able to spar again. Mr. Fisk would take care of him, though. He was good about that sort of thing. Netto's daughters would never know how close they had come to losing their father, but they hadn't lost him. They hadn't gone through what Maya had. They'd been spared.

Once she thought about it that way, she decided she would never think about it again. She would lock it away with all the other things best not remembered.

What did Mr. Hoang tell him? What had upset Mr. Fisk?

Sometimes he confided in her. Sometimes he didn't. Maya didn't like to be left out—she would never betray Mr. Fisk's trust in her. At the same time, she didn't think she could be of use to him if he kept her in the dark about so many things. Mr. Fisk was all about compartmentalizing. He was ruthless in business, tender with his wife, indifferent to the suffering of competitors, generous with strangers. He would do anything for Maya and yet, with someone like Netto, who had been a loyal employee for years—

But no. That was something she had decided to put away. Returning to her suite in Fisk Tower, she went into the bathroom and reached into the shower stall to start the water, but then curiosity got the better of her. She could shower later.

Maya woke up her laptop and let her fingers dance over the keys, digging up the hidden program and entering the string of passwords. Then the feeds were live.

She admitted to herself that it was wrong to spy on Mr. Fisk, the man who had rescued her, who had given her everything. She told herself she only wanted information, so she could be of better use to Mr. Fisk. Also, she was just plain curious. Why did he hide so much from her? Did he think she wasn't ready? She knew he had a dark side. She knew he would blur the line between right and wrong in order to serve the greater good. She could help him if he would let her.

Maya could help him make better choices.

She was sure of it.

There were three cameras hidden in Mr. Fisk's office, but the feed had its limits—the angles could be tricky, and that meant she couldn't always read lips. She had an idea of adding a hidden microphone and connecting it to voice-recognition software. Yet more technology meant more risk, and she hated to think what would happen if Mr. Fisk found out about her surveillance.

He was alone there now, sitting, holding a glass of water in one hand, looking at a video feed on his own computer. Maya was able to zoom in to get a better view of what had his attention. It looked like surveillance footage. Filtered through her own camera, the feed was fuzzy at best, and it took Maya a moment to sort it out.

It looked like the roof of a construction site. Two figures were fighting, but this wasn't normal fighting. They were leaping in the air, spinning, covering impossible distances. One of the figures was dressed all in black. The other...

The other was the man who had murdered her father.

SEVEN

SHE barged in without knocking.

Still sweaty from her sparring, and still wearing her athletic clothes, Maya looked out of place in his large and cheerless office. Most likely she wanted to talk about what he'd done to that fool who couldn't follow orders. The girl was too soft-hearted. She wasn't ruthless in the way he needed her to be. There was still time to mold her, though. He felt certain she would become what he needed.

Fisk reached to turn off the video feed, but it was too late. She had already seen it. The expression on her face told him all he needed to know.

"What is that?"

"I've asked you to knock," he said.

She was kind-hearted, but not soft. She deflected his deflection without missing a beat. Moving around to the side of the desk—as if this was her space as much as his—she gestured toward the video screen.

"Is this what Mr. Hoang came in to tell you about?"

"It's not important." Fisk switched off the monitor and turned to see if she would defy him.

"It's important to me," Maya insisted. She pointed an accusing finger at the now blank video screen. "That… that *thing* killed my father."

"And we will bring Spider-Man to justice," Fisk said. "I've promised you that, but we must wait for the right time. With everything we have in play, an all-out battle with a costumed vigilante isn't in our best interests. Once we've achieved our goals, when we have the power and influence to do as we please, then we will crush him. I've given you my word, and I intend to keep it."

"Who was he fighting?" Maya demanded. "That man in black moved just like him."

Even recalling her uncanny powers of observation, he was surprised that she had seen so much, so quickly. She could recall anything she'd even glimpsed, recreate any image in the smallest detail, but this was something new. Perhaps for her a fleeting image was like a photograph that could be studied from every angle. Was her mind truly so acute?

Fisk sighed inwardly. This wasn't something that should involve her. He wanted her to remain passionate in her hatred of Spider-Man, but sometimes that passion, that single-minded focus, became more a burden than an advantage. Yet boxing her out at this point would do more harm than good.

"Close the door and have a seat," he told her. "I'll tell you everything."

○━━━━━━━━━━━○

HER gambit worked.

She worried that she'd let slip too much, but Mr. Fisk seemed not to notice. He regarded her ability to observe and remember and mimic as a kind of magic, and anything she did with those tools seemed possible.

Once she sat, Mr. Fisk pressed a button to turn on the monitor. He hit a few keys and began the feed from the beginning. Maya watched intently, learning, remembering. She was only vaguely aware of how the air felt cool against her damp skin. When it was done, she turned to him again.

"Spider-Man is a problem that is not going to go away," he said, "until we make him go away."

"And I will be part of that," she said. "You told me so."

"You will be," he assured her. "After what he did to your father, you know I would never take any final action without your involvement. We will expose his crimes and we will see him punished—but at the right time."

"Then who is that man in the feed?" she asked. "He moves just like Spider-Man."

Though she didn't say it aloud, Maya knew that *she* could move just like Spider-Man as well. She couldn't cling to walls, and she couldn't shoot webs, but she could match him blow for blow, punch for punch. When the time came to face her enemy, he would not be able to touch her—but she could touch *him*. She had watched every clip of him she could find, and knew his fighting style better than he did.

It was at the level of instinct now.

"The man in black is someone I've found, someone I've trained to match Spider-Man," Mr. Fisk said.

"*I've* trained to match him," Maya countered.

"Indeed, your abilities inspired me to pursue this approach, but I don't want you exposed. Especially not now, when I need you by my side. This… contractor will absorb all of Spider-Man's attention, while we focus our efforts in other areas."

"How did you train him to leap like that?" Maya asked. "His abilities—"

"I have many interests, many investments, some in countries with more relaxed laws concerning medical experimentation," he said, interrupting her. "I would never allow you to be subjected to the same processes, Maya. You are important to me. This man is nothing—a tool to be used and, if need be, used up."

She steadied her dark eyes on him.

"What is his name?"

Mr. Fisk sighed. "I would refuse to tell you, but if you want to know, you'll find out. Your tenacity can be a trial, though it's what makes you so valuable. The man's name is Michael Bingham." He gestured toward the computer. "If I agree to send you a redacted file on him, will you let the matter drop?"

Maya gave this some thought, and nodded her head. She didn't know if she meant it, though. At that moment, she would have said anything to learn more.

"I'll email you the documents tonight," he said. "In exchange, I want you to keep away from him. He is dangerous. From what I know, he was never quite stable, but the training he underwent has further unbalanced him."

"Of course," she said. *Let the record show*, she thought, *that I haven't actually agreed to anything.*

"Until we achieve our goals, Spider-Man is Bingham's problem, not yours."

Maya nodded. She rose from her seat and moved to open the door, but first she turned back to her mentor.

"When Mr. Hoang brought you the news about this, why were you so upset?"

His mouth twitched in that way that said he was trying to hold his temper.

"Mr. Hoang brought me news about something else." She started to speak, and he held up a hand to stop her. "An import agreement with the Russians. Nothing you need concern yourself with."

He was lying. When she'd checked on him, just minutes after they left the gym, he'd been reviewing the video—not grappling with oligarchs. Bingham might be a solution, but he was also a problem. That much was clear.

Maya would review the documents when she received them, and then she'd decide her next move. Despite her loyalty, nothing was off the table—not where Spider-Man was concerned.

EIGHT

"IS the work boring you?" Theodore Peyton asked.

"I'm awake!" Peter jumped and sat up at his workstation, pushing away sleep. As he began to focus, he let the humiliation wash over him.

How much easier it would be, he thought, if he didn't have to conceal his life as Spider-Man. All those times his Aunt May thought he was forgetful or unreliable or flighty—wouldn't it be refreshing to tell her he hadn't forgotten to run that errand, or meet her at the bus. No, he'd been saving lives! All those times Harry thought he didn't take their friendship seriously. And now the lab administrator thought he had been out partying too late to get a good night's sleep.

Even on a Sunday, Theodore Peyton was wearing a suit with a bow tie pulled tight enough for the edges to slice bread—maybe even saw through wood. He was thin and tall, and with his severely parted hair and round little eyeglasses, he looked like a nineteenth-century schoolteacher. Not a nice one, either. The kind of schoolteacher who liked to whack his students with a stick for not conjugating their Greek fast enough.

Peyton, like Peter, was a scientist—but he was also in charge of the lab's finances, so it could never be predicted if he was going to be wearing a lab coat over his suit or sitting in a corner somewhere balancing numbers on a spreadsheet.

The lab's director—the man who had been Peter's mentor in science since his undergraduate days—was in charge of the real science, but Theodore ran the business end of things. He pinched the pennies, and made sure he wrung every last bit of work out of the underpaid employees. Peter put up with it because he loved the boss and he believed in the science, but there were times when he wasn't sure if that was enough.

"I'm sure there are places you'd rather be on a sunny Sunday afternoon," Peyton droned. "Science may not be sufficiently glamorous for you. That said, we don't pay you to sleep here."

It wasn't as if Peter was getting paid by the hour, and he'd put in at least sixty hours in the past week. He'd come in because there was work to be done, and he was glad to do it—at least abstractly. He did agree with Peyton on one point, though. There were places he'd rather be.

The lab was like a larger, more scientific version of Peter's apartment. There were workstations, mechanical equipment, computer monitors, tools, and prototypes in various stages of completion. They were everywhere. The place had a mad scientist vibe if ever there was one.

"Point made, Theodore," Peter said. "I was just up late, but I'll get back to work."

"Trouble sleeping again?" Peyton asked, but there wasn't a hint of kindness. Peter had been using that excuse for as long as he'd worked in the lab.

Peyton wasn't buying it now, if he ever had.

The thing was, Peter really didn't mind working on a Sunday. New data had come in from their synthetic neural relay tests, and numbers had to be crunched. Peter loved the work. It was exciting, and it was important. The place was on the forefront of the science that would lead to sensitive, fully functional prosthetic limbs. They were doing things that no one had ever done before, things that would make a difference for millions of people. The applications for wounded veterans alone would be staggering.

Being Spider-Man was important, but this was different.

Peter had never asked for his amazing abilities. He'd never yearned to be a costumed crime-fighter. He'd *always* wanted to be a scientist, though. Sure, with great power there also came great responsibility, but wasn't an aptitude for science a great power? Didn't he have a responsibility to pursue his abilities here as vigorously as he did on the street?

He loved being Spider-Man—most of the time. In a way, Peter never felt more liberated than when he was in that suit. Lately, though, he'd begun to worry that being a web-slinger wasn't just part of his life, but getting in the way of his life. He spent so much of his time fighting bad guys, and those bad guys always seemed to come back.

Of course, he'd saved a lot of lives but if he'd stayed home and watched television last night, Andy would still be alive. What about the people who suffered when nutcases like Electro or the Scorpion or the Shocker came gunning for him? Was Spider-Man a deterrent, or a magnet for the crazies? By being out there, was he making things worse?

"If you're not up to the task," Peyton said, bringing him back down to earth, "I could replace you with someone who is willing to dedicate their time to this important work."

"There's no need to dip into the endless pool of scientific slave labor," Peter said. "Give me half an hour, and I'll have the data ready."

THIRTY minutes later, with the work done, Peter walked into Peyton's office and found him reviewing computer models that represented artificial neural pathways.

"The results have been uploaded," Peter told him.

Peyton nodded and then opened a new file on his computer. His slender fingers began flying across the keyboard as he located the data Peter had generated and integrated it with the model he was running. Peter watched as animated arms appeared on the screen, then attached themselves to animated stumps. Flowing lights—representing the transfer of data from the subject's brain to the artificial limbs—began to flow down the arms and back again. A few more keystrokes, and the hands clenched and unclenched.

"You seem to have managed to get the job done," Peyton said. "I hope your nap time wasn't too severely inconvenienced."

"The boss's work is amazing," Peter said. He hardly even heard Peyton's snide comments anymore. "This is exciting stuff."

"Yes," Peyton agreed. "I have to admit, you contribute a great deal to the effort, Parker. Your mind is first-rate, you know. I have no complaints about your abilities. It's your efforts I find wanting. You must remember that we are serving a higher cause here, and I'd hate to see sloppy work habits get in the way. You truly are your own worst enemy."

Given the kinds of enemies he'd made over the years, Peter wished this were true. He'd rather face himself than the Rhino pretty much any day.

"Point taken, Ted."

"My name is Theodore, as you well know, and your glib responses will not insulate you from the larger point. Anyone else would have been gone a long time ago, but the director likes you, and you add value when you make an honest effort."

Peter had been so caught up in watching the computer models on the screen—and ignoring Peyton—that he hadn't noticed that someone else had entered the lab. He wished, not for the first time, that his Spider-Sense would tingle for embarrassing situations as well as danger, because he felt pretty sure that this attractive young woman had heard him getting chewed out.

"Ah, excellent," Peyton said when he spotted the woman. "Peter, this is the new undergraduate assistant, Anika Adhikari. She is, among other things, technologically competent, and she will provide assistance for our data analysis. Anika, this is Peter Parker, former undergraduate assistant, now an employee."

"You make it sound so exciting," Peter said.

"Hi," she said, grinning noncommittally. Peyton, as usual, was oblivious to the awkwardness of the moment.

"Peter, please show Anika around," he suggested. "Get her familiar with the lab and maybe have her start collating the test results from the models I just ran. That should help bring her up to speed. The sooner we can put her to productive use, the better."

"Will do," Peter said.

He was just going to have to pretend he didn't notice how insanely pretty she was. Not that she was trying. Her long dark hair was tied in a loose ponytail. She wore old jeans and—in the category of things that definitely didn't help—a faded Spider-Man T-shirt. No matter how rumpled she'd managed to make herself, it didn't do much to conceal those enormous brown eyes, and a heart-shaped face that seemed to radiate kindness.

"Sorry I heard you get raked over the coals," she told him as they walked away from the office. "I mean, I heard it, and you know I heard it, so it's best to get your embarrassment out in the open, right?"

"And you're in the sciences, you say?" Peter countered.

She laughed. "You got me. I just hate awkward situations. I know the project's lead scientist thinks highly of you, but that guy…"

"Theodore Peyton," Peter said, "but more like 'Pain-ton.' Am I right?"

"That's the best you can do?"

"Hey, I'm warming up here," he replied. "He's actually not a terrible guy, but he lives to balance budgets and squeeze every last drop out of our resources. Sometimes I want to strangle him, but the fact is we'd have a hard time keeping the lights on without him."

"And he thinks you're a slacker," she said with an easy grin. "Got it. Now let's see the cool stuff."

"Cool stuff it is," Peter agreed as he began to show her around the lab. "It's quiet today, being Sunday and all, but more often than not a lot of the action happens at nights and on the weekends. I'll give you my number, in case you need to reach me then. The boss pretty much never goes home, never sleeps, and never stops working. He's relentless, which is great and scary and intimidating. If you're here, it's because you're super smart, but when he starts talking, you're going to feel like he made a mistake and you're out of your league. Resist this feeling. It's a rite of passage. Besides, unlike Peyton, he's really nice, and he doesn't do it to make you feel small."

"Believe me, I'm ready to be humbled," she said. "I've read his papers on theoretical electroencephalography. I still can't believe I got the internship."

"Where do you go to school?"

"Empire State University," she said.

"My alma mater," Peter told her. "Cool T-shirt, by the way."

"I'm wearing it ironically," she said. "Scientists are the real super heroes."

"They stand among them, yes," Peter replied. "Anyhow, that's the kitchen in there. Don't eat the frozen granola bars. Peyton loves them for some reason, and he always knows exactly how many are supposed to be there."

"Not much of a chance, but thanks for the heads-up."

Once they'd finished the tour of the lab, Peter sat her down at a workstation, set her up with a login and a password, and showed her the files on which she was going to work.

"We'll start with something basic," he said. "Nothing you do today is going to challenge you, but it'll help get you familiar with the terms of the work, which will make it easier for you to dive into the good stuff. Keep that in mind when you're thinking about all the better things you could be doing with a Sunday afternoon."

"If I weren't here, I'd be studying," she said. "That's life in the city." She paused for an awkward moment. "How about you? Do anything fun last night? Hot date?"

This was the time to mention MJ. That would be the right thing, but it would also be a little awkward because they both knew she was fishing, and he didn't want to shut her down.

"Just hung out with a friend."

There'd be plenty of time to tell her his story.

Later.

NINE

MJ LIKED how quickly things moved in journalism. It suited her.

She'd spent most of Sunday writing and rewriting and rewriting some more, and early Sunday evening she'd sent her piece to Robbie Robertson at the *Bugle*. His secretary called Monday morning to say Mr. Robertson wanted to meet with her that afternoon.

Here it was, 2:05—less than twenty-four hours after submitting—and she was standing outside the editor-in-chief's office.

"He's running a little behind," the secretary told her, "but not as behind as usual, which means he's running ahead. So you're in luck. It should only be a few more minutes."

MJ didn't mind. If half an hour later she was still sitting here, politely sipping burned and cold coffee from a chipped Styrofoam cup, she might mind then, but not yet. For the moment she was soaking in the journalistic energy all around her. The phones ringing, the voices shouting, the endless clacking of fingers on keyboards.

A woman ran through the newsroom clutching a sheaf of papers. It was like something from a movie, and she knew that nothing extraordinary was happening at that moment. There were no political upheavals, no superhuman battles in Times Square, no scandals bursting wide open. Just another day at the races, and soon—maybe tomorrow—she'd be part of it.

She had to think so. Mr. Robertson wasn't going to call her in, waste her time and his, just to let her know that she hadn't done well enough. He was going to offer her a job. That had to be it. She was going to be a writer for one of the most important papers in New York City.

MJ had written for her high-school paper, and then for the paper at ESU, where she'd studied journalism. Yet somehow, after graduation she hadn't immediately tried to land a job. Her life had been crazy, in large part because she'd been Peter's girlfriend. That would sound pathetic for any other woman, but Peter needed help. He needed a full-time manager, if she was going to be honest, and she'd tried to step in and fill that role because he was off saving the city on an almost weekly basis.

Having a front-row seat to Spider-Man's heroics had been thrilling at first. It was thrilling now, but there was more she wanted to do—things she wanted to accomplish on her own.

Through it all she'd kept writing—mostly freelance pieces for the city's numerous weeklies, and some investigative long-form pieces she'd placed in some high-profile online publications. That had been a step toward a larger goal. Online journalism could be a solitary existence, and she wanted the buzz of the newsroom, that coiled feeling of something uncontainable about to break free. She wanted to be on the front lines of what mattered, digging up the truth.

Truth be told, it was hard to be around someone like Peter—who made a difference every day—and not want to make a difference yourself.

"You're MJ, right?"

She looked up to find a familiar-looking woman grinning at her. The woman had dark hair, a serious expression, and she was holding her hand out.

"Let me take that for you," she said, looking at the coffee cup. "Everyone's too busy around here to notice that they're giving you coffee from Friday. I hope you didn't drink too much."

MJ surrendered the cup, trying to fight the sour feeling in her stomach.

"Not as much as I might have," she said, standing, "but more than I should have. Have we met...?"

"Betty Brant," she said with an easy smile. "I remember you from when Peter Parker used to take photos for us. You're his wife, right?"

Her hands now free of the cold coffee, MJ held them up as if to ward something off.

"Don't rush it," she said wryly. "Girlfriend."

"Robbie passed your piece over to me." Brant shifted the conversation without missing a beat. "He was that impressed. I'm an editor at the city desk, so I took a look at it." She paused, then added, "I have to say, he was right."

"Wow," MJ replied. "Thank you."

Brant nodded. "He's going to offer you a job. I read some of your work in *Breakthrough* and *Wrecker*, so I know features isn't where you want to spend the rest of your life. This job is a foot in the door, so don't sweat it. I started out answering phones and typing memos, so believe me when I say hard work and a passion for news will get you noticed."

MJ felt herself blushing. After spending so much time in Peter's shadow, it was great to be noticed for being herself.

"It's very nice of you to say all that."

Betty laughed. "I'm being selfish, though. Though things have improved a lot since I started, journalism is still kind of an old boys' club. Our previous editor, J. Jonah Jameson, didn't consider change a priority. Mr. Robertson's a whole lot better, but I still want to stack the decks with as many badass ladies as possible." She raised the coffee cup in salute, and then dropped it into a trash can. "You need anything, let me know."

As she turned to leave, Robertson's secretary motioned MJ over.

○────────────○

"I like this a great deal," Robbie Robertson said. He was in his early forties, graying at the fringes, glasses sliding down his nose. He had the look of a man who had seen it all, like he came from journalism central casting. Despite that, there was a friendly crinkle at the corners of his eyes.

He had printed out her piece, a clear sign that

he'd come of age before going paperless became second nature. Notes and underlines and comments, all in red pen, filled the margins and spaces. She didn't mind being edited—she *liked* being edited by someone with a good eye—but there was close to being more note than text on the page.

"You're a talented writer," he said, "though there are some passages that feel forced, like you're gunning for a Pulitzer. Nothing wrong with swinging for the fences, but you still need to keep things crisp and clean. Let the story win the prizes, and not the flowery language."

"Of course," she began. "I still have a lot to learn…"

He waved her comment away. "Yes, you do," he agreed. "So do I. I've been in this business a long time, and I'd never think of printing a word that hadn't been slapped around by a smart editor with a bug up his ass. Or hers. If you don't like to be told you can do it better, the *Bugle* is the wrong place for you."

"I understand—"

"The job is for a features writer," he said. "You'll be running down specific assignments, but there will be time for you to pursue your own leads. *Features* leads, Miss Watson. I recognize an opening move when I see one." He gave her a meaningful look. "I've read your online pieces. You want to go after Fisk, don't you?"

"There's an angle," she said. "I'm sure of—"

"Look, I've got a whole building full of people who want to go after Fisk," Robertson said. "And they've put in their time, built their credibility. As much as I need hard news, we also need to fill pages with exercise fads and organic farmers' markets and the latest trends in SAT prep. *That's* the job I'm offering. It's *not* chasing down the Kingpin of Crime." He rose from his seat. "That's someone else's job, and if you're doing someone else's job, you won't be doing what we hired you to do." That look again. "Are we perfectly clear on that?"

"Perfectly," MJ said, meeting his eye. She understood the rules of the game, but she wasn't going to let herself be intimidated.

He smiled, and she relaxed a bit.

"Do what we hire you to do, do it well, and you *will* rise through the ranks. The best always do." He handed her the marked-up story. "You're not the best, Miss Watson, but you're very good, and I expect you to get better. There's no reason you can't be the best, eventually, but you have to put in the time and the work and pay the dues."

"Yes, sir," she said, rising to stand in front of him. "Thank you, sir."

"Robbie, unless I'm mad at you," he said, "which I am not… currently. Now read my notes, learn from what's helpful and ignore them where I'm wrong. Be here at eight o'clock tomorrow, check in with my secretary, and please close the door on your way out."

MJ smiled, clutched the printout, and left.

She'd done it. She'd landed the job.

It wasn't exactly the job she wanted, but she was on her way. And she completely understood Mr.

Robertson… *Robbie's* point about needing her to do features. That was why she'd been hired, and she'd do what she was hired to do. She would do it well.

As for what she did in her own time…

BETTY Brant poked her head into Robbie Robertson's office.

"I have a good feeling about her," she said.

"She's going to be a pain in my ass," he said. Then he flashed a grin. "So, yeah, me too."

TEN

SHE'D been there since just before sundown, binoculars around her neck, dressed to be ready for anything—black exercise leggings and a long-sleeved spandex top. The leather parkour gloves exposed her fingers, allowing for precision, but protected her palms from rough or jagged surfaces.

While preparing herself, Maya had been thinking about her dreams. In them, she bore the handprint on her face. Perhaps it could become a trademark—*her* trademark, like her hated foe's spider symbol, black on his chest. She'd dismissed the idea, yet she couldn't let go of it altogether.

She had a bag of raw cashews, in case she needed a quick high-protein snack, and two bottles of water because dehydration made her sleepy. She couldn't afford to let her guard down. Not with this guy.

The skyline loomed in the background as she trained her binoculars on the apartment window. The file Fisk had given her had been more than a little redacted. It contained Bingham's name, his nearest living relatives, where he'd gone to school, and little else. Even his address had been excised.

Fortunately, Maya knew her way around the system. Fishing for more information was a good way to be found out, but locating an original version of a redacted document was fairly easy, and likely to go unnoticed. The unexpurgated version hadn't told her much more, though.

In the two hours she'd been camped out, she'd caught a couple of glimpses of him, but nothing of substance. Maybe what she was doing was absurd. Mr. Fisk had asked her to leave it alone, and so she ought to do as he asked. He had his flaws—she knew that—but she trusted him to act in her best interests. He might try to conceal things from her, but he would never do anything that might harm her.

Still, why did he need someone else who could move like Spider-Man? Did he not trust her to do what needed to be done? Did he think she would be unwilling to do what he required her to do?

Sometimes Mr. Fisk hurt people. She'd visited Netto in the hospital just that afternoon, and it had served as an unwelcome reminder of his temper. Despite his own tendencies, however, Mr. Fisk had never asked her to hurt anyone.

Then why all the training?

Did he think she wasn't ready?

Life wasn't black and white. It was gray, and she had faith—absolute faith—that if Mr. Fisk wanted someone to be hurt, they needed to be hurt. Because she knew that, she could be the right hand he needed her to be. All she had to do was show him how far she was willing to go to further his cause.

Yes, his methods could be brutal, but this was a

brutal world. Maya knew that more than anyone, and Mr. Fisk was making the city better, more prosperous, more livable for everyone—not just the rich and the privileged. It was a mission worth pursuing. It wasn't simply good, it was *just*, and Maya was prepared to do what was needed for the cause.

If hurting Spider-Man was part of the package, then that was just a bonus.

Mr. Fisk often said that he thought Maya could do anything, that he never factored in her deafness when considering her potential. Yet here she was, on the sidelines, while some stranger was doing what ought to be her job. Not only doing it, but doing it in a way that somehow infuriated Mr. Fisk.

Why would he allow that?

She would find out what this man was up to, and she would show Mr. Fisk that there was nothing he couldn't trust her to do for him. She would show him that whatever this Bingham person could do, she could do it better.

o———————o

AN hour later, Bingham climbed out his window. Wearing a Spider-Man suit.

It was a good one, too. Thanks to her Oscorp military-grade binoculars, it was as if she was standing two feet in front of him. The suit looked real—like a second skin, the way the real Web-Slinger's suit looked. The colors were right, but there were a few imperfections. The web lines were a little too close together, though she doubted anyone without her skills would notice.

Spider-Man himself probably couldn't tell the difference.

So why hadn't Bingham worn this suit during the fight at the construction site? What was he up to now? She watched as he leapt off the fire escape, shot off a strand of some sort and swung off into the night.

Well, there's only one way to find out…

She set the binoculars down, broke into a run, and leapt to the adjacent roof.

IT wasn't easy keeping up with him. Bingham moved fast—faster than she could, though if she'd had access to web shooters, they'd have been on more even ground. She tried not to think about that. Mr. Fisk had access to web-shooting technology, and he'd given it to Bingham.

Not to her.

This isn't the time for that, she thought. Her focus had to be on following Bingham. Besides, it was better when her doubts shut down, and she could live in the burn of her muscles. This was going to take everything she had.

New York did not provide a continuous supply of level roofs, which meant tailing a guy who could swing from building to building presented challenges. Maya leapt from the top of a building to a fire escape, scrambled up to another roof, dashed across the top, and hurled herself to grab onto a drainage pipe, barely taking the time to hope it was properly affixed. She bounded over air-conditioning units and crumbling brick walls. She clambered up a wall using windowsills and missing bricks as handholds.

Fortunately, he didn't go far. There was a side street with an Italian wine bar that offered outdoor seating. Bingham clung to a wall—something else she couldn't do—and watched, as Maya crouched in the shadows. Nothing much happened until a panhandler came by, asking the upscale wine bar patrons for a handout.

Bingham leapt into action. He swung down and pointed his web shooters at the panhandler. With a *thwap* the man was hurled across the street and webbed against the side of a building. Patrons screamed in horror and surprise. One indignant woman began to shout at Bingham to stop assaulting the poor man. He didn't pause, though. Without a word he jumped upward, webbing his way into the night.

Instantly Maya was on her feet, intent on keeping up. She *had* to see what came next.

YET that was it. Bingham went back to his apartment, entering the way he'd gone out, through the fire-escape window.

What's his game?

What could he hope to accomplish?

Bullying some homeless guy wasn't exactly going to bring Spider-Man to his knees. A handful of people might decide that he wasn't the hero they thought he was. The story might make the newspapers, though that was less likely now that J. Jonah Jameson wasn't at the *Bugle*. He'd been the one journalist willing to call Spider-Man out.

So, if it hadn't been about dealing a blow to Spider-Man's reputation, what had been the point? Was it the panhandler himself? Unlikely. If those webs were like the real thing, they'd dissolve soon enough. Otherwise the cops would cut him down.

Whatever this was—a trial run, an equipment test—it couldn't be an endgame. And that meant the real plot was yet to come.

○————————○

MAYA had two options—stealth, or the direct approach.

She'd already collected a lot of information. More than likely, she ought to go home, do a little more digging around, perhaps even confront Mr. Fisk with what she'd learned. He might be impressed with her tenacity, her ability to keep up with a man who possessed superior abilities or technology, or both. Yes, the best thing to do would be to call it a night.

Forget that.

If she opted for stealth, she could try sneaking into Bingham's apartment. That didn't seem viable, though. A pizza delivery guy had arrived shortly after he'd returned, and that suggested a night in. Besides, while Maya didn't like to limit herself, and she believed she could do anything a person with hearing could do, she wasn't unrealistic. No, breaking into a man's apartment while he was home would be foolish.

That left the direct approach.

ELEVEN

IT was a truth universally acknowledged that a man with pizza would want something to drink. She knocked on his front door holding a six-pack of SwillCo cola.

He came to the door wearing a tank top and sweatpants. He wasn't a huge guy, but he was wiry and covered with a defined layer of muscle. He had a low forehead with thick eyebrows that came dangerously close to touching, a wide nose that had clearly been broken more than a few times, and thin bloodless lips.

It was the eyes that struck her most, though. They were pale blue, and small and strangely cloudy. As if he was thinking about something else, even while trying to process the meaning of the beverage-laden stranger at his door.

Maya gave him her best smile. She wasn't exactly dressed to impress, and she hated—absolutely hated—using her looks to sway men. On the other hand, there was nothing wrong with being friendly.

"I thought you could use a drink to go with that pizza."

He squinted at her, and looked as if his mind was a thousand miles away.

"You a neighbor or something?" He stuck his

head out of the door and looked around. "I don't like neighbors. I don't like nosey neighbors especially."

"I'm not a neighbor," Maya said, keeping the smile going but thinking this might have been a really bad idea. Still, she'd started it, so she might as well go for broke. "I'm just a person who thought you might have worked up a big thirst swinging around the city."

There was a blur of movement, the bags clamored to the floor, and she was inside Bingham's apartment. Her arm hurt. She was backed against a wall—he had grabbed her, lashed out like a viper, and pulled her inside. One of the soda cans had cracked open and its hissing contents pooled on the floor.

Bingham slammed the door shut and spun to face her. His eyes were no longer cloudy, no longer distant.

"Who sent you?" he demanded, moving closer.

Maya was in her element. She'd seen him fight—on the video-camera feed. It hadn't been much, but it had been enough. He swung at her, hurling a fist like a barroom brawler, but connected only with air. As he turned she was in his blind spot, behind him, dealing a sharp blow to his kidneys. He let out a hissing breath and staggered forward.

Maya took a step back and held up her hands.

"I just brought drinks," she said. "I'm not here to hurt you."

Then she looked around. There was something weird about this apartment. There was no real furniture—just some plastic folding chairs and a table. The pizza box was propped on one of the chairs. No television, no books or magazines. Nothing to keep him busy except clear plastic stacking boxes, and they held very peculiar things.

A container of paper clips, another of rubber bands, a third of unused hotel soap bars. And those were the less disturbing ones. There were containers of dirt, of frayed shoelaces, of crumpled balls of tissue. There were jars, too. Some of them contained liquid of various shades of yellow. Maya didn't want to think about those. Another contained what had to be hundreds of dead cockroaches.

Under no circumstances did she want to be in an enclosed space with a cockroach collector.

Without saying a word he came at her again, fast and deadly. Like her father's killer, he had incredible skills, but he fought much more conventionally. He lashed out with a fist. She made as if to return the punch, but stepped back instead. She wasn't there to prove herself. She wasn't there to beat him. She wanted information. If she damaged him, it might make Mr. Fisk very, very angry with her.

"Stop. We're on the same side," she said. "I work for Mr. Fisk. Just like you." Bingham took another swing at her but caught only air. He then stopped.

And *laughed*.

"How do you do that?" he asked, his body language a little more relaxed.

"I'm fast," she said. "We're both fast, right?" She wasn't nearly as fast as he was, but she could fight a whole lot smarter than this guy. If she had access to his technology, to his "training"—whatever that had been—she could only imagine the things she could accomplish. Avenging her father was at the top of the list. Making Spider-Man pay was the first thing she would do, but after that—she could be whatever Mr. Fisk needed her to be.

He stood and lowered his hands, keeping them clenched into fists, she observed.

"Who are you again?" Bingham asked. The fight over, he turned to grab a slice from the box of pizza. He took a long time choosing his piece, then he snapped around, grinning at her.

"You want one?"

"No thanks." She couldn't imagine eating food that had spent any time in this apartment.

He turned to study the fallen beverages. This seemed to occupy him for some time. Maybe he wasn't as bright as she'd thought. After a moment, he grabbed a can of soda.

"Something to drink?" he said, grinning again.

"I'm good," she said. "Just want to talk."

"You can't hear anything." He smiled broadly. "You're a deafie! You've been watching my lips."

Then it struck her. He'd asked her the same questions—about the pizza and the drinks—when he'd had his back to her, and she hadn't known. Maya didn't make a point of hiding the fact that she was deaf. Let people make of it what they would. If they wanted to underestimate her, they did so at their own peril. Still, she felt as if she'd given up a weakness he could exploit.

"How come you don't have that deaf-person voice?" he asked earnestly, as if it was a reasonable question.

"Because I've worked hard to sound like someone who can hear," she said, crossing her arms. "Now, would you mind if I asked you a few questions?"

"Are you here because *Mr. Fisk* sent you?" he said, tearing a piece out of his pizza as if he was imagining biting someone's head off. "You can tell *Mr. Fisk* that sending his little deaf girl over here wasn't part of the deal."

Maya frowned. This would be a lot easier if they could relax, and she wished Bingham would invite her to sit—though now that she thought about it, she wasn't sure she'd want to sit in any of those chairs.

"I think we got off to a bad start," she suggested.

"I don't know—it was fun when I grabbed you," Bingham said. "Yanked you inside. That was a good start." He scowled. "It wasn't so good after that."

"I just need some information," Maya said. "For Mr. Fisk."

Bingham snorted. "Too bad, because I'm not a Fisk bootlicker. I don't work for him, deaf girl. I'm a contractor. *Con-trac-tor*," he repeated, dragging the word out. "You understand? That means he asks me to do a job. If I want to do it, and the price is right, it'll get done. If I don't like it, I don't do it. That's how it works. But there's nothing I can't do. Did you know that about me? Did you know I'm special?"

"No," Maya said sweetly. "I mean, I'd heard you had an impressive skill set…" She left it at that, to see what he'd say.

"You don't know anything," he replied. "Thief, assassin, safecracker, infiltrator, human dynamo, space explorer. Black ops and wet work. You want it, I've done it. I've been trained." She thought he puffed out his chest a little.

The world was a strange place, but Maya was willing to gamble it all that this guy had never been in space. And what exactly was a human dynamo? Regardless, Mr. Fisk was trusting Bingham to do a job, so she could assume the thieving and safecracking were real.

"So, what was your mission tonight?" she asked. "For Mr. Fisk."

"If you don't know, I ain't gonna tell," he replied belligerently. The grin was long gone. "You're real pretty, but I'm not dumb enough to let anything slip. How do I even know you work for Fisk?"

She took a business card out of her pocket and handed it to him. He stared at it for a moment, then screwed his face up in a smirk.

"Anyone could print these up," he said. "But you know what… I believe you. You want to know why I believe you?"

Because you're a human dynamo?

She just shook her head.

"It's how you talk about him," he continued. "See, people give things away with how they say stuff, and you sound like you'd be happy to spend all day, every day, licking his gigantic shoes. That's how I know you're the real deal. So, what I think is this, *Miss Special Assistant…*" He waved her business card around. "I think you're maybe not as special an assistant as you'd like to be. I think maybe the Kingpin hasn't told you nearly as much as you'd like to know about my business.

"Maybe you asked him and he clammed up," Bingham added. "Maybe you didn't have the guts to ask him. You clearly have guts, but when it comes to him—I ain't so sure. Still, you've got the guts to come here and spy on me, and then ask me about it—go toe-to-toe with a guy who could wipe the floor with you. That's what I think."

Maya narrowed her eyes. Bingham wasn't terribly smart—of that she was certain. At the same time, he had a kind of animal cunning that made him dangerous. It wouldn't do to underestimate him again.

Yet she could use him to her advantage. A person like this, who likely had struggled in school, who had spent his whole life knowing he wasn't smart enough, would have weaknesses she could exploit.

"Very good," she said. Best to soft-pedal it. "You're not wrong, but just because Mr. Fisk hasn't chosen to tell me everything, you don't have to make the same choice. We could come to an understanding." Even she wasn't sure what that might mean, but his reaction could speak volumes.

He snorted. "Nice try," he said, "but I'm not saying anything that might affect me getting paid. I need money… for my things."

"Okay, then at least tell me this," she said. "Where

did you get those moves? How did you learn to imitate Spider-Man, and do it so well?"

"Imitate?" Bingham choked out the word. "I'm not imitating anyone. I *am* Spider-Man."

Maya stared at him, not sure what to say.

"Look—look at this." He lifted his shirt. At first glance he appeared to have a bandage strapped across his stomach. Then she realized it was a pouch, the sort nervous travelers wore when in strange cities, so they wouldn't have to leave their passports in hotel rooms or risk having them stolen out of pockets or backpacks. Bingham reached into the pouch and pulled out an old black-and-white photo, unfolding it. It was brittle and held together by tape, where folds had split long ago. He handed it to her.

The photo showed Spider-Man swinging through Midtown. He was facing toward the camera, as if he knew it was there. There was something about the angle and the composition of the image that made it appear as if he was looking right at the viewer. No, it was something more than that. It felt as if he was looking *into* her.

Maya refolded it quickly. She couldn't stomach even the *illusion* that Spider-Man might read her thoughts. He'd know them in the end, though. She would be the last person he saw when she avenged her father.

There was some small printing on the back of the photograph. It was a *Daily Bugle* logo and a date from six years earlier. She handed the print back to Bingham, letting go the moment his fingers made contact. Maya didn't want him touching her. He was creepy.

"Do you see it?" he asked.

"Honestly," she said, "no, I don't."

He snorted and put the photo back in his secret pouch. "They never do. Not until it's too late. Soon it'll be too late for you, deaf girl." Abruptly he waved toward the hallway. "Now get out of here while you still can." With that he turned his back on her, and Maya had the distinct impression he was still talking to her, deliberately saying things he knew she couldn't hear.

Opening the door, she walked out of his apartment, more confused than ever. What was Mr. Fisk thinking, putting his trust in someone so unpredictable? What could be so important? He was a man who never took chances, who mapped out every move like a chess master. Why on earth would he introduce such irrationality into his oh-so-rational world?

Yet experience told her not to doubt. There had been times in the past when she'd been unable to see her mentor's grand strategy. Though she was ashamed to admit it, there had even been a time when she'd doubted his innocence. Yet he'd always proved himself prescient and precise and just. Here again, she might doubt—but eventually she'd see the wisdom of his actions. She knew it to be true.

But she also knew she could not let it go.

TWELVE

AFTER finishing at the lab, Peter took a few hours to patrol the streets as Spider-Man. It was important to make an appearance every day, if possible. If he gave himself any time off, rumors would begin to fly. Was he hurt? Had he been killed?

The *Daily Bugle*, back when J. Jonah Jameson was in charge, had been inclined to go to extremes. Once, when he'd gone on a long weekend trip with Aunt May, the *Bugle*'s headline pronounced: FAKE HERO TOO BUSY FOR FOUR-ALARM FIRE.

Now, with his suit packed away in his backpack, he met MJ for a late dinner. It was nowhere fancy because Peter considered himself a man of simple tastes—at least that's what he told himself when faced with the cost of eating out in New York City. He picked a sandwich place just off Times Square because it was shockingly good, reasonably priced, and relatively unknown to tourists.

"You sure know how to show a girl a good time," MJ chided as they waited on line to order.

"You love this place," he reminded her.

She smiled at him. "I love this place."

With overstuffed sandwiches, filling bursting out of the bread, they found a seat toward the back. Peter was starving. His enhanced metabolism required a lot of food, and he often had to hastily down energy bars during the day, just to keep his mind focused. He wanted to make this sandwich submit to its new master, and quickly, but he'd learned from experience that even the most understanding girlfriend frowned upon eating food like a starving barbarian.

Besides, MJ had a serious look on her face.

"What's going on?" he asked her.

She smirked at him. "I feel like I'm in a cartoon, and you see me as steaming platter of chicken," she said playfully. "Why don't you get friendly with your dinner before we talk?"

He knew that tone, and he didn't like it.

"That sounds ominous."

She flicked her fingers at his food.

When she wouldn't say another word, Peter gave in and took a big bite. It was as good as he remembered.

"I'm in at the *Bugle*," she said.

"That's so great!" He burst into a grin, and then clamped his mouth shut. Shards of bacon were probably sticking out of his teeth like broken fence posts. He swallowed quickly, then said, "I know much you've wanted this—and how hard you've worked. You must be ecstatic."

"You have no idea," she said. "I think this is it, Peter—what I'm supposed to be doing. I don't mean in some kind of cosmic sense, but people can have a calling, a thing they're better suited for than anything else. You have yours."

Peter wished he had that same kind of confidence. He was sure MJ meant his career as Spider-Man, but she didn't know the doubts he'd been experiencing—that web-slinging might be getting in the way of his calling. And this wasn't the time to tell her. This was her moment.

"There are some things we really need to talk about," she continued.

Uh-oh.

Talks that included a preamble were never good. Peter didn't always feel as if he knew a lot about life, but he knew that much.

As he began to respond, his phone buzzed. Peter had tinkered with his phone so that Yuri could contact him without ever knowing his real number. It had meant setting up a second line on the same cell phone—something that wasn't supposed to be possible, but there were a lot of things that were supposed to be impossible, yet people did them all the time.

He gave MJ an apologetic look.

"Take it if you need to," she said without a hint of irritation. She knew who and what he was, what kind of responsibilities rested on his shoulders. While she could be disappointed or frustrated with how that affected them as a couple, she was never angry. In fact, she was always supportive. That, he knew, was a rare thing.

"Lieutenant," he said. He tried to sound calm and wise, but came off like the villain in a spy movie. "What's up?" he added—not, in his opinion, making things any better.

"This new partnership of ours," she said. "I need you for it."

"Like right now?" he asked.

"Are you busy saving the world or something?"

"No, I'm having dinner with my girlfriend."

"You have a girlfriend?"

"Is there some reason I shouldn't have a girlfriend?"

"I don't know," she replied. "I just never imagined you having a normal life—just figured when you weren't swinging around the city you went back to, I don't know, your lair or something. Besides, you sound kind of dorky."

"I'm a normal person," he said. "I'm so normal it would terrify you. I'm also very non-dorky."

MJ just shot him a smirk.

"Then tell your long-suffering girlfriend you have to go," Watanabe said. "I'll text you the location."

"Is it important?"

"Only if you want to get Wilson Fisk," she said, and hung up.

Peter looked over at MJ.

"You have to go," she said.

"I'm really sorry, MJ," he said. "Can you maybe say what you need to say before I run out?"

"It can wait," she said. "You go do your thing."

Sometimes it was unnatural how reasonable she was. Whatever she wanted, whatever she needed, he would take care of it.

He gave her a quick kiss, wrapped up the remains of his sandwich, and headed for the door.

Then he turned back to her.

"Don't even *consider* doing a write-up of this place for the *Bugle*," he said in his most serious *I mean it* tone. "It'll get too crowded."

"Tough call," she said. "I don't want to be remembered as the reporter who somehow missed the big sandwich story."

He dashed out.

BINGHAM zoomed into the tracking device's location. A restaurant off Times Square.

Perfect.

A busy location would provide just the right kind of attention, and if the false Spider-Man liked this place, then he'd take it personally.

It was exactly what he needed. He headed for the fire escape.

"SO *this* is your idea of a good place for a little chat?"

They stood on a rooftop in the west fifties, overshadowed by Fisk Tower. Watanabe wore a long coat, and her short hair fluttered in the wind, but she didn't look in any way uncomfortable.

"Seemed like a good place to talk without being seen or overheard," she said, "but I guess we could meet in a diner next time, if you want."

"Good point," he said. "I guess I don't have a lot of meetings."

"We all have our shortcomings," she said. "Now, do you want to help me get Fisk or not?"

"What do you have in mind?"

"I've been spending a lot of time thinking about what I can do with direct access to Spider-Man." When he started to protest, she held up a hand. "Don't interrupt. I asked myself, what value can you bring to the investigation? Well, like I said before, you have access I don't, to places and things."

"You can't get a search warrant?" he asked. "Isn't that the way it's supposed to work?"

"The way it's *supposed* to, yes, but this is the real world. Fisk has a lot of influence inside the department. I'm not sure how much, and I don't know who I can trust, but I have my suspicions about a number of people—including my immediate supervisor. I've been warned about freelancing on this case, and if I'm found out, then it could mean my job."

"So why not let someone else deal with it?" Spider-Man asked. "Why take the heat?"

"Because no one *is* dealing with it," she said. "I don't know if it's because Fisk has greased the right palms, or because the last time we tried to get him it was a PR fiasco the department wants to forget. Now that he's trying to play himself off as Saint Wilson, brass seem even more gun-shy. The bottom line is that if I don't do this, it won't get done."

"But why *you*?" Peter pressed.

"I was involved in the case eight years ago," she said. "I was just a rookie, but I played a small part.

When the authorities were closing in, and Fisk got scared, he had to shut up a lot of people. I worked my share of those murders, and I'll never forget them. There were spouses and kids and neighbors who got caught up in the mess.

"Fisk is still walking around. That's why me."

"So what do you have in mind?" Spider-Man said.

"Fisk might have people in the police department, but I have people in the Fisk operation," she said, staring at the looming tower. "No, don't get excited. It's no one high up—a mail clerk here, a marketing flunky there. People who can give me snippets of information for me to piece together." She turned to face him. "I've got a line on something now. It won't look like much—it's a payroll file—but I think it'll fit with some of the other data I've collected."

"You want me to break into Fisk Tower just to steal a file?"

"Not steal," she said, "copy. I can give you a camera if you need one."

"I've got one," he replied. "That's not the point."

"The file's been left on a desk," she said, without letting him continue. "It'll have to be put away by the morning. My contact could lose her job if they discover she left it out, so it has to be tonight. You're not afraid of going into Fisk Tower, are you?"

"Of course I'm not, but do you really need Spider-Man for this? I mean, I hate to toot my own horn, but honestly, there's a principle here. You could hire a private detective to do this sort of thing."

"Gosh, have I offended your dignity?" Watanabe asked. "If you know a PI who could get into Fisk Tower tonight, and not leave a trace, please, give me his business card." She took a step closer. "Look, I'm sorry this isn't glamorous enough for you. It's not as exciting as fighting rhinoceros people or leaping lizards, but this is how cases get made."

"You really think you can do this?"

"I've studied what went wrong last time," she said. "I know exactly what we need and what we can do. If you help me with these kinds of surgical strikes, I think we can build a case against Fisk in a year, eighteen months tops."

Eighteen months. Peter had been hoping for something more like the Thursday after next. If he was going to quit being Spider-Man he'd been thinking—in the back of his mind—that a Fisk arrest was a fitting conclusion to his career. Fisk was the one who got away. If he could put that guy behind bars, maybe the city wouldn't need a web-slinger anymore.

But eighteen months.

He'd never really thought about giving himself some kind of retirement date. Suddenly the idea of doing this for another year and a half seemed exhausting. Still, how could he say no? How could he refuse to help this detective who knew what she was doing, and who had a plan.

"I'll do it."

"What a prince," she said.

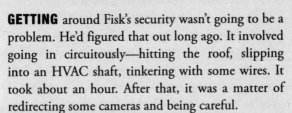

GETTING around Fisk's security wasn't going to be a problem. He'd figured that out long ago. It involved going in circuitously—hitting the roof, slipping into an HVAC shaft, tinkering with some wires. It took about an hour. After that, it was a matter of redirecting some cameras and being careful.

There were some places in the tower he wouldn't dare attempt to go without more recon and planning, but the cubicle farm on the 48th floor should be safe. The Web-Slinger slipped in, found the desk number Watanabe had given him, and used his suit camera to copy the twenty-plus pages of the document.

Piece of cake.

A call came in just as he was finishing up. He didn't recognize the number, and it went to voice mail. He decided to check it to see if it was anything important.

"Hey, Peter." It was Anika. Uh-oh. *"Just, you know, calling. Uh-huh, that's what I'm doing. Using the phone to talk about science stuff. Yeah, I have some questions about procedures at the lab. I guess. I don't know. Anyhow call me back if you get a chance… or, if not, I'll see you at the lab. It's fine either way. Sorry about interrupting your evening. You don't have to call back. Unless you want to. Okay. Bye."*

Well, that was adorable, but also kind of problematic. Could she be interested in him? He was going to need to let her know he wasn't available, and as soon as possible. The trick was to avoid making her feel embarrassed. He liked her, and he didn't want her being weird and uncomfortable around him.

That was a problem for another time, though.

He began the process of slipping out the way he'd come in, which meant more wriggling through air shafts—no one's idea of a good time. He had to pause a few times along the way because he was afraid of being noisy. Once he had to stop because he heard voices. He was about to move along when realized he knew one of the speakers.

It was Fisk.

He recognized the depth and the cadence of it, but he couldn't make out the words. It was impossible to pick out from the distance and through the walls. The smart thing to do would be to keep going.

He couldn't do it.

Quietly, Spider-Man removed the grating from the shaft, and slipped out onto the floor. He wasn't entirely certain where he was, so he did a quick scan for security cameras. There were plenty and they were everywhere—though none were pointing in his direction—so he figured he had to be on one of the executive floors.

There was a light coming from one of the offices, which meant the conversation was probably coming from there. He had to get closer.

He looked at the cameras. If he used just a little bit of webbing on each one, he could freeze them in place and work around their range of vision. The devices oscillated slowly enough that the security guards might not even notice for hours, by which time the webs would have dissolved. Even if they did notice, they'd first assume it was a system failure, not a physical obstruction. Again, it should buy him plenty of time.

Choosing his first target, he aimed and webbed. Within minutes the cameras were safely immobilized, and he zigzagged across the room to crouch just outside the office door.

It was ajar, so he was able to peer through. Fisk sat behind his desk talking to an attractive young woman in her early twenties. Her back was to him, and from what he could see she had high cheekbones and dark hair pulled back into a ponytail.

"This is not a neutral topic for you," Fisk was saying, "and it should not be. I would never advocate walking away from something like this. It is merely a matter of choosing the right time."

"That's not what you're advocating," the young woman responded. "You're choosing the right time for me, without my input."

Fisk summoned a tight little smile from somewhere. "I'm choosing the right time for both of us. Your father was my friend, and I haven't forgotten what was done to him. The price will be paid, but only when it is safe for us to act."

Without context, Spider-Man couldn't make head or tail of their discussion. What was more interesting was the way Fisk was acting with this woman. He had never seen anyone push back against him, and have Fisk take it in stride. There was no anger, no temper tantrum. She was pretty, but they weren't giving off any kind of romantic vibe. Even the worst monsters had a soft side, he supposed, and Fisk was touchingly devoted to his wife.

No, he wasn't flirting here. There was something almost fatherly in his tone. Yet he'd mentioned her father...

"There's still too much you haven't explained to me."

"Knowledge is power, Maya," Fisk responded, "and whoever surrenders power is a fool."

"You have to trust me if I am to aid you," the woman answered.

"It's not about trust, it's about protection," Fisk told her. "You win at chess not by charging ahead, but by outthinking your opponent. When you get to checkmate, there is no countermove. I've isolated you from some of the details because there are people involved, and people behave unpredictably. That is something I never do, by controlling the board in such a way that no one will be able to touch me.

"The press will present the facts the way we want them to," he continued. "They won't even think about criticizing me or suggesting I might be involved in anything improper."

The woman laughed. "You'll be too big to fail."

There was a moment of silence, and then Fisk let out a short laugh. It was abrupt and violent. Spider-Man thought of a seal in pain.

"That's exactly right," he said. "Too big to fail. I like that analogy—it's perfect. And once that becomes true, it will be checkmate, and we will have no reason to hold back."

"SO then she's like, *'We'll be too big to fail,'* and he's like, *'Ha ha ha'*—evil laugh— *'yes, that's exactly right, my loyal minion.'* It was weird. There's something big happening."

Spider-Man was waving his arms around while talking, and decided to adopt a more composed posture. He leaned casually against an air-conditioning unit, the way dignified people did.

"Did you get the file?" Watanabe asked.

"Yes, I got the file," he replied. "I've already sent the images to the email address you gave me. That's not the point."

"It's *exactly* the point," Watanabe said. "That Fisk is up to something bad? That's not news. Doing terrible things that hurt people and make him money is what gets him out of bed in the morning."

"I know that, but this seemed to be of a different order."

"Maybe." Watanabe didn't sound convinced. "It could just be bluster, or it might be he's about to hatch some new plot. But something that could make him untouchable? Not likely, and it doesn't matter, because we have to stay the course. Gather evidence we can use to force the issue, and get someone to prosecute the guy.

"We can't let ourselves become distracted."

Spider-Man nodded, because he knew it was true. Fisk wasn't a costumed clown he could knock down and let some mysterious government agency cart away. They had to stop him legally, or they wouldn't stop him at all. He knew she was right.

It still left him frustrated.

"The woman he was talking to," Spider-Man said. "He called her Maya. Does that mean anything to you?"

She shook her head. "No, but I'll look into it." She paused, then added, "Hysterics aside, you did good work tonight. I know it's not glamorous, but this is how we'll get him. I promise you."

"It just feels like drops in the bucket."

"Give yourself a break," Watanabe said. "You're only one person. You can't change the world by yourself. You're part of an effort now, and that effort is going to succeed in the end."

He hoped she was right. Turning, he dove off the roof and swung into the night, wondering what the city would look like if the Kingpin's operation really did become too big to fail.

MR. Fisk received a call, then excused himself and left the office. His wife, Vanessa, was overseas, but she apparently had something she wanted to discuss. His devotion to her was one of the many things Maya admired about him.

She stood in the middle of the floor, looking at

the oscillating cameras that were not oscillating. There was nothing to be done, not tonight, so she decided not to alarm him. She would tell security, and they would investigate.

They would find nothing.

She took a pen from one of the desks and poked at the substance around a camera. It was sticky.

Webbing.

Something would definitely have to be done. It would have to be done soon.

THIRTEEN

THE plan had been to meet Aunt May for breakfast, but Peter somehow managed to sleep through the alarm he'd set on his phone. When he called his aunt, she laughed and suggested he come to F.E.A.S.T., where she worked, and they could grab a quick coffee.

This was exactly the sort of thing that left Peter feeling vaguely uneasy. His aunt had grown so used to his being unreliable, it hardly even registered with her that her nephew, the boy she had raised and treated like a son, really ought to show up on time. She had long since decided he was flighty or distracted or a kooky science type. The truth was, Peter really *wanted* to be considered reliable. He wanted to be someone people trusted to honor his commitments. Unfortunately, when he didn't blow those commitments to fight a villain or rescue someone, it was because he was exhausted from living two incredibly demanding lives.

It didn't take long to get from his apartment to the F.E.A.S.T. shelter in Little Tokyo. When he walked through the door, he immediately heard his aunt's voice, talking in soothing tones. Her work at F.E.A.S.T. was supposed to be administrative, but—as with all charitable organizations—there were always more tasks than there were staff members, which meant everyone had to do whatever was needed at any given moment.

In this case, Aunt May was talking down a homeless man in camouflage clothing and whose missing left leg meant he got around on crutches. They'd attracted a crowd, and several of the onlookers wore frightened expressions.

Peter resisted the urge to rush in and stayed back to watch her in action. In doing so, he was reminded just how awesome his aunt could be.

"Everyone has bad days, Steve," she was saying in a firm voice. "Everyone gets frustrated, and we're all tempted to take it out on the people who are trying to help us, but that doesn't make it right. Now, you owe this young man an apology for yelling at him."

The man in camouflage turned to Harris, a clerical worker who usually affected hipster nerdiness. At the moment, though, behind his impossibly chunky glasses, he wore an expression that combined fear of the man in camo with awe at Aunt May for taking control of the situation.

"I'm truly sorry, young fellow," the man said in a rumbling bass voice. It practically rattled the windows, but it was still full of contrition. He leaned on one of his crutches and removed his hat. "I sometimes have a problem with my temper, but I ought not to have spoken to you as I did."

The clerical worker nodded.

"Now," Aunt May said, "let me show you where you can get something to eat, and while you do that

Harris here will review the paperwork and see if we can't straighten out the problem with your benefits."

"After I change my underwear," Harris mumbled.

○————————○

"YOU were pretty fearless in there," Peter said, sitting at a nearby tea shop sipping a steaming bowl of matcha.

"What, with Steve?" Aunt May waved a hand. "He's mostly bark, very little bite. I've dealt with his outbursts before. He gets emotional, and I can't say I blame him, but he always feels bad afterward. If it were someone I didn't know, I'd have taken a much more cautious tone."

"It's amazing the way you take the time to know the people who use the shelter."

"A job at a place like F.E.A.S.T. is always about keeping the lights on. That's pretty much what's on everyone's mind all day, every day—but we can't forget why we're there. The point is not just to keep going, but to help people. When I start letting the people we serve suffer because I want to get back to the job, then I might as well find something else to do."

Peter took another sip of the green tea. He loved its earthy flavor, and wondered why he didn't order it more often. Oh, that's right. Because he was usually too busy to hang out in tea shops. The fact that he was only a few hours behind schedule with his aunt, instead of canceling entirely, meant that he was having a pretty good day so far.

"I'm really sorry about this morning."

"I know you're busy," she said, "and you've always been easily distracted, but your heart is in the right place. I never doubt that, Peter. So how are things at the lab?"

Peter gave her the rundown of the work and the latest updates concerning MJ, whom she adored. She listened and smiled and took genuine pleasure in hearing about his life. He wished he had the time to be a better nephew, and *far* less irresponsible. He wasn't sure he'd ever be as forgiving as Aunt May.

As they walked back to the homeless shelter, Peter realized this was exactly what he'd needed. He'd been feeling so unmoored in his own life, wondering about what mattered, about where he was putting his energy. Then she reminded him. *People* were what mattered. His family, his friends, and MJ. Aunt May got it intuitively. The little problems and frustrations never seemed to distract her from what was important.

He walked her back to her desk and was about to leave when a smiling man in an impeccably tailored suit approached them.

"This must be the nephew I've heard so much about," the man said.

Aunt May seemed to glow with pride. "Peter, I'd like you to meet Martin Li, our benefactor."

He'd heard a ton about Mr. Li, mostly from his aunt. He was a self-made man who'd become one of the city's most successful businessmen. From what Aunt May had said, Martin Li was essentially the anti-Fisk. Rather than wanting to wring money from suffering and trying to pretend he was a philanthropist, Li was determined to give back to the city that had provided him with an opportunity to make something of himself.

"It's great to meet you," Peter said. If there were more Martin Lis in the world, he thought, then there might not have been the need for a Spider-Man. "What you do here is so important."

"We wouldn't do much of *anything* here without your aunt," Mr. Li said. "She holds this place together."

She waved her hand again and laughed, but her eyes crinkled with pleasure. Raising him must have felt like banging her head against a wall, Peter mused. Now she had an opportunity to work hard and see the results of her labors.

"Your aunt tells me you're quite the scientist."

"I've been very lucky," Peter said. "I ended up working with a great innovator, and I'm learning an incredible amount from him."

"Gratitude is an important component of success," Mr. Li said. "I'm sure you must be busy, but if you have any free time, consider volunteering a few hours here and there. I think you'd find it rewarding, and it would give you even more insight into how remarkable a person your aunt is."

"I'd like that," Peter said. He wished he could commit right then and there, but he didn't want to let yet another person down. They shook hands again, and Li walked into the back.

"He seems like a good guy," he said to his aunt as he hugged her goodbye.

"Oh, there's no doubt about that," she agreed.

＿＿＿＿＿＿＿＿o＿＿＿＿＿＿＿o＿＿＿＿＿＿＿＿

HE had just enough time to get to the West Village to make his appointment with Harry Osborn. It wouldn't be long before Harry was off in Europe, and when he wasn't around Peter would hate to think he'd missed the opportunity to spend time with his friend.

They were meeting at the Coffee Bean, a place on Bleecker Street where they'd hung out since high school. Peter passed by a creepy old mansion that had freaked him out when he was still young enough to wonder if a house might be haunted. Maybe he was still young enough, because there was no way to look at that place without wondering if something supernatural was going on inside.

Just as he reached the door, Peter checked his watch and saw he was still two minutes early. This was turning out to be a remarkable day. When he entered he saw Harry already seated at the table, waiting for him.

"I thought I'd finally beat you somewhere," he said, shaking his friend's hand.

"And here I was kicking myself for being punctual when meeting you," Harry replied. "But you're actually early. The end times are upon us."

Peter smiled and sat down. He'd learned to act like his unreliability was just a goofy part of his personality, but there was no getting around the fact that Harry, like his aunt, thought of him as unreliable.

"You caught up with MJ the other night?"

"Yeah, and she got the job at the *Bugle*."

"I know," Harry said. "That's great, right? You must be thrilled for her."

"I am," Peter said, "but, I don't know, I get the feeling that there's something off between us right now. She seems kind of distant, somehow?"

"Have you talked to her about it?"

"We were going to talk last night, but—" Peter stopped himself. "I haven't, but you have, haven't you. You totally know what's going on, don't you?"

Harry held up his hand, palm out. The three of them had been friends for years, and Harry had elevated third-wheeling to a sublime art. He could be friends with both MJ and Peter, and each could confide in him, but they'd learned to respect that he had to protect himself from becoming a go-between.

"Peter, if it were something you needed to hear from me, I would tell you," he said, "but I'm not going to play couples counselor."

"But I heard your rates are reasonable." Peter made a conscious decision not to worry. Couples had disagreements all the time, and whatever was bothering MJ, they would work it through. He was determined to enjoy his time with his friend.

Asking Harry about his travel plans, he allowed himself to relax and listen. When he'd been younger it had been hard not to feel envious of Harry. Even now, the idea of picking up and spending months in Europe seemed like a fantasy. He couldn't even consider something like that. It wasn't because of the money—not that he had any—but because of the things that tied him down here in New York. He'd never consider walking away from his obligations, but the thought made for a nice daydream.

They'd eaten lunch and were on the second coffees when the atmosphere in the restaurant seemed to shift. All conversations stopped at the same time. There were several gasps. Peter felt himself tense. He knew from experience how people responded when something terrible was happening, but at the same time his Spider-Sense hadn't so much as twitched.

Peter looked up and saw what had happened, and it was only with the greatest effort that he kept himself from groaning. Norman Osborn, the mayor of New York City, and Harry's father, had just walked into the Coffee Bean.

FOURTEEN

HARRY made no effort to conceal his displeasure as the mayor slowly made his way over to their table. Slick as oil in his bespoke suit, Osborn had to stop to shake hands, pose for selfies, and sign autographs. That gave Harry plenty of time to put on his game face. He didn't seem interested in doing so.

"So you had no idea he was going to show up here?"

"Are you serious?" Harry responded. "I don't even know how he found out where I was going to be. Sometimes I think he's having me followed."

It wouldn't be the first time, Peter knew. Norman had arranged surveillance for his son years ago, but that was when he was the son of a famously rich innovator and attending public school. Peter didn't think Norman would have a good reason to keep an eye on his adult son, but at the same time he wouldn't put anything past the man either.

Norman had a tendency to do what he wanted.

"Peter!" the mayor cried happily when he finally ran the gauntlet of constituents and reached the table. He embraced Peter in a hug. His son got a clap on the shoulder.

"How did you know where to find us?" Harry asked coldly.

"What makes you think I knew?" Norman shot back while they sat. "Just grabbing a cup of coffee. These kinds of coincidences happen in the big city every day."

That was certainly true. New York was the world's biggest small town. At the same time, the mayor hadn't actually denied anything. He'd simply proposed an alternative theory.

"So, what's new with you?" he asked Peter. "Still slaving away in that salt mine of a lab?"

"He's working on a number of interesting things right now," Peter replied, knowing that his mentor would want him to keep things vague. "It's exciting stuff."

"No doubt, no doubt," Norman said, "but I've seen his funding, and I know he can't afford to pay you what you're worth. You could be making a fantastic salary if you wanted to come over to Oscorp."

"Can you just leave him alone one time?" Harry put his hands to his face and groaned.

"It's very kind of you, Mr. Osborn," Peter said. This was the usual role, trying diplomatically to keep these two from each other's throats. "But I first started working at the lab when I was in college. I'm going to see things through."

"I get it," Norman said. "Is Theodore Peyton still working there? He used to be one of Oscorp's, you know. A strong head for numbers, but a bit difficult to work with."

"I understand his need to keep the budget in line," Peter said.

"Budget is less of an issue at Oscorp," Norman continued. "But I won't press the point. You don't want a handout from your friend's dad. You've always been a go-getter, Peter. I appreciate, even admire that you want to make your own way, but part of making your own way is letting the people you impress smooth things over for you."

"He doesn't want to work for Oscorp," Harry said. "How many times do you have to put him on the spot before you get that?"

Norman laughed as if Harry had made a joke. "Point taken, gents."

"So, how's the mayoring going?" Peter asked.

"It's less work but more frustration than running a company, I can tell you," Osborn said. "Everyone wants something, but no one actually expects to give anything in exchange. It's been an eye-opening experience."

"I'll bet," Peter said, trying to keep conversation on this neutral footing. "So, Harry's trip sounds pretty exciting."

"Yes." Norman dropped the smile. "Harry's trip. I think the issue here is less what Harry is going to do on his trip, than what he's going to do *after* it. It's a mistake to see this trip as a suspension from real life, when it could be an opportunity to make plans for that life."

"Well, this has been a great time, Peter." Harry slapped his hand on the table and stood up. "Time for me to go."

"Come on, Harry." Norman shook his head

theatrically. Peter could imagine him having done it in countless board meetings. "Don't act like a child."

"Seriously," Harry said. "I'm leaving." Without even waiting for a response, he was out the door before Peter could figure out what was going on.

"I am sorry about that," Norman said. "He hasn't been himself lately. Maybe you've noticed."

"I guess," Peter said. "I mean, he's always been a little hot-tempered."

"And there's nothing wrong with that," Norman said, "as long as you direct that heat toward the things that matter." He looked at his watch. "Unlike my son, I really do need to be places, but you were going to tell me how things were going at the lab. You said something about a new breakthrough."

"I'm pretty sure I never said that." Peter would never share anything about research, especially with another scientist.

"No fooling you," Norman said. "I appreciate your loyalty, but don't forget that loyalties can change."

"I should really go too," Peter said.

"Thanks for keeping an eye on Harry," the mayor told him as they rose.

"He's my friend," Peter responded. "I'm here to help him."

"I know you've known each other a long time," Norman Osborn said, meeting Peter's gaze with an unexpected intensity. "But helping him is my job."

o————————o

IT was a late start at the lab, and Peter found Peyton in a good mood. At least Peter thought he might have been. He was never more animated than a statue, but his suit looked extra pressed and his bow tie was a little brighter than usual. That had to count for something.

"You are late as usual," he said, "but at least you don't appear to be excessively fatigued." He then gave Peter a series of tests to run for the day.

"I'm trying," Peter said. "It's just, you know, life and all that."

Peyton gave him a stern glance. "Yes, I have some familiarity with the concept of life. Now please proceed with the data I've provided."

Peter got to work, running a group of computer model simulations, and by the time he was ready to begin the analysis, Anika had shown up to lend him a hand.

"So, did you get my message the other night?" she asked casually.

"Oh, yeah. Sorry about not getting back to you," he said. "I sort of got distracted."

"It's fine." She began to twirl her black hair nervously. "Can I ask you a question?"

"Is it about the toilet not flushing properly?" he said hesitantly. "Because I had no idea that was a problem."

She laughed and put her hands behind her back, and then clasped them in front of her, and then shoved them in the pockets of her jeans.

"I never saw the note on your desk to call the plumber," she said. "But we'll stick a pin in that conversation. I've been looking at some of the data you've been running, and your analysis is brilliant."

"Thank you, undergraduate assistant."

She gave him a playful smack. "I'm serious. Although I would never have worked the data the way you did, that doesn't mean I can't recognize how clever your analysis was. I mean, it's fantastic work, and even Theodore recognizes that you're really smart…"

"So why is he always giving me a hard time?"

She shrugged.

Peter felt a strange, almost unhinged, urge come over him—to confess to being Spider-Man. *I can trust her!* he thought out of the blue. The fact that this urge came packaged with a vision of him giggling uncontrollably was a sure sign that he probably ought to resist it.

There was no reason to start trusting new people, let alone someone who was almost a complete stranger, but he was so tired of lying—even in conversations that were supposed to be completely honest. How many times had he done that with Aunt May, with Harry, even with MJ—both before he told her about being Spider-Man, and even after? Sometimes it was better for her not to know just how much danger he'd been in, or how much the odds were stacked against him.

Would it really be so bad to trust someone new?

Not now, obviously, but she was supposed to be a technological whiz. Maybe she could help him with his suit. Wouldn't it be nice to have someone who had his back, instead of always being on his own? And knowing his secret wouldn't really put her in danger, would it? Not unless someone else found out she knew.

It wouldn't be like telling Harry or Aunt May— that would just relieve his guilt about lying to them. It would be selfish, because he would be doing it so they didn't think he was a flake.

No, with Anika he would be building his support base. She was intelligent, energetic, optimistic, ridiculously pretty—no, that last one didn't matter.

But the rest were real plusses.

The idea was nuts, and he knew it. He was having some issues with MJ—whom he loved, by the way. Throwing out that little PSA there. He was feeling vulnerable, and this was how normal people reacted in that kind of situation. He'd read about normal people, and he thought he had a pretty good understanding of how they worked. The tiny male brain sometimes saw an attractive woman as an escape, but flirting with Anika wouldn't make his life any easier.

So, time to lie, he told himself.

"I've just been kind of distracted," he said, hearing how lame the excuse was, even as the words left his mouth. It made him sound lazy, but he'd never been able to think of a way of deflecting the truth without telling a bigger and more complicated lie. "And I've never been the best at time management. I think Peyton is getting tired of taking the good with the bad."

"In other words, you're not going to tell me?"

she asked, putting her hands on her hips.

"What do you mean? I just did."

"*I've been kind of distracted,*" she said, mimicking his tone. "That's not an answer. That's a non-answer. Who'd buy something that lame?"

Pretty much everyone, he thought. Teachers who were indifferent or too busy to press, close friends and family who respected his privacy, people who just couldn't be bothered. Maybe they hadn't been satisfied, but they'd accepted it.

"Talking about things can help," Anika said. "But if you don't want to talk about it with someone you don't know all that well, then you should just say so."

"No, that's not it," Peter said. "I mean, if there was a stranger I'd talk with, it would be you. You'd be just the right kind of stranger." He was babbling now, and digging himself a hole.

She smirked. "I like to think so."

"It's nothing bad—like drugs or gambling or whatever—but I have a lot of responsibilities outside of work." That sounded reasonable. "I have obligations I can't walk away from, and sometimes it's like I'm living two lives, I guess. I have to do these other things. I mean, I think I do. I'm not sure anyone else will if I won't, and there are things I need to see through, but at the same time, I'm just so tired of not being able to give my full attention to the work here, which I love."

He sat back in his chair and let out a long breath. This was as close as he'd come to being open and honest with anyone other than MJ for as long as he could remember. It felt good.

Anika sat across from him. "It feels good, doesn't it?" she said, as if she was reading his thoughts. "Even if you didn't tell me anything at all, really."

"Exactly!"

"Would you like some advice from someone who's lived fewer years and has less experience than you?"

"I'll take what I can get."

"Okay, so I've been where you are, when I first started at ESU," she said. "I won't go into the details, because we're not there yet, but I was being pulled in two different directions. Your complexion suggests to me that neither of your parents are Indian, but let me tell you, when your mom and dad come from another country, and work incredibly hard their whole lives so their children will have opportunities they never had, they sort of expect you to get good grades.

"My older sister obliged," she continued, "and they went through the roof when I didn't. It's perfectly reasonable, and I couldn't tell them *why* I wasn't getting good grades, just like I'm not telling you. So of course they didn't buy my excuses."

"So what happened?"

"What happened was I figured out what's important to me. I took some time to decide what I want to do with my life—not what other people expect of me, but what *I* want. It turned out I really *did* want to go into the sciences, and I refocused my energy. I can only hope that when I apply to grad school, that B+ in

'Intro to Medieval European History' won't sink me."

"Yeah, it sounds like you bottomed out."

"It was a crisis," she said without missing a beat, "even if I managed to contain the worst of the damage."

It wasn't exactly a direct comparison, he thought—medieval history versus the Vulture—but it was still good advice. He'd been skirting around the issue for a long time, but hadn't really confronted it. He'd been asking himself about the value of being Spider-Man, but he hadn't asked himself if he *wanted* to be Spider-Man. He was going to have to confront this sooner or later—but not, he decided, until he saw this Fisk business through to the end.

"Well, my parents weren't from another country," he said, "but it was kind of complicated." He told her about being raised by his aunt, and that led him to talking about Uncle Ben, about how he could have stopped a thief and didn't step in, thinking it wasn't his problem. The thief who killed his uncle.

He'd learned to tell the story without crying, but it was still hard to talk about, to remember. There were moments, he knew, that stuck with you forever. Some regrets would never go away.

"Every time I have to make a choice," he said, "I feel the weight of making the right one—not just for the moment, not just for me, but for how my decisions will affect everyone. I'm terrified I'll do something, or *not* do something, and the consequences will be terrible."

Her eyes were wide.

"You can't live that way," she said. "You couldn't

foresee the consequences with that, that thief. What if he'd been stealing to pay for medicine for his dying child, and by stopping him you'd have condemned a child to death? You never know how things are going to play out, so you can only make the best choices based on the information you have available."

"But I made the wrong choice," he insisted. "On that day."

"Stop it. You didn't know you were making the wrong choice," she said. "It's not like letting a murderer or a terrorist run free. When something looks trivial, you can't know it will turn out to be important."

"I'm not sure I agree," he said.

It was a crime. I should have stopped it...

"It's common sense," she said, giving him a frown. "If you worry over every decision, try to project every possible ramification, it must drive your friends crazy. Or your girlfriend," she added. "If you have one."

Anika was fishing now. While it seemed like a bad time to tell her about MJ, he knew it would be cruel not to. They had a connection, and in a different world who knows what might have happened with the two of them, but he wasn't living in that world.

"Yeah, I do have a girlfriend," he said, "and I think she does find me kind of difficult to be around sometimes."

He couldn't quite read her expression, but he thought it was disappointment. She went silent, and they didn't talk for a few awkward moments.

She changed the subject, and they talked about

some of their favorite places to eat in the city. Peter mentioned the sandwich place in Times Square, and she made fun of him, but in the end she agreed to try it. It was an awkward transition, but Peter was happy he'd talked to her.

It had been a lucky day when she'd showed up in the lab.

FIFTEEN

MR. Fisk always had his reasons.

Maya knew that, but this time she wasn't certain he was right. Moreover, she was pretty sure he was wrong.

"He was in this building last night," she said. "To steal, or to spy on us."

The security detail had been useless. Fearful of the consequences, they had told her to go directly to the boss.

Mr. Fisk nodded, looking thoughtful. At least he gave her concerns due consideration.

"There is no harm that he can do us here," he said, remarkably calm. "And there is nothing of consequence for him to find that is not securely stored inside a safe."

"He might have overheard our conversation."

"And what if he did? We said nothing specific. There was nothing he could use against us."

"It's a mistake not to take him more seriously," she insisted.

"I take him very seriously," he told her. His eyes were narrow, and his voice dropped a register. "That was why I deployed Bingham."

Maya worked hard to control her expression. She couldn't let him know she had gone to speak to Bingham. Maya had little experience lying to Mr.

Fisk, and those few transgressions she had committed, when she was much younger, had left her feeling small and ungrateful. She owed everything to this man—but she still believed he was wrong.

"I've crossed swords with these costumed vigilantes before," Fisk said. "They all thrive on attention, on feeling as though they are at the center of something important. If you push back, that only feeds the delusion."

"Spider-Man is already a problem."

"He is a nuisance," Fisk said with a wave of his hand. "But if I were to attack him, then it would quickly escalate, perhaps beyond what we want."

"You may be underestimating how much he—"

The slab of Mr. Fisk's palm came down on the desk. Papers, pens, photographs flew like debris in the wake of a bomb blast.

"*Enough*," he said. "You are very clever, Maya, but you still have much to learn. Unless Spider-Man directly assaults us in some way we cannot ignore, we shall not speak of him until after we have completed the project." He pinned her with his gaze. "Is that understood?"

"Yes," she said, rising to her feet. "Absolutely." She ignored the field of debris that surrounded the desk. Once, when she was younger, she had scrambled to pick things up, but that had only made him angrier. He didn't like attention called to his temper.

Without another word between them, she left the office. On the way out she spoke to Mr. Cisneros, the first-shift secretary.

"There was an accident in Mr. Fisk's office."

He nodded, springing from his chair. "I'll tend to it right away." Just then, a smartly dressed young woman entered the foyer.

"Hi," she said. "I'm Mary Jane Watson. I have an appointment with Mr. Fisk."

"Yes, of course," Mr. Cisneros replied. He looked conflicted.

"I'll take care of this," Maya told him. The longer Fisk sat with his items on the floor, the more he would brood. She turned to Miss Watson. "I'm Maya Lopez, Mr. Fisk's special assistant. Mr. Fisk will be with you shortly." She gestured. "Please have a seat. Can I offer you some coffee, or water?"

"No, thank you," the woman said as she sat.

"May I ask what this is regarding?"

"I'm with the *Daily Bugle*," she explained. "Working on a series about the low-income people who stand to benefit from mixed-unit apartment projects, and since Mr. Fisk is part of that movement…" She allowed herself to trail off, most likely thinking it was charming.

"Mr. Fisk *is* the movement," Maya corrected, moving a step closer. "Others may be trying to ride on his coattails, but they offer fewer units of less quality, trying to benefit from the good press without making a real contribution to the city. The work of the Fisk Foundation is changing this city for the better. I hope you will include that in the story."

"If it turns out to be true, I certainly will."

Maya turned to leave. Then she stopped and

turned back to face the reporter.

"In the past, reporters have come here claiming to be working on one kind of story, but they were working on something else—something designed to twist Mr. Fisk's work so it appeared to be something dark and illegal." She paused, then added, "You wouldn't be doing that, would you, Miss Watson?"

"I've just started at the *Bugle*," she said. "As a features writer. It wouldn't be wise to do anything other than what I'm told."

"No, it wouldn't," Maya agreed. "Reporters who do that sort of thing find their careers taking unfortunate turns." Then she smiled brightly. "Good luck, Miss Watson."

Maya left the office, a frown coming to her face. For some reason, this reporter hadn't seemed troubled by the implied threat. Perhaps she wasn't smart enough to understand it. Or she was more dangerous than she appeared.

That gave her a thought…

○──────────○

MAYA had wanted to meet at a coffee shop, the way normal people did when conducting business outside of the office. But no, he insisted on meeting at a hot-dog vendor's cart two blocks from Fisk Tower. She sent a text.

Do you think it's too dangerous to meet indoors?

He'd responded immediately.

HOTDOGS

they have the best damn hotdogs in the city
if I'm going to be near there, i want one

She arrived a few minutes early, but he was already sitting on a bench near the metal cart. He was about halfway through one dog and had another resting on his briefcase.

"Get a dog," he told her. "You won't regret it. Don't forget the relish. Even if you think you don't like relish, get it. This guy's relish is incredible. He makes it himself."

She sat down next to him. "I'm not here for hot dogs."

"You don't have to be here *for* hot dogs to enjoy a hot dog," he told her. "Life is full of misery and hardship, so grab your pleasures where you can."

Maya didn't like eating while on the street. It distracted her, and city streets were chaotic places. It was best not to be distracted. Plus, she wasn't about to eat processed meat and buns made of refined flour. She trained hard and was fanatical about what she consumed. No hot dogs for her.

A few people who passed by glanced in their direction. The man she was meeting wasn't exactly a celebrity, but New York was a media-driven town. It didn't help that his flat-topped brown hair with its graying wings, his stubby mustache, and massive eyebrows all gave him a distinctive look.

"Let me be clear that I appreciate what you're offering," J. Jonah Jameson began. "The *Bugle* didn't have the guts to let me continue telling the truth. That's why I got the boot. I want to be able to tell the people what's really going on in this city, especially when it comes to that menace Spider-Man."

"And we want to help you," she said.

"I'm sure you do, but I'm a little suspicious about your anonymous benefactor's motives."

"I represent an organization in which people at the highest levels appreciate your work," she said. "It's that simple."

Even simpler. Maya wanted to make Spider-Man's life miserable. If she couldn't do it physically, she would do it psychologically. She would wear him down, so that when it came to direct confrontation—and she had no doubt that it would—he would be that much weaker.

"It's really not," Jameson said. "Simple, that is. I didn't get to run a paper like the *Bugle* by being an idiot. I came up the hard way, as a reporter, so I know that your people at the 'highest levels'—which translates to a bunch of greedy fat cats—aren't going to throw money at me unless they think there's something in it for them."

Maya did her best not to appear concerned. "The people I represent want to do business in a city that isn't plagued by the sort of chaos you've spent your career condemning."

"That's it, huh?" He looked dubious, and took another big bite, chewing theatrically. It made it difficult for her to tell what he was saying.

He was playing the gruff newsman. Maya knew he was posturing, but people postured all the time. She was doing it herself.

"Mr. Jameson, we believe the city is poorer since your voice has been silenced, and we are prepared to give you an even bigger megaphone than the one you had with the *Bugle*. A radio broadcast of the sort we envision would put you everywhere in the city—in homes, in stores, in taxicabs, in offices. Would you refuse such an offer because you don't like the idea of anonymous backers?"

"Maybe," he told her. "Understand up front that no one tells me what to say or what to do. You get me, you get pure Jameson. Straight—no water, no ice. If anyone starts whispering in my ear that I need to say this or not say that, I walk away. If that's not in the contract, then the contract doesn't get signed."

"I will pass that along to the lawyers and get you the contracts by the morning."

Jameson finished his hot dog and wiped his hands on a paper napkin. Then he reached out to shake Maya's hand.

"Then it looks like you've got a deal," he replied. "When can I start making Spider-Man's life miserable?"

"As soon as possible," Maya said, accepting the handshake. "Start to organize a staff and plan out your schedule." With that she stood and walked away, pulling a little bottle of hand sanitizer out of her purse.

As she walked back to the office, she couldn't help but feel pleased with herself. Mr. Fisk would be furious if he found out, but only because he'd told her to stay away from all things Spider-Man. In his anger, he might not see how good this plan really was. No one was better than J. Jonah Jameson at whipping up the public to turn against Spider-Man.

She'd been encouraged to explore her own projects, and it wasn't hard to find a slot for Jameson on one of the most high-profile talk radio stations. All they had to do was wind him up and let him go. Jameson's hot air would take care of the rest.

SIXTEEN

SHE couldn't tell what Fisk's secretary was doing in there. There was a lot of scraping and some thumping, and what sounded like growling.

MJ was glad she'd turned down that cup of coffee, yet she also regretted it. It would have helped to settle her nerves, but she didn't need caffeine jitters when she was interviewing Fisk.

Her phone buzzed, and she considered ignoring it. Her instincts told her not to be on the phone when the secretary came out for her, but then she reconsidered. It would make her look like a busy reporter, and could only help to give the impression of someone who needed to be in touch with others at all times.

Besides, it was Peter.

She hated how she'd left things with him last night. *"There are some things we really need to talk about."* Not a good note on which to end a conversation. It wasn't her fault, of course, and Peter could take it, but even so… It was something important, and something he wouldn't want to hear, but if they were going to survive together, they needed to have this conversation.

Until that happened, she didn't want him to worry too much. So she hit "accept."

"Hi," she said when she answered. "I can't talk long. I'm about to go into an interview."

"You report, girl," he said. So this was just a chatty check-in, not an *I-have-to-go-to-Iceland-to-fight-robot-assassins* conversation. "Who are you interviewing?"

"You promise not to freak out?"

"Of course."

"Wilson Fisk."

A brief silence.

"I'm freaking out."

"Peter…" MJ groaned.

"Reporters who try to expose him vanish," he said. "You know that."

"I'm just doing an interview—getting to know him."

"So you can expose him later," he snapped. "Don't tell me I'm wrong." His tone irritated the hell out of her.

"And don't tell me how to do the right thing," she said. "I don't tell you."

"You tell me plenty," he countered.

"No, I offer you advice, and you're welcome to do that, in return—but that's not what this is. You're setting limits."

"I'm not setting limits," he said. "I'm trying to keep you safe."

The door to Fisk's office opened.

"I've got to go."

"Wait!" Peter said. "If you get a chance, ask him where he keeps the evidence of his crimes—"

MJ disconnected, slipped the phone into her purse, and stood up.

"Mr. Fisk will see you now," the secretary said.

O———————————O

HE was big.

Everyone knew Wilson Fisk was a large man, but nothing MJ had read, none of the news clips she'd seen on television, none of Peter's stories about trying to dodge his massive fists, prepared her for the real thing.

It was like she was standing next to a creature out of folklore, or from another world. He was tall, yes, but broad and built on a more massive scale than anyone she'd ever seen. When they shook hands, she had a memory of her father playing with her when she was a little girl pretending to shake a troll's hand. The difference in proportion wasn't simply notable—it was absurd.

For all that, he had a kind of charm that surprised her. He dressed well in suits that were—of course—bespoke, and his manner was relaxed. He projected a kind of aura that suggested there was nothing he would rather be doing than this interview with—literally—the *Daily Bugle*'s most junior reporter.

MJ had no illusions that he'd researched her employment history. He would know what she'd written, and when she'd been hired. She and Peter had been careful to make sure there was no public record of the two of them being involved. Peter had been closely associated with Spider-Man when working as a freelance photographer, but it wouldn't surprise her if Fisk knew about their relationship, too.

If he hadn't bothered to dig deeper yet, she thought, he would later on—before she was done with him. But not today. Today was going to be pleasant. Today would be about paving the way.

"So, tell me about your story," Fisk said. "How can I help you?"

MJ had prepared what she wanted to say, and let it come out with the air of spontaneity. She was new at the *Bugle*, she said—he would know this already, and the fact that she wasn't trying to conceal it might encourage him to let his guard down—and writing stories about working people who stood to benefit from what Fisk was promising in his new apartment projects.

"Not just promises," he told her. "Mixed-income projects like these have been tried before, but they always fail because of the greed of everyone involved. If you can give ten units to the working poor, they suppose, then why not five and pocket the extra money? If there's a profit to be had, why not more? During my time of... exile, I realized I was as guilty as anyone of this sort of avarice. Maybe more than most. No amount of wealth would ever be enough, I thought, so I never stopped thinking of ways to make more money."

"But that changed?" MJ prompted. "Because of the trial?"

"The trial, my time in Japan, where I dedicated myself to meditation and reflection. I'm not quite ready to give up my material wealth, of course, but now I strive for balance. I want to make money, but I'm willing to find an amount that's enough. I don't need five yachts, or fifty sports cars. No one does. Admittedly I'm enough of an egotist to seek a certain kind of grandeur, so rather than indulging my worst impulses I'm channeling them into something more productive. Rather than simply growing richer, I want to be a force that helps the city grow its own riches."

"And you want to be celebrated for that?"

He smiled. "I am, by nature, an ambitious man, and because I cannot change my nature, I can change the manner in which I express that ambition. Already other developers are modifying their practices to make them more like mine. Building affordable units for working people. Offering higher wages for workers. Better benefits. That's all happening because I have changed the standard. Other people are stepping up their game. Without my example, I doubt we'd see anything like Martin Li's F.E.A.S.T. operation, which is revamping how we help the homeless."

"Doesn't F.E.A.S.T. predate your return to New York?" MJ asked. Maybe it was a mistake to contradict him, but if she didn't push back a little, he'd either think she was a worthless sycophant or suspect she was after a bigger story.

"It may have existed," he said, "but if you check the timeline, you'll find that he significantly increased his funding, and the scope of his operation, after I began my programs and launched the Fisk Foundation."

MJ wasn't sure this was true, but she wrote it down. She'd do the research later and decide how to handle the claim.

"This is how change occurs," Fisk continued. "This is what people who are fortunate can do for the city. In the end, history will judge businessmen like me much more kindly than, say, the costumed vigilantes. Even if some of them try to do the right thing, they end up sowing chaos more often than they help anyone."

MJ wrote this down, all the while keeping her expression neutral.

"You disagree with me," Fisk said. "I can see it on your face."

She flashed him her most disarming smile. "We're here for me to listen to *your* opinions, Mr. Fisk."

"But I want to hear yours, as well." He moved his massive hand back and forth between them. "If there is to be any kind of relationship between us, and a relationship is necessary if you are to be a successful journalist, I must know something of you. So tell me what you think of Spider-Man and the others of his ilk."

She nodded. "It's well-known that you have particular reason to dislike costumed crimefighters, but I'm not convinced we can live without them. There are bad people with incredible powers and abilities as well, and we need someone who can push back against them."

"Perhaps," he said, "but I believe they seek each other out. The so-called good ones fight the so-called bad ones. It's a public gladiatorial spectacle. They have their fun, and the rest of us clean up their mess. My belief is that if we stop encouraging them, they will go away."

I'll remember that next time Electro takes down the power grid, MJ thought, but she said nothing.

"My fundamental concern is that the way this city is run can't be arranged for those with special abilities, or any persons who are identified as extraordinary," he pressed. "The city must be made a place where ordinary people can live."

"Do you consider yourself extraordinary?"

He laughed—a bass rumble that MJ felt in her bones. "I suppose I set myself up for that question. In some ways, yes. I made my fortune, which was nearly ripped away from me by an overzealous and misused justice system. I managed not only to move past that difficulty, but to grow. I have become a better person through adversity."

Suddenly MJ felt as if she was the one who had been set up. That answer felt polished. As she considered this, he looked at the clock on his computer monitor.

"I'm afraid that's all the time I have for you, Miss Watson," Fisk said. "However, I appreciate your coverage of this subject."

"My pleasure." MJ stood up. He did, as well, and once again engulfed her hand in his.

"I like you," he told her. "You don't hesitate to ask the questions *or* express your opinions, but you don't seem to be looking for kill shots. Far too many reporters walk through that door seeking to trip me up, to set a trap that—in their minds—will end with me admitting I'm some kind of criminal mastermind."

"Oh, don't get me wrong," MJ said. "I'm very ambitious."

"I don't doubt it," he said, "but there are many paths that lead to the top. Crossing Wilson Fisk isn't one of them. You show a great deal more wisdom."

"Thank you," she said with her best smile.

As she stepped out of the office, she felt like she needed to take a shower—but MJ also felt quite pleased with herself. She'd rolled the dice, and was pretty sure the gamble had paid off. Wilson Fisk would seek to manipulate her to his advantage, but she was going to be one step ahead of him. She'd be the one manipulating Fisk.

SEVENTEEN

HE was in the lab when his phone buzzed. It was MJ, proposing that they try again to have that "talk."

"How about the sandwich place," he said. "For the sake of consistency?"

"You don't fool me," she said. "You just like their pastrami."

"Guilty. How'd the interview go?"

"Really well." The excitement was obvious in her voice. "I think he likes me."

This is one of those times, he told himself, *when I need to take a moment to consider what I'm going to say.* Then he started talking without doing any more considering.

"MJ, you're playing with fire," he said. "There are only two ways to push up against a guy like him. You're either co-opted, or you're destroyed."

"Or you beat him," she said. "Aren't you trying for door number three?"

"I have certain advantages."

"So do I," she said. "Peter—" She cut herself off. "You know what, let's save this for later. I don't want to fight with you right now."

"I don't want to fight either," he said, "but I can't just sit here and let you put yourself in danger."

"You don't *let* me do anything," she said sharply. "I don't need your permission, Peter."

"That's not what I'm saying," he replied. He couldn't win. "I feel like you're twisting my words to score points, rather than hearing me. But you're right—we won't talk about it now. We'll discuss it later, without arguing."

"We won't argue if you don't say dumb things," she said, and they set a time. "See you then."

HAVING a crush at work, especially on an older guy, was a bad idea. Having a crush on an older guy with a girlfriend was a worse idea. Anika decided that she wouldn't have a crush on Peter anymore. That was her decision, and she was sticking to it.

That didn't mean she couldn't be friends with him. There was nothing that said you couldn't be friends with an older, smart, funny, impossibly cute guy you worked with. In fact, it would be an effort for them *not* to be friends. Clearly they were on the same wavelength, had a similar sense of humor, many of the same interests. They got along great. It wasn't her fault that he already had a girlfriend who obviously didn't get him or appreciate him or want to be supportive when he needed it.

At least that was what it sounded like, when she accidentally listened in on his phone conversation. She was checking on a neural simulator they'd ordered to see if it had been shipped. Peter was sitting on the other side of the terminal she'd been using.

The right thing to do would have been to walk away. Eavesdropping was *not* admirable behavior. As she wrestled with the conundrum, she heard what she heard. That done, there was no putting that toothpaste back in the tube, so now she had to figure out how best to act, knowing that his girlfriend was totally wrong for him.

Anika chewed on it all day. Most of her tasks were menial, which left her mind free to go this way and that. At times it came back to the work they were doing, which was pretty amazing.

She had a great-aunt who lost a leg in a car accident, years ago. Her aunt was close to eighty now and still got around pretty well with her prosthetic, but Anika loved to imagine what the lab's research would mean for people like her. The ability to move with the same ease and flexibility that she'd had before the accident—that was some seriously life-changing stuff. She was thrilled to be a part of it.

A lot of what she was doing was data entry and fact checking, but she also helped Peter run some tests. They'd had a number-crunching session when there'd been a problem with one of the formulae for the synthetic neural relay. Anika had been the one to figure out where a number had been transposed—a simple clerical error that had thrown everything off. It would be one thing if she'd just spotted the error through proofreading, but she'd deduced where the mistake had to be and backtracked it to the source.

Both Peter and Theodore had watched her do

it, and they'd both been impressed.

Anika could see herself working in the lab for a while. Definitely for the rest of the year, and maybe longer if she decided to take some time off before applying to grad school. There was no way she could stick around all that time if things weren't comfortable with Peter, and that meant being honest and being his friend. That seemed perfectly reasonable to her.

Maybe she was sort of stalking him, too. But if she *knew* she was doing something sort of creepy, did it mean she wasn't really being creepy? That seemed to make sense. She was just... exploring her feelings. That was the best term for it.

Late in the afternoon, Peter headed for the door. Closing up a file she'd been finished with for fifteen minutes anyhow, she grabbed her backpack so she could leave at the same time.

"Good work today," he told her while they were waiting for the elevator. "You saved us a ton of headaches."

"Anyone could have done it." She brushed some hair away from her eyes.

"It didn't look like that to me," he said with a grin. "That was some crazy math wizardry there."

She felt her cheeks burning. "Thanks."

The elevator doors chimed open, and they stepped in.

No point hesitating, she told herself. *Just dive right in.*

"Look, I didn't mean to, but I sort of overheard your fight with your girlfriend."

"It wasn't really a fight," he said. "More of a disagreement with a side of vehemence." He laughed a little nervously. He probably wished this super-awkward conversation wasn't happening.

In for a penny...

"Well, I don't want to pry," she continued, "but if you need someone to talk to... I mean, we've already talked some, right, and it would be more like continuing to talk than starting a new conversation. I'm just saying that I'm a good listener. I'm also rambling, which I promise not to do if you actually talk to me about anything important."

"Thanks, Anika," he said. "I appreciate it."

He didn't sound like he appreciated it, though. He sounded like he was really uncomfortable and was desperate for the conversation to end. When the doors chimed open, he said good night and bolted off.

Now she'd done it. Now he was going to be super uncomfortable around her. She wished there was some way to figure out the right approach, but she had no idea what that might be. If she had some insight, knew how things *really* were with his girlfriend, it would probably make things easier. But there was no way for that to happen.

Unless...

They were going to the sandwich place—the one he'd mentioned. It was in Times Square. A fact-finding mission. Gathering data.

This wasn't, she knew, the sort of thing normal people did. She certainly couldn't make a habit of it, but if it was just this once, and she never did it again, she figured she could live with herself. A one-time incident could be filed as "enthusiastic" rather than "creepy."

She waited a few minutes. The last thing she wanted was to run into him on the subway. Then, walking slowly so she would be on the train after his, she began her research.

IT had been a particularly contentious meeting with a neighborhood association. Not everyone was pleased with the idea of mixed-income housing, and it had required a great deal of self-control to keep from knocking heads together. Fisk's third-shift secretary hadn't yet arrived, or had gone to relieve himself or some other excuse, so he had no idea if there were any important messages.

On top of that, Michael Bingham was in his office when he walked in.

Fisk supposed he ought not to be surprised that a man who had nearly identical abilities to Spider-Man should be able to get past security, but this was a serious breach of protocol. It wasn't at all what Fisk had agreed to.

If the man had been sitting and waiting patiently, that would have been one thing. It would have been outrageous, certainly, but perhaps not beyond the pale. As it happened, Bingham was rifling through his desk drawers.

"Wilson," Bingham said as he looked up. He

wore faded jeans and a tight T-shirt that showed off his physique. "I was wondering when you were going to show up." He took a handful of paperclips, slipped them into his pocket, and closed the drawer. "You'll want to sit at your desk, I guess. I don't know. I've never had a desk, but it seems like people like to sit at them." He nodded toward the big chair.

Fisk approached him. He was so accustomed to intimidating people with his size he hardly even noticed he was doing it anymore, but he noticed it now. This insignificant worm was attempting to assert dominance. Over *Wilson Fisk*. It would have been laughable, had Bingham not been so dangerous.

It was important not to show too much concern.

"What is it you want?" he asked as he lowered himself into his desk chair.

"Just thought I'd drop in," he said, "to give you a progress report. We don't really chat so much, and I guess maybe it's my fault. I'm not as social as a lot of guys. People make me uncomfortable."

Fisk simply stared, making a point of not inviting Bingham to sit.

He made a point of sitting anyhow.

"I'm not entirely certain this relationship is working to our mutual benefit," Fisk said. "You've acted on several occasions without my consent. It may be time to rethink our terms."

"You can do all the thinking and rethinking you want," Bingham said, "but I'm going to show that phony who the real Spider-Man is. Keep your TV on tonight,

Wilson. There's going to be some great entertainment."

"I haven't approved any action for tonight," Fisk replied. "Any more than I approved what happened at the construction site. What was the point of fighting him in that ridiculous outfit? And why there?"

That truly rankled Fisk. No one knew the building site was his property—it was registered in the name of a satellite company—but even the most complicated labyrinth of shell companies and LLCs could be unraveled by someone with enough time and determination. How had Bingham lured Spider-Man there in the first place? How had he hired those henchmen? This project, though only just begun, already seemed to be spiraling out of control.

"It was a dry run," Bingham said. "I wanted to make sure I could take him, but I wasn't ready yet to show the world that he ain't the real deal. Soon they'll know, though. *I'm* Spider-Man. That's what they'll see."

"I think that before you act again," Fisk said, "you had better submit any plans you have to me for approval."

Bingham leaned back again.

"We both know I don't work that way, Wilson," Bingham said. "I'm a free spirit. I told you that from the beginning. Maybe you think I'm, I don't know, too loony to remember what we talked about, what we agreed." He twirled his finger around his ear. "Maybe you don't think I'm playing with a full deck, and you can just say whatever you want, but it ain't how it works."

"Then why are you here?" Fisk asked, his voice turning into a growl.

"Like I said, I wanted to let you know what was going on." He stood up quickly. "Professional courtesy, let's call it."

"I could keep you from ever leaving this building."

Bingham grinned again. "You could try."

He turned and moved toward the door.

"Stop," Fisk said. "This can't continue." He needed to sound calm, even agreeable. If he pushed, Bingham would push back. Most people could be intimidated, but not everyone. "If we are to be successful, we must work together."

Bingham turned. "I thought that's what we were doing." Then he kept going. He opened the office door and walked past Maya Lopez. She stopped in her tracks to watch him pass. Bingham put a hand alongside his mouth, and cupped it.

"Good evening, miss!" he said loudly, enunciating slowly. Then he cackled happily and made his way to the elevator.

Fisk clenched his fists and observed Maya for a moment, holding his temper by dint of great effort. She watched the disgusting individual leave, then continued into his office and closed the door.

"What was he doing here?" she asked. "Who was he?" she added hastily.

"Someone who needed to provide me with some information," Fisk said in a flat tone that meant he didn't want the conversation to continue. He was clenching and unclenching his fists and blinking rapidly, all signs that he knew that he was losing his temper. He needed to get himself under control. He needed to get this situation under control.

"It didn't look congenial," she said. "Are you sure you can trust him?"

"I will decide that!" Fisk snapped. His rage was a living thing beneath his skin, trying to break free. He had never let himself loose, not fully, around Maya. There had been some minor incidents, of course, but nothing serious. He could feel himself slipping, though. He could imagine his fists pounding down on his desk, breaking it in half while she looked on in horror.

Maya was one of the few genuinely good things he had to show for his life. Not simply successful, but *good*. Her loyalty to him, her devotion, was like a testimony to what he hoped to achieve. Not this ridiculous business with giving apartments to poor people. That was just for show. It hardly mattered. All the handouts in the world wouldn't eradicate poverty. The only way the city would ever improve was with better leadership. Not elected fools like Osborn, but real leaders.

Fisk had done things in pursuit of this goal that had crossed lines from which he could not go back. Yet there were two people who saw him for who he really was. Vanessa, his wife, and Maya, who was not his daughter, but she was as close to it as anyone in this world. He did not like to let the beast loose while she watched.

Something else troubled him.

Something he had seen.

How had Bingham known she was deaf?

He turned to Maya. "That man who left my office," he said. "Have you had any dealings with him?"

"I've reviewed his file," she said. "Nothing more."

Fisk had no reason to doubt her. And yet...

"If you have, tell me now," he said. "I will forgive you if you are honest, but if you hide the truth from me, then we will have... difficulties. Tell me."

Abruptly he realized he was towering over her. He hadn't meant to approach her, to menace her. Now he took a step back.

"Tell me," he said, this time more quietly.

Maya shook her head. "I haven't..." she said, her voice quavering. "I wouldn't." She sounded afraid, but of course she was afraid. She had seen him hurt people when he was like this. She had to fear that he might hurt her, if he lost control. He hated that.

Even more than he hated that, had she answered the wrong way, he might have given her *reason* to fear.

"I need to go," she said.

"Then go," he told her, his voice controlled. "Close the door on your way out." He waited until she would be far away from his office, then he looked at his desk.

Fisk raised his fist.

He should hold back.

He should constrain himself.

Then rational thought was gone, and he let his true nature take command.

EIGHTEEN

PETER had pastrami on his mind.

Yes, he was also a little worried about how things were going with MJ, but he knew they would work things out. They'd been together for a long time, and each had to bend if they were going to grow together. She'd already put up with things that were beyond what any girlfriend should endure. Whatever she needed from him, he'd find a way to make sure she got it.

She was already waiting for him and on line when he walked through the door. He checked his wristwatch just before he gave her a quick kiss.

"You're living dangerously," he said, "showing up early."

"And you're on your best behavior, showing up almost on time."

"*Exactly* on time," he said, tapping his watch. Wearing one made him a bit of a relic, he knew, but it had belonged to Uncle Ben, and he liked having it close.

The line ahead of them was pretty long, and it only took a few minutes for it to begin snaking behind Peter. He looked around, hoping they'd be able to find a place to sit.

"So," he said, "maybe this isn't the best place to

have a serious conversation, but since we're going to work things out anyhow, maybe we should talk about it now."

"So your sandwich pleasure isn't in any way diminished?"

"It's a good sandwich," he admitted. "I'd hate for anything to ruin it."

"I'm glad you have your priorities straight."

"Absolutely."

"Okay," she began. "Well, I think you're right that it doesn't have to be a big deal, as long as you actually hear what I'm saying. But this is serious, Peter, so you really have to hear me—not just agree, but *hear* what I'm saying and make changes based on it."

"Right," he mumbled, but he was already distracted.

Looking annoyed, MJ glanced around and saw why. There were a pair of cops ahead of them on line. They were, in fact, about to get their sandwiches, but one of them said something into his radio and they rushed out, leaving dinner behind. Another pair of officers ran down the street past the shop's windows.

"Something big is going on," Peter said.

"You want me to order you something?"

"Would you mind? Put it in your fridge. I'll come by later if I can."

"Not too late," she said, "or it might not have survived the wait."

"I'll take my chances." He gave her a kiss and rushed out the door. Something hovered quickly in his peripheral vision, like a familiar face, but he didn't have time to sort it out. This wasn't exactly the moment to say hi to whomever it might have been. If it was someone he should have recognized, they'd have to deal with it. One of the advantages of being famously flakey was that no one was surprised when you flaked.

THE moment she stepped into the sandwich place, Anika felt sure she was making a mistake. Then she looked at the menu posted over the counter and decided she could probably live with the consequences.

To the far right, people were collecting the sandwiches they'd ordered—some to-go orders in bags, others on trays—and once she caught sight of them, there was no way she was turning around. This place really did look good.

There was Peter, talking to a woman with red hair. She really was pretty. Anika had hoped she would look mean, but she didn't. There was no sign of them arguing, either. They seemed entirely comfortable with each other. Just a normal couple having normal couple problems.

Anika decided she needed to get out more. She'd worked so hard at school that she'd lost perspective on how normal people lived. She'd get her dinner, go spend some quality time with her cat, and rethink her life. She needed more time with the menu, though. The line wasn't moving fast, but she wanted to be prepared when her turn came.

Then she noticed a commotion. Policemen started shouting into their squawking radios and dashed out of the restaurant, joining up with other officers running past outside. A few seconds later Peter took off, running right past her but not even noticing her.

Why would he do that? she wondered. *What does he have to do with the police?* She'd have to run some theories by her cat when she got home.

Anika sighed. At least now she didn't have to worry about being spotted.

WOULDN'T *it be nice*, Peter thought, *if I could actually spend a little quality time with my girlfriend and a delicious sandwich?* It was as if the city was conspiring against him. He hadn't been patrolling or listening to a police radio. He'd even had his phone turned off.

But no, the crisis had to go waving its arms right in front of his face, and of course he couldn't just ignore it. If anyone ended up getting hurt, just because he'd wanted to enjoy some time with MJ—well, no point in even thinking about it. Peter didn't work that way.

Ducking into the shadows of a niche between buildings, he dodged a pile of trash and clambered up a wall and onto the roof. Once there he changed into his spider-suit and monitored the police chatter through his mask. West of Central Park, over at an auction house called Rosemann's, some nuts had taken a bunch of people hostage. There were children in there—or there *might* be children in there. There were conflicting reports about the number and type of hostages, as well as the perpetrators. Someone said it was a lone wacko with a gun. Another said it was someone with super-powers.

By the time he arrived, the logistics of this thing were still a mess.

It was always a risk to interact with cops—occasionally he encountered one who was overzealous, and wanted to be the guy who captured Spider-Man. Still, he needed more information if he was going to help, and he spotted a solitary officer who'd just helped to clear the perimeter. A couple of teenagers had tried to push their way through, and this guy had ushered them away, but he'd done it without being a jerk about it. He seemed to be sympathetic with the fact that teenagers were, by nature, going to do stupid things.

So it was worth a shot.

He leapt down and landed on a brick wall right next to the police officer.

"Holy crap!" The guy took a step back. "You're Spider-Man!"

"Got it in the first try," Peter replied. "And you?"

"Jeff Davis," he said. "You know what's going on in there?"

"I was kind of hoping you could tell me—so we could see if there was any way I could help."

"The whole thing feels hinky to me." The cop shook his head. "We got a bunch of conflicting reports, but so far no hard information. The infrared and sound-mic guys are set up, but so far they haven't been able to pick up anything. It's a big place, with its own warehouse, but that doesn't explain it—there are still some itchy questions."

"Like who takes hostages in an auction house at night?"

"Exactly!" The cop touched his nose. "Something's fishy."

"You said it," Spider-Man replied. "Thanks for your help." He pushed off and leapt upward, bounding back and forth between two buildings until he reached the roof. From that vantage point he looked down at the auction house and its storage facility. There were a few points of entry, including one on the roof, and they all looked quiet.

He was grateful that the cop had been so helpful. He wished now he'd been paying attention when he'd said his name. Jefferson, or something like that?

○———————○

INSIDE Rosemann's, everything was completely quiet. There weren't even any security guards, because they'd all been evacuated. After doing extensive recon, Spider-Man took out his phone and called Yuri Watanabe.

"You hear anything about this Rosemann situation?" he asked her. "I'm inside, but I don't see anything. It's completely deserted."

"You shouldn't be messing around with a

hostage situation," Watanabe said.

"That's my point," he answered. "There are no hostages. No hostage takers. No one at all."

"Are you sure?" she asked. "Half the department is down there. They're treating this like a major crisis. They've even called in a hazmat team. There's a rumor that a dirty bomb might be involved."

"Maybe a dusty bomb," Spider-Man said, running his fingers along the wall. "It's possible something could be hidden in one of these crates, but there's no sign of anything bad-guyish at all. It feels like a complete false alarm or—"

He stopped himself, pretty sure Watanabe was thinking the same thing.

"A decoy."

○━━━━━━━━━○

ANIKA watched MJ on line ahead of her. She hadn't seemed angry at all that Peter had run out on her. Then she ordered two sandwiches—presumably one for him—and waited for her food. She leaned against the wall and poked at her phone, but didn't gripe or look angry or call anyone to complain. She seemed nice, just like Peter was nice.

Isn't that just terrific? she thought wryly.

The girlfriend picked up her order around the time Anika placed hers. She went and stood where the girlfriend had been, vaguely monitoring the atmosphere for nasty vibes but not picking up on anything. She took out her phone and began scrolling through her news feed. The best thing she could possibly do was distract herself from the fact that she'd been stalking.

Then she heard the screaming.

She looked up and one of *them* was in the restaurant—one of those people who wore costumes, and not one of the good ones. He had on a yellow puffy suit that almost looked like a winter jacket, and a yellow hood with an orange stripe down the middle. There was a mechanical contraption on his back, and he had metal gauntlets that seemed to be wired into the device.

"I am the sinister Shocker!" the man cried in a voice muffled by his mask. "Here to cause mayhem and destruction!" He turned to the door and bursts of teeth-rattling vibrations emanated from his gauntlets. The metal around the door buckled and folded in around itself, leaving everyone trapped inside.

Anika felt panic welling up.

"Let's just calm down," a man said, stepping forward. He was dressed like he'd just come from the gym, and his muscles were bulging out of his tank top. It looked like he wanted to play the hero, but he was also being cautious, approaching slowly with his hands up. "We can talk about this."

"This isn't a time for conversation!" Shocker proclaimed. A burst exploded from his gauntlets. The man flew backward and landed on the floor, twitching but still alive. It was as if he'd been tased or bludgeoned or something. That was a sign the Shocker didn't want to kill anyone. At least she hoped it was.

Her phone was in her hand anyhow, so with trembling fingers Anika opened the camera app, turned it to video, and began recording. The police were going to want to see as much evidence as possible. She could show them when this was all over, and if she didn't make it—well, people would say she'd been a thoughtful citizen until the end.

"Prepare for the worst!" Shocker cried out, as if he was trying to make sure they could hear him in the cheap seats. It was like the guy had never dealt with people before—but wasn't he a known villain? "There will be violence. You there!" He pointed to a teenager wearing a hoodie. "Do you have a heart condition?"

What on earth…? Anika thought.

The kid shook his head.

The Shocker hit him with a blast from his gauntlets.

"Let that be a taste of my power!"

There was something very wrong about this, and Anika wasn't the only one who seemed to be aware. People were looking around with obvious confusion. No one said anything though, trying not to draw the lunatic's attention.

Then Spider-Man showed up.

He leapt in from the back room, sailing across the restaurant and slamming feet first into the Shocker's chest. The villain staggered, and the device on his back struck the wall with a crunching sound.

"Hey!" Shocker shouted. "Be careful!"

"Forget that," Spider-Man said. "I'm gonna mess you up, Shocker."

"I have a room full of hostages here, Spider-Man," the villain answered back. As loud as it was, his voice was as empty of actual emotion as a fourth-grader reciting lines from a school play. "If you attempt to apprehend me, I will kill them."

"You think I care about these losers?" Spider-Man asked, gesturing toward the huddled civilians. "They're not rich or famous. What I care about is getting the credit for stopping you. If some people have to die along the way, that just means I've bagged a bigger fish."

"You won't take me in," Shocker said. "I've wired this restaurant with a bomb. If you try to stop me, we'll all die."

"Not me, with my enhanced reflexes," Spider-Man replied. "I'll get away. If you're dead, what do I care if you take the hostages with you?"

"I'm done with this!" one of the hostages shouted. A burly man wearing a windbreaker, he picked up a trashcan and threw it hard against the window. The glass shattered and he—along with a dozen other people—raced out of the restaurant.

Anika wondered if she could make it. She'd have to cross Shocker's line of vision to get to the window, but he didn't seem to be paying attention to his hostages anymore. He was more interested in circling around Spider-Man—if it really was him.

That was starting to seem unlikely. Anika had

been too busy with school to pay attention to the costumed heroes who always seemed to be cropping up, but she'd always kind of liked Spider-Man. In the news footage he was always cracking jokes and saving kids who wandered in front of traffic. She supposed this man's claim not to care about the victims might be an act—something to throw the Shocker off his game—but that didn't feel right to her.

"Your hostages are getting away," Spider-Man said. "Don't you think you should do something?" He looked over at a man cowering near him and grabbed him by the wrist. Yanking hard, he tossed him at the villain, who dodged out of the way. Then the two of them began to grapple.

That was her chance. Other people were climbing through the broken window, yet she felt as if it was somehow important to record this—to preserve the data. That's what she did. It was a piece of a puzzle, and even if she didn't know what that puzzle was, someone was going to need to see it.

Still—restaurant wired to blow.

It was better not to ignore that sort of thing, so she began moving toward the gaping hole in the window, but slowly, holding up her phone so she could record the two men fighting. Or pretending to fight, maybe. More and more it looked fake.

Suddenly the Shocker looked up.

"We need to go," he called out, and the two of them dashed into the kitchen—together.

Oh, no…

Anika lowered her phone and moved quickly toward the window.

If I can just—

There was a flash of light.

Then there was nothing.

NINETEEN

IT didn't seem real. Didn't seem possible. While the actual restaurant smoldered behind him, and first responders combed the scene and put out fires, Spider-Man perched in the shadows and watched a massive Times Square television streaming news coverage of the event. Though it was usually silent, they'd turned on the sound.

The restaurant he'd been in. Destroyed.

People were dead.

AS he finished combing the antiques warehouse, Spider-Man's phone rang with a call from MJ.

"I'm fine, I'm fine," she said when he picked up the call.

"Why wouldn't you be?"

"Oh my God, you haven't heard."

The chatter on the police band had been too much to let him focus on the task at hand, so he'd muted it. Now he turned it back on, and immediately a picture began to form. An explosion. Casualties. The Shocker—and Spider-Man.

And it all happened at the sandwich place where he'd been just a little while ago.

"I need to check this out."

"I know," she said. "Just… be careful, okay. Something weird is going on."

———o———o———

"HE called himself the Shocker," a woman said as she stared into the interviewer's camera. "He'd set a bomb in the place, and then Spider-Man came rushing in and they started fighting. Spider-Man said he didn't care who got hurt. He even used one guy as a weapon—tossed him at Shocker."

The Shocker wouldn't set an explosive. His weapon was vibrations, like a concussive blast. Strictly a second-rate villain, and not a bomber.

That wasn't the most inexplicable part of the story, but it was the one on which he focused. It was solid, concrete. It was something he could work with. Why would the Shocker, who loved using his gauntlets, set a bomb? What would it get him?

Then, on the giant TV screen, the woman's face was replaced by J. Jonah Jameson.

Oh, that's just great.

"Spider-Man is a menace," Jameson said, and it boomed across the square. "I've been telling the people of this city for years how dangerous he is. Even those who didn't want to accept it will believe me now."

"Tomorrow, on my new broadcast, I'm going to break down how this latest affront isn't anything new for the web-shooting maniac," he said, "but a continuation of the dangerous criminal practices he's been using all along. It's time for people to wake up and acknowledge him as a threat to public safety!"

His face disappeared, and the screen showed wobbly cell-phone footage of the fight between the Shocker and Spider-Man. It was definitely the Shocker—he'd recognize that puffy suit anywhere. And in a completely surreal way, it was as if he was looking at footage of himself. Whoever it was in the costume moved like he did. It was the same one from the shipyard. It was close, very close, but not quite his spider-suit.

"This is footage from a cell phone found at the scene," a news announcer said. "The camera belonged to one of the persons who remain unknown and may still be trapped under the rubble." They showed an image of first responders covering a still body. It was just an instant, but Peter knew the face. He knew it. It was Anika.

The breath caught in his lungs.

"Emergency personnel are still combing the site, and if anyone knows the identity of the person who took the video, please call the number on your screen."

Anika. How was that even possible?

He had to do something. He didn't know what it was, but he had to act.

HE was at the scene—combing through rubble— before he'd even realized he'd made up his mind to do so. There were emergency workers everywhere, digging through debris that was soaking wet in some places, smoldering in others. Peter was lifting bricks and support beams and chunks of wood. He didn't even notice it at first.

People were screaming at him.

"You haven't done enough?" someone shouted.

"Back for more?" another person called.

"Get the hell away from here, you creep!"

Then he saw it. A stretcher being wheeled away. Anika's face, covered with dirt and soot and blood, visible for just a second before the EMT pulled the sheet over her face. It didn't seem real. It couldn't *be* real...

Then there was a grip on his wrist.

"Let's go," a cop said. "You're gonna have to answer some questions."

He felt himself shifting back to reality. Light reflecting off of handcuffs. A few other police officers moving closer, some reaching down to unbuckle their firearms. He had to go. People were dead. Anika was dead. Someone had done this—someone who looked like him. He would have to deal with it, but he couldn't if he allowed himself to be arrested.

"Sorry, but you've got the wrong guy," he said. With his free hand he shot a web out to a nearby building, pulled free of the officer's grasp, and launched himself upward.

○———————○

YURI Watanabe was silent. The site of the explosion was a few blocks away, but clearly visible from the rooftop on which they stood.

"How could anyone do something like that?" Spider-Man asked, staring out into the space between the buildings. "It's so senseless, so random. People are dead, Yuri, and someone wants me to take the blame."

"Not someone," she said, her voice angry. "Fisk. This is all him. You fought the fake Spider-Man at his construction site. We know now that it was his— the records weren't as well hidden as he thought." She made a noise that sounded like a growl. "That can't be a coincidence. Fisk set it all up."

"He must have been watching me," Spider-Man speculated, but his voice sounded distant, even to his own ears. "It was like he knew I wouldn't be able to resist checking out such an offbeat crime. Then, when I showed up at the snake shop, that set everything in motion. But why? What does he get out of this?"

Watanabe shook her head. "He wants the public believing that you've gone bad," she said. "That's the only logical assumption. It doesn't matter why— he's got a million reasons. Motive is for the cops on television. Real cops deal with evidence, and that means we need to stop Fisk before he pulls another stunt like this."

Spider-Man tried to focus. The fake hostages, the Shocker, the bomb, Anika. MJ. If it had gone down just a *little* differently, MJ could have been killed in the blast. His thoughts kept working in circles, going nowhere at all.

"I'm going to get him," he said, clenching his fists until it hurt. "I'm going to take him down. Now."

"No," Watanabe snapped. "Listen to me. What if he *wants* you to come after him? The way things stand right now, that might make him into even more of a hero. Don't play into his hands. You can't let him call the shots."

"So we do nothing?" he asked. "What about justice for the people who died tonight?"

"We'll have it." Watanabe put a hand on his shoulder. He twitched. "I promise you. It may take more time than we'd like, but if we keep going, we'll put him behind bars."

He took a deep breath, tried to clear his thoughts, but the best he could do was to focus on a single point—a bright and burning ball of fury. Revenge. Justice. Retribution. Whatever it was called, he knew he couldn't rest until he'd dealt with Fisk. It would be the most important thing Spider-Man ever did. Maybe it would be the *last* thing Spider-Man would ever do. But it would get done.

"Okay," he said. "Let's do it. Let's take him down."

Watanabe nodded, and then turned back toward the site of the explosion. The area around the blast crater was lit up like daylight, and a hint of smoke still rose above the rubble. There was an acrid smell in the air, like a burning pot left on the stove. They remained there in wordless testimony, their silence more powerful than any spoken vow.

o————————o

FROM his own rooftop, Bingham watched the weak

Spider-Man imposter. Though his face was hidden behind the mask, Bingham could imagine the fury, the rage, and maybe even some fear. Fear that his world was starting to crumble.

The false Spider-Man had gotten away with pretending for so long that he'd probably come to believe he was the real thing. Confronted with the truth, facing the power of the true Web-Slinger, he wouldn't know what to do. He would run here and there, go this way and that, and still he would be powerless and helpless and weak. He was pathetic, and Bingham felt nothing but contempt for him.

That woman next to him. Even in the dark, Bingham could see the badge clipped to her belt. A cop. The pretender needed a cop's help. It was so pathetic it was sad.

Still…

A cop could spell trouble for Fisk. The fat man would want to know, but Bingham wasn't about to tell him. Let Fisk solve his own problems. Bingham didn't work for anyone—regardless of what they thought. He was his own master. Anyone who thought to control him would find out the hard way.

As for the fake web-spinner, Bingham could take him down any time he wanted. Right now if he wanted. There was nothing to it, but it wouldn't be any fun that way. He wanted to watch the fish flop on the hook for a while. He'd stalk and hunt and torment, and when the time was right, Bingham would make his kill.

TWENTY

THE cup of coffee in his hand was cold, and Peter carried it to the microwave to reheat it for the third time. Maybe the fourth. He stepped over piles of clothes, stacks of books, discarded computer equipment. Usually he chastised himself for the mess. Today it didn't even register.

When the microwave's chime rang out, he took the cup back to his bed and turned again to the TV. He clutched the cup as if for warmth, but didn't lift it to take a drink.

Peter had been up all night, unable to sleep. It seemed frivolous, disrespectful, even to try. Wilson Fisk had murdered someone he knew, someone he worked with. He'd killed eleven other people—people with friends and family and children and parents. He'd targeted that restaurant for a reason. There was no way it could be a coincidence. Maybe Fisk hadn't set that bomb or detonated it personally, but that didn't matter.

Fisk was going to pay.

"Spider-Man is going to pay," someone on the television was saying. A construction worker, it looked like. It was a man-on-the-street interview—and for a final insult, a sign for Fisk's development company was visible in the background. "He can't just run around doing whatever he wants, hurting people, and expect to get away with it."

They switched to another man, an ice cream vendor in Central Park. He shook his head. "If Spider-Man did it, he should be punished, but I heard the recording. It didn't sound like him." Then the image cut to a woman behind the wheel of a delivery truck. "Wasn't Spider-Man. Guy sounded totally different. Had to be a fake."

They switched to a panel discussion, and J. Jonah Jameson was one of the speakers. They were weighing in on the topic.

"Shocker has no history of using bombs." That was a professor who had written a book on super villains. "He seems fixated on the vibrations his devices are able to produce. Based on everything we know about him, planting a bomb doesn't fit his profile. Perhaps even more mystifying, Spider-Man's behavior was inconsistent with anything we've seen from him before."

"His voice was different," another panelist said. It was a woman who was an expert on super hero psychology—though Peter was unsure how somebody acquired that expertise. "I think it's worth stating the obvious," she continued. "These people wear costumes that conceal their faces, which means there may be no stable identity behind Spider-Man or the Shocker. Both personas may be inhabited by a number of different 'performers,' if you will. Alternatively, one or both of the people in that restaurant might have been imposters, taking on the role of the Shocker or the Spider-Man persona."

Another woman, an author, cut in. "I'm not prepared to comment on Shocker, but that was not Spider-Man," she pronounced. "We saw footage of Spider-Man coming to the scene, looking for survivors, because that's what he does. The real Spider-Man is a hero."

The screen split between the four panelists and the host, who remained silent. Jameson now leaned into the camera, and it looked like he wanted to punch it. The television was filled with his image.

"We're talking about people who put on masks to terrorize the city," he said loudly, as if to drown the others out by sheer force of will. "Call them 'heroes' or 'villains,' they're all criminals. The heroes are the first responders who risked their lives to help the survivors. Policemen and firemen."

"*Police officers* and *firefighters*, you mean," the author said. "Though you may not be aware, some first responders are women."

"You know what I'm saying," Jameson snapped. "Maybe I'm not the most PC guy in the world, but I know the real heroes—the ordinary citizens who carried the wounded out of the blast zone. Spider-Man isn't a hero, he's a troublemaker and a fraud. As for his voice, we're talking about a nut who wears a mask and pretends he's a bug. Disguising his voice doesn't mean a damn thing."

Peter snapped off the television. He'd had enough.

THE lab felt like a funeral home. Even Theodore Peyton seemed shaken.

"This is a most unfortunate day," he said, his voice quiet. "Everyone is devastated."

Peter nodded. "It's just hard to process." Then he looked up and saw two strangers standing by Anika's workstation. They were clearly older, and the man looked astonishingly like a middle-aged male version of Anika. They had to be her parents.

He had no idea what he could possibly say to them, but he knew he had to try to say something. He went over to the workstation and introduced himself.

"I didn't know her long," he said, "but she was smart and funny and great at what she did. I can't imagine what you're going through, but if there's anything I can do, please let me know."

"Thank you," Anika's mother said, and then she began to cry.

"She liked to take risks," her father said. "She went skydiving and rock climbing, and we worried terribly about her. But for something like this to happen at an ordinary restaurant…" He shook his head.

Peter nodded and tried to hold back his own tears. It was impossible to see these grieving parents and not want to do something, but there was nothing to be done. Not now and not yet.

The time would come, though.

He would make it happen.

TWENTY-ONE

FISK sat in his office while Bingham was shown in. The man had demonstrated his power and his defiance, but in the two weeks that followed he had remained relatively quiet. Perhaps he had purged it from his system. Or perhaps he had exhausted the limits of his imagination. There was a chance, he thought, that Bingham might yet be brought to heel.

The attack at the restaurant had been brutal and sloppy and wholly amateurish. The fact that anyone considered it remotely possible that the real Spider-Man had been involved was a testimony to the public's credulity and the vehemence of certain voices within an easily manipulated media. These were the same forces—those with the desire to bring on "experts" who could debate opposing sides of any issue—that had enabled Fisk to rehabilitate his reputation.

Was Bingham clever enough to have anticipated this, or simply lucky enough to have wandered into a process that worked in his favor? It was difficult to know. There was no doubt that Fisk himself was responsible in part for Bingham's success. After all, he had funded some of those voices who denounced Spider-Man. The most powerful of these was turning out to be J. Jonah Jameson, whose new radio show led the charge against the web-spinner.

The irony was that, when he ran the *Bugle*, Jameson had been no friend. There was no one he enjoyed bashing more than Spider-Man, but Fisk himself had been a close second. Now Jameson was playing right into Fisk's hands.

This was how the game was played, and it was why he won. Sometimes force was required, certainly. Sometimes there was no choice but to use threats and violence in order to terrify, and manipulate, but he liked it best when he could bring people into line without them even suspecting they were serving him. If his new scheme succeeded—and it would—then the entire city would serve him, and never even suspect.

As for Bingham, the man needed to be reined in, but it would be a mistake for Fisk to overplay his hand. The man didn't respond well to threats, and while he was not bright, he understood his own chaotic power. While the man was artless, and very probably insane, he managed to get the job done.

When Bingham came into the office, he looked around as if he'd never been in there before, taking in the furnishings and decorations as if he was in a museum. He hadn't dressed to show any respect, however, wearing jeans, a black T-shirt, and a leather jacket.

"What do you want?" Bingham asked when he sat across from Fisk. "I'm a busy man."

"The effort at the restaurant was clumsy, but… effective," Fisk began. "You certainly attracted the target's attention, but it could have been done in a manner that didn't raise so many questions. I'd like to suggest some ways to help quiet those voices in the media who don't believe you are the real Spider-Man."

"But I *am* the real Spider-Man." Bingham's eyes narrowed. "That's what I'm showing them."

"Point taken." Fisk forced a tight smile. "Please allow me to clarify. Many people believe it wasn't the person they have traditionally believed to be Spider-Man."

"If they're that stupid, it's not my problem," Bingham said, stretching out his legs. "Guys like you, you're all into—what do they call it?—messaging. I don't care about messaging, about how to get the word across. I care about the message itself. You get the difference, right? Sometimes smart guys don't get anything. You one of those smart guys, Fisk?"

Fisk felt his smile grow heavy and brittle, like ice about to shatter.

"It would be useful if we could review what you plan next," he said evenly. "Hiring the Shocker was... innovative, but it came with certain risks."

Bingham took out a cell phone and began tapping and swiping. From where Fisk was sitting, it looked as if he was scrolling through messages on his phone.

"Perhaps," Fisk continued, "if you brief me on what you have planned next, I can offer some feedback to help you control the operation more effectively."

Bingham thumbed his way down the phone's screen for a few minutes before looking up.

"Wilson, I'm not a flunky," he said. "I'm a force of nature. You wanted an earthquake, and now the ground is rumbling. Too late to complain about the dust that's falling into your soup. You want to do something to make your life better once the earthquake starts? Take shelter."

MAYA couldn't believe what she was seeing.

As she watched the meeting through her hidden cameras, Bingham behaved dismissively and disrespectfully, and Mr. Fisk simply took it. She'd seen him hospitalize men for less, and while she was happy that Mr. Fisk had mastered his emotions, she wasn't sure she understood why he would do so now.

She applauded, albeit reluctantly, Bingham's efforts to undermine the myth of the benevolent Spider-Man, though the deaths concerned her deeply. Mr. Fisk clearly felt something had to be done, but he seemed unable to put a collar on this lunatic.

"This adversarial posture doesn't serve either of us," Mr. Fisk said. "We share the same goal—destroying Spider-Man's reputation. If you allow me to guide you, we can achieve that goal much more efficiently."

"Are your ears too fat to hear me?" Bingham asked. "I *am* Spider-Man. I'm showing New York what the real Spider-Man is all about. I've got plans, fat man. Big plans that involve things you don't know about. You can just sit there and stuff your face and watch."

Bingham took a photograph out of his jacket pocket. It was folded, and when he opened it, holding it so Mr. Fisk couldn't see, it showed Spider-Man on a rooftop talking with a woman. Maya had to strain to make out the detail, and realized she had a badge clipped to her belt.

So, Spider-Man was working directly with a person or people inside the police department. Either he had lied to them, or corruption was rampant within the department. Either way, it was impressive that Bingham had discovered this key information. Perhaps he wasn't as useless as he appeared to be.

He folded the paper and put it back in his jacket pocket.

"What do you mean, things I don't know about?" Mr. Fisk asked, an edge to his voice.

Bingham laughed. "Oh, a little of this, a little of that," he taunted. "Or maybe a lot." He looked around. "I wouldn't mind an office like this. How come you get an office and I don't? I come in here and tell you what to do, and you have to take it. How come I don't get an office?"

Maya gasped, and felt her heart pounding. Bingham didn't say anything about the cop, and that was information Mr. Fisk needed to have. She couldn't tell him, though, because then she'd have to admit she had been watching him.

Why was Mr. Fisk letting Bingham treat him this way? Yes, the man had impressive abilities, but that shouldn't be enough. Mr. Fisk was deliberately restraining himself. She knew that look on his face, understood her mentor was playing a long game, but to what end?

She started to wish she'd never set up these cameras, never gotten herself involved with Bingham. She was in too deep, though, and she had no choice but to see it through.

○────────────○

BINGHAM had agreed to the meeting because he liked the idea of Wilson Fisk sucking up to him. It was also possible that the fat man would have something important to say, but it was nothing like that.

Fisk was just afraid. Everyone was afraid of him now, and that was how Bingham liked it. Things had been different when he was younger, but back then he hadn't known that he was Spider-Man. It was possible, he knew, that he might have gone his whole life without realizing he was Spider-Man. He might have lived all those years imagining he was someone else. He might never have been himself.

"I've got things to do." Bingham stood up. "You're wasting my time."

Fisk didn't move. *He squirms like*—Bingham had to struggle to think of something—*like an octopus in a little rock cave*, he thought. That's what Fisk was like—a slimy fish with tentacles. It was disgusting.

"Not until we arrive at an understanding," the fat man said. "You must agree to let me know before you act again."

"Not how this works, Wilson," Bingham said. He loved calling Fisk by his first name. It reminded the guy who had the power.

"If I can't count on you to cooperate," Fisk droned on, "then I will have to reconsider our arrangement."

"Reconsider all you want, Willie," Bingham said. He pushed himself out of the chair with a theatrical little leap—just to remind the guy who had moves, and who was a big lump—and walked out of the office door. At the last moment he turned back. "Can't you hire any girls to sit at your desk? Men secretaries— that's what's wrong with this city. Everything is the opposite of what it oughta be."

○───────────○

HIGH school had been hard for Bingham. It shouldn't have been that way. His name was Bingham, and he grew up in Binghamton. That meant it should've been his town. He'd always said it when he was little, and people told him how funny he was. They'd loved it, and he'd kept saying it. In high school, though, people didn't love it anymore. Worse, they didn't respect him. Kids would mess with him in the halls.

"Whose town is it, Mikey," they'd say, shoving him or surrounding him. Big kids—bigger than him, thinner than him.

"This is my town," he'd answer. They'd laugh. *Laugh.* Sometimes he'd lash out, and usually he got beaten—but that wasn't what bothered him. It was the constant laughter.

They put him in a special class with other kids— ones who had problems. Kids who weren't smart or had something wrong with them, and even those kids were mean to him. Julie was deaf, and he thought she'd be nice to him. She talked all the time like she had a cold, so other kids made fun of her, but that didn't make her sensitive. Julie was the meanest of all to him. She called him fat, which wasn't nice.

People couldn't help what they looked like.

He'd never had a father, so Bingham always kind of thought of the city itself as his parent. It taught him things. Binghamton had seen better days. It was falling apart and had little to look forward to, but that made it no different than a lot of the fathers he saw around.

Sometimes his mom invited men to stay with them, and each time Bingham wondered if he would have a new father. Most of them didn't want to talk to a kid, though. Sometimes they were mean to him and called him words Bingham wouldn't repeat because they were bad. One of them had been nice, though. He was a big man named Rick who laughed a lot and who said he used to be a fighter. He decided to teach Bingham to fight, and they would spend hours with their fists up, circling each other.

"A man has to be able to defend himself," Rick would say, but Bingham couldn't imagine actually hitting someone, even though sometimes the other kids hit him. Sometimes they knocked him down. He hated the pain, but even more, he hated the feeling of powerlessness. He'd never wish that feeling on anyone else.

Rick went away, though. They all did, and then his mom stopped having men stay with them. She became tired and sad, and he preferred the memories of what she had been instead of who she became.

He remembered her making him the special grilled cheese sandwiches he liked and taking him to the movies. He remembered her hugging him. He remembered asking how he knew if she really loved him, and she would say that true things didn't need to be explained. He liked remembering those days.

Bingham's mother became thin and her skin grew brittle. She worked long hours cleaning rooms at the motel, and when she wasn't working, she was out with friends—that's what she said, but Bingham never met any of them—or she would just sleep the hours away in her room. She'd turn on the TV, get under the covers, and sleep. The time of day didn't matter. Once he realized he couldn't remember the last time he'd seen her eat anything. She didn't make him sandwiches anymore.

Then she got sick, and the doctors said they weren't going to help her. Maybe they said they couldn't help her, but it sounded the same to him. They didn't care about her and didn't care about him. Whatever actual words came out of their mouths, it all added up to the fact that she was going to die and he was going to be on his own.

Not exactly on his own, because he was too young for that. The city sent a mean woman with a lot of freckles. This woman walked like she was older than she looked, and she came to talk about what she called his "choices." It sounded to him like he didn't have any. He didn't have relatives, so he'd have to live with some stranger or go to a group home. When people talked about choices, they were usually lying.

There was only one choice, and you had to take it.

That's when Bingham discovered he had a power. They gave him one choice, but what if he didn't take it? That meant rethinking everything, like walking away when kids were mean. You didn't have to stand there and listen, he told himself. You could go somewhere else.

It felt weird leaving Binghamton. It was his place, but he told himself he'd be back some day, and things would be the way they were supposed to be. Maybe his mother wouldn't die. Maybe when he came back, she'd still be lying in that hospital bed, and he'd tell her she wasn't sick anymore and she would stand up and walk right out of there. Maybe Rick would come back and show him some more about how to fight.

It would be his town, like it was supposed to be.

He wanted to go to Syracuse, because he knew there was a place called Syracuse in ancient Greece, and he liked the idea of one city being in two different places, two different times. He didn't know how that could work, and he wanted to see it for himself.

The woman at the ticket counter spoke with a heavy accent, though, and she kept accusing him of mumbling even though she was the one who was hard to understand. There were decisions he had to make, and they were so confusing, and he ended up just agreeing to something she said so the conversation could be over. That's how he ended up buying a ticket to New York City.

When he realized what he'd done, he'd been upset. He'd wanted to cry. Things like this shouldn't happen in his city, but they did whether he wanted them to or not. It seemed like bad things were all that happened anymore, so maybe going very far away was for the best. Maybe he should go where the ticket told him to go.

So Bingham went to New York City.

It was terrible, and also familiar. New York was a place from the television and the movies. He'd seen it so many times that going there almost felt like stepping into a memory. But people were busy and rude, and he couldn't find a place to live. He hadn't even thought about that. He'd imagined he would walk around, look for houses with signs in the windows advertising rooms for rent. That was something he'd seen in a movie once, but there weren't houses in New York—just buildings, and to rent an apartment you needed identification and references. You needed a job, and you needed more money than Bingham could imagine.

A very impatient man in a real estate office explained it to him and then demanded that he leave. And so he'd ended up sleeping in the subway until the police made him leave. Then on a bench. Then on some flattened cardboard boxes, where someone stole his shoes. It was getting cold, and it was hard to go around with bare feet, so he stole someone else's shoes.

That person hadn't been sleeping, but he looked like he owned a house that had more shoes in it. Bingham wished he hadn't resisted so much.

He tried to remember everything Rick had taught him about keeping his hands up and using his feet and punching behind his target. When he had to do it, though, it wasn't like dancing, the way Rick had taught him. Fighting turned out to be less about footwork and more about pounding fists and elbows and knees. It was about knocking people down and kicking their faces.

Then you took the shoes.

That's all you needed to know about fighting.

He ran off with his shoes and hid in case the police came. They didn't.

○———————○

ONCE, when Bingham looked up, he saw a figure swinging from rooftop to rooftop. It had to be the person they called Spider-Man. It was dark, and Bingham couldn't see his face, but he knew Spider-Man was looking at him and was scared of him.

The idea came into his head all at once—that they had switched places somehow. Bingham was supposed to be the one swinging through the night, and that guy in the Spider-Man suit was supposed to be stuck on the cold ground. He didn't know how he knew it, but he didn't worry about it, because true things didn't need to be explained.

That winter was very cold. Maybe it wasn't as

cold as the winters got in Binghamton, but back home he'd been able to spend more time indoors. He'd never had to sleep outside during the winter before. That made it seem colder. Knowing that Spider-Man was out there with his stolen life made things colder, too.

He had to ask people for money and food. Sometimes he got it. He found a cat and put it on a leash, and that helped him get more money and food. People liked the cat, but the cat ran away, so that only got him through a couple of weeks.

One day, there was a pretty lady standing in front of him.

"Can you give me any money or food?" he asked. "I'm hungry, and I don't have any money."

"I can take you to a place that's warm," she said, smiling. "There will be plenty to eat, and we can help you—if you are willing to help us."

"Help you do what?"

"We want to give you some medicine and see if it makes you better or worse."

Bingham thought about that. He didn't think he could get any worse, and the idea of being warm, of having plenty to eat, sounded much better.

"Okay," he said. "I'd do that." He went with the pretty lady, and he started taking the medicine. It made him worse at first, and then a whole lot better.

That's when he met the man who changed his life.

TWENTY-TWO

ALL this effort didn't seem to be making things any better.

Spider-Man had searched two more Fisk buildings since the blast, copying files, securing data. Lieutenant Watanabe told him it was making a difference, building their case, but he didn't feel it. He hated that people had died so that Fisk could play his head games, and he hated that people blamed him for what had happened. Not everyone, and the debates still raged in the media about whether or not it had been Spider-Man who fought Shocker, but enough people were willing to think the worst of him.

"That doesn't matter," the lieutenant said during one of their meetings. "I know it hits home now, but it will blow over. Another story will distract them, and people will go back to seeing the good you do."

Spider-Man wasn't so sure. Tonight he'd rescued a teenager from a mugger, and both the mugger and the victim had fled from him in terror. How could he help people if they were afraid of him?

For that very reason he'd been keeping a low profile. Crime victims, accident victims, people trapped in burning buildings—it didn't matter if the walls were coming down around them. They still treated him like he was the threat. Meanwhile, his doppelgänger was spotted two or three times a week, not exactly giving random citizens wedgies, but causing minor mayhem and generally spreading the idea that Spider-Man simply didn't care about ordinary people.

"Keep your eye on the important things," Watanabe said, but he had two eyes. He could keep one on her data hunting, but he had his other eye on someone else. Again and again he watched the footage of the fight between the Shocker and the imposter. One thing was clear—the Shocker was in on it. He wasn't the brightest light out there, and if he could just be nabbed, getting information out of him shouldn't be hard.

Watanabe didn't know about this plan, because he wasn't in the mood to be talked out of it.

○——————————○

IT felt strange, walking into a place like an ordinary person, but in costume. Not swinging, leaping, or tumbling—just… walking. His search for the Shocker had hit a dead end, and it was time to start questioning some people who might actually know.

The establishment known as the Bar with No Name was familiar to the police, but even if they were looking for criminals with enhanced abilities, it wasn't worth the danger to try to get inside. It was also well-known to people like Spider-Man, but good guys in costumes generally kept out unless there was a solid tip. J. Jonah Jameson claimed that super villains did what they did because super heroes egged them on. There might be an element of truth to the notion. Thus, going into one of their safe places could quickly escalate.

So he would go in mellow. He would follow the rules, and there would be no problems.

He knocked on the door and an eye-level slit hissed open.

"So, I'm selling cookie dough for a fundraiser," he said. "Any interest?" He leaned forward and said in a whisper, "You don't even have to use it to make cookies. You can eat it right out of the tub."

"Sorry." Only a pair of eyes could be seen on the other side. "This is a no-trouble zone."

"No trouble intended," Spider-Man said, showing his empty hands—as though that actually meant anything. "I know how it goes in there. I just want to talk."

The panel slid shut, and there was a muffled conversation. He had the distinct impression the guy at the door was talking it over with someone. Then the door clicked open.

When he entered there was the usual hubbub of a bar, and a guy stood in the back holding a microphone. As soon as he was through the door, the effect was instantaneous.

Silence.

Conversation stopped as if a switch had been flipped. All eyes turned toward Spider-Man. He decided he would play it cool, act like he didn't notice, and strolled up to the bar, taking note of everything he saw along the way.

Like, for example, Electro hanging out at a table, and the Scorpion standing nearby. There were lots of other people without costumes. They could have been anyone, from some crime boss's henchman to gang members to villains Spider-Man had fought—difficult to recognize without their usual getups.

"Chill down, villainous people," he announced with the same meaningless empty-hands gesture he'd used outside. "Bar with No Name. No fighting. I get it."

Spider-Man walked calmly across the room. He reached the bar and smiled at the bartender—though it didn't do much good. The guy was tall and wore a tank top that exposed arms that looked like they could punch through walls. He also held what looked like a glowing green baseball bat—some kind of tech that could stop someone with enhanced abilities, or at least slow them down.

"There are rules, and as long as you follow them, you get to come in," the bartender growled, "but it's a bad idea you being here."

"Why, have prices gone up?"

"I'm serious, bro. We're all on thin ice."

"Relax," Spider-Man said. "I'm just here for justice and vengeance. Nothing can go wrong. What do you have that's good filtered through a mask?"

"Come on!" a simian, and frankly hairy, shirtless guy shouted. "Let's get on with it!"

Ugh, that guy, Spider-Man thought. "Hey, Gibbon. 'Sup!"

"Just cool your jets," the bartender told Hairy.

"I'll deal with this." Then he waved to the guy with the microphone. In turn, the man in back leaned into the microphone.

"What is…" he began in menacing tones, "the largest lake in Africa?"

At their tables, people began talking among themselves and scribbling. The noise level went quickly back to normal.

"It's trivia night," the bartender explained. "What do you want?"

Spider-Man looked around the room. The Scorpion—Mac Gargan—hissed at Electro, loudly enough that "Lake Tanganyika" could be heard. Electro shut him up.

"It's not Tanganyika," Spider-Man said to the bartender. "I'm looking for a guy who hangs out here. Average height. Wears a puffy suit. Backpack. Vibro-gauntlets. Goes by the name of 'Shocker.' Ring any bells? Does it—" Peter forced a fake snicker "—jolt any memories?"

Before the guy could respond to his witty repartee, a shadow stretched across the bar. Someone was looming behind him, but his Spider-Sense wasn't tingling, so he chose not to react. In his peripheral vision he could see that the Scorpion had come over—no easy task with his giant spiked tail sticking out. Gargan put a massive gloved hand on Spider-Man's shoulder.

"You're disturbing game night, Web-Head," he said. "I'm gonna have to escort you out the back way, whether you like it or not." Then, much more quietly, he leaned in and whispered, "Play along, but don't go too quietly."

Still no Spider-Sense, so all signs, however improbably, suggested that the Scorpion was sincere. He struggled a bit, then let the big man in the bigger costume shove him forcefully through the bar, past the bathrooms, and into a storeroom. Just before the door closed behind him, he turned back to the room and shouted:

"It's Lake Victoria!"

He was met with a chorus of boos.

Once outside, the Scorpion moved him a safe distance away, then stepped back and folded his arms.

"Seriously?" he said. "Sauntering in here like it's an old private eye movie. What if Electro and I decided to, I don't know, team up against you? Kick your ass?"

Most of the time these guys couldn't agree on the time of day, much less have the discipline to team up, but he wasn't going to antagonize the Scorpion by saying that.

"I need to find Shocker."

"Yeah, I heard that," Scorpion said. "And I'm gonna help you."

"Ooooo-kay," Spider-Man said cautiously. "I mean, I'm not complaining, but why would you do that?"

"Because there are weird things going on in this city," Gargan replied, and he sounded sincere. "People moving into territories that don't belong to them. Guys disappearing who people like you would never miss, but it messes with people like me. And honestly, I don't like this fake web-slinger."

"I'm touched," Spider-Man said. "So you knew it was a fake?"

"Of course I knew," Scorpion said. "What, do you think I ain't got eyes? Guy didn't talk or act anything like you. Plus the suit was wrong—any idiot could tell. The web lines were too close together."

"I'm not all that comfortable with how much I agree with you right now, so maybe you could tell me where to find Shocker."

Scorpion jabbed a thumb toward the far corner of the storeroom, where a man sat slumped on a wooden chair, eating miserably out of a bowl. "He hates trivia night," Gargan said in a quiet voice. "He gets everything wrong."

The guy looked like the embodiment of depression. His slouched posture, red and watery eyes, the slack expression on his face as he mechanically spooned something into his mouth.

Herman Schultz. Shocker.

And out of his suit, which seemed like a pretty good deal, as far as Spider-Man was concerned. He felt the anger begin to build inside. Here was the guy who had blown up the sandwich place, who had killed all those people, who had killed Anika. Spider-Man wanted to grab him, to drag him out of that bar. Let Scorpion or anyone else try to stop him.

He controlled himself, however, because he was there for answers. He had agreed to play by the rules, because something had been totally wrong with that operation from the beginning. The guy on the video feed hadn't seemed like Shocker, hadn't talked like Shocker, and there was no way Shocker would cause mayhem—certainly not with bombs, when he could be using his gauntlets. He loved those gauntlets.

"Herman," he said, walking over, "quit stuffing your face for a minute and tell me everything you know, or we're going to have a major problem."

"I already got major problems," Schultz said. "Someone stole my suit."

Spider-Man folded his arms. Okay, this made sense. It would certainly explain a lot if that had been a fake Shocker, fighting a fake Spider-Man.

"When did this happen?"

"Maybe a month ago," Schultz said. "I've been trying to get something new put together, but it's complicated 'cause the cops are looking for me. Not just for the restaurant thing. I commit a lot of crimes."

"You say that as if we're not already friends," Spider-Man replied.

"Hey, you seem like you know a lot of science stuff," Schultz said. "Maybe you could help me get a new suit."

"Yeah, wait right there. I'll call my tailor." He paused, then added, "What can you tell me about the one you lost?"

"Some guy all in black came at me from behind... and above," Schultz said. "Never saw it coming. He actually kind of moved like you, but he punched like a boxer. If I could've gotten one good shot at him, I'd have taken him, but he didn't fight fair."

"That's a bummer alright," Spider-Man agreed.

"It wasn't just the suit, though," Schultz said. "He took over my website. Shut me out of the thing. I put in my name and password, but it says I'm wrong. I mean, I can't make any money if I don't have a suit, but there's a principle here."

"You have a website?" Spider-Man said.

"You gotta be all modern these days," Schultz explained.

"Can't argue with a tautology," Spider-Man agreed. "Did you try tracking the IP address of the hacked website, to see if you could locate the guy?"

Schultz blinked at him.

"You're just making word-like sounds as far as he's concerned," Scorpion said.

Spider-Man turned to Gargan. "Didn't you guys try to get his suit back for him?"

"We're all sort of on the same side here," Scorpion said, "but it's not like we're on the same *team*, if you get my meaning. Besides, after that restaurant fiasco, Shocker is red hot. None of us want to go anywhere near anything that has to do with his suit."

Better for me, Spider-Man thought.

It might be too much to hope for, but he knew his way around a computer. If he could find out who was running the Shocker's website, then he'd be one step closer to finding out who had partnered with the false Spider-Man.

He shrugged at the Scorpion. "This has been a

surprisingly productive use of my time. I'm not really sure how to say this, but thanks."

"I oughta rip you in half for answering that trivia question," the Scorpion said, "which I knew, by the way, but I get it. You're trying to protect your reputation, so I'll give you a pass."

"What does it matter to you, me trying to protect my reputation?"

"Because it's selfish," the Scorpion said with a grin. "That means you're just like the rest of us."

○────────────────○

HE wasn't being selfish.

Sure, he had a personal motivation for not wanting the world to hate him, but it made it a lot easier to be one of the good guys. Ultimately, that was the important thing. Probably. In any case, it was a philosophical question, and Spider-Man had other issues to address.

His first priority was tracking down the owner of the stolen suit, so he made a quick detour to his apartment and pulled up Shocker's website, which was pretty basic—means of contact and methods of payment through third-party systems. There were a whole host of ways to hide an IP address, but there were also plenty of ways to crack those protections.

Turned out it wasn't particularly well-hidden in the first place. In less than half an hour, he had a location in Turtle Bay, right around the corner from the Wakandan Embassy.

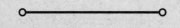

UNFORTUNATELY, his digging couldn't get him an apartment number, so Spider-Man was reduced to peering into the windows of the converted brownstone. He hoped he didn't see anything embarrassing. The last thing he needed was to be labeled a Peeping Tom.

Many of the apartments were dark and empty. In one, a couple were watching TV. In another, a man was playing with his dog. In yet another, a man in a Shocker suit stood before a full-length mirror, posing.

"I am the sinister Shocker!" he announced in a voice muffled by the suit.

Something tells me this is the place.

The man in the Shocker suit turned suddenly. He must've caught a glimpse of Spider-Man in the mirror, because he unleashed a wave of vibrations from his gauntlet. The Web-Slinger simultaneously pushed himself back and twisted to the side. As he tumbled through the air, he shot a line of webbing at an adjacent—and much taller—building, pulling himself high in the air to give himself a moment to formulate a strategy.

When he looked back, the fake Shocker was standing by his open window, peering out like he was admiring the view.

There's my strategy, Spider-Man thought, torpedoing the fake Shocker with two lines of webbing. Then he pulled hard as he fell. The Schultz impersonator tumbled out the window headfirst.

Tumbling downward, Spider-Man put out protective webbing below the man in the Shocker suit and then sent out another line so he could swing, rather than plummet, to the ground. When he landed, the fake Shocker was lying on his back in the web, trying to sit up. He managed to raise his arm enough to send out a blast, but the Web-Slinger backflipped out of the way.

This guy is no Herman Schultz.

He used his webs to pin the imposter's arms. He lay there trapped in—Spider-Man thought about this for a moment—a hammock of despair. Yeah, that felt right.

But it wasn't nearly enough, he told himself. This was the murderer, then. This was the guy who committed crimes too horrible even for the Shocker.

"Stop!" the imposter cried out. "Don't web me anymore. I don't want to fight."

"Then why did you *start* fighting?"

"You startled me—and then you pulled me out of my window!" The guy actually sounded scared and, well, harmless. He didn't sound like a cold-blooded killer.

"The bombing," Spider-Man said. "Tell me everything."

"I didn't know!" he shouted. "Look, my name is Phil. Phil Simons. I'm an actor. I mean I want to be. I've had a few roles. I even had the lead in—"

"Focus," Spider-Man snapped.

"Look, the suit came in a package, along with the password for the website. Then jobs started coming in. I needed the money, and then came the thing at the sandwich place, and a note saying I had to do it or they'd turn me over to police. I was never really a bad guy, just playing one."

"In real life."

"It was good money!" Simons protested. "And I kept getting threats. He said I had to keep on being the Shocker. I didn't know what to do. You have no idea what it's like not to be able to pay your rent."

"Yeah, that's outside my experience for sure," Spider-Man said. He didn't expect the guy to catch the irony.

"I swear, all the jobs I've taken have been about intimidating people. I'd never hurt anyone." His voice rose as he talked. "And at the sandwich place—he said it was just to make a scene, to make you look bad. I had no idea there was a bomb. I'd never want to hurt anyone. I'm just an ordinary guy."

"You could have called the police."

"I needed the money," Phil whined. "I told you that already. And it was a great role. You've fought the real Shocker, right? You'd never have known it wasn't the real thing. The Spider-Man guy—it was like he wasn't even trying to be you. But I inhabited that role. I *was* Shocker."

"How do I find the guy?" Spider-Man demanded. "People died there. I need answers."

"I have no idea. He contacted me. I never had a way to get in touch with him. I'd help you if I could, but I don't know. Please, you have to let me go."

Down the street there was the warning bleat of a police car, which didn't surprise him. He hoped that cooperating like this might begin to repair his reputation, at least a little.

"Sorry, Phil," Spider-Man said, "but it looks like this is going to be the role of a lifetime—or at least about twenty years."

Cars pulled up on either side of him, and cops tumbled out, guns already drawn.

"Hands up, Spider-Man!" one of them shouted.

"So it doesn't make a difference that I caught the sandwich-shop bomber?" he asked, slowly raising his hands.

"On your knees, slowly, clasp your hands behind your head!"

"This is the Shocker," he replied. "Or a guy pretending to be the Shocker. Whatever. This is the guy involved in the explosion. He'll tell you—I didn't have anything to do with it."

With that he leapt straight up, faster than they could react, shot off a web and swung himself out of there. He hoped the police would have the good sense not to fire at him.

TWENTY-THREE

SHE sat in Fisk's office again. MJ had been trying to reach Peter all morning, but they kept missing each other. At least his messages said he was okay. The story in the paper wasn't clear, but it seemed like both he and the Shocker had been cornered the previous night, although Spider-Man had escaped.

According to the report, Peter fled the scene as soon as the cops arrived. The Shocker wasn't the real Shocker, but he did seem to be involved in the bombing. The police were still trying to sort it all out, even while they downplayed Spider-Man's role in the arrest.

Ever since the night of the explosion, they'd struggled to find time together. Peter was throwing every spare minute into his efforts to bring down Wilson Fisk. They'd never even finished their conversation, but that was largely MJ's decision. He was struggling, which made it a less-than-ideal time to fine-tune their relationship.

The relationship would survive. She hoped.

For now she had to get her head in the game. Fisk had invited her in after another of her stories had run. It had outlined some of his plans for upcoming development projects, but had taken more of a hard news angle than her editor had originally wanted. MJ had compared Fisk's projections with plans filed with the city, and she'd interviewed some of the contractors. The bottom line had been that it seemed like reality was going to fall far short of Fisk's promises.

Robbie Robertson had called her into his office.

"You are a features writer," he'd said. *"Features. If you have a lead like that, you let someone know, and they'll pass it along to an appropriate reporter. If it checks out, you get to participate. You do not choose for yourself which stories to write. Are we clear?"*

MJ had nodded.

Then he'd grinned. *"I'll also say that this is a hell of a story. You're going to make an outstanding reporter."* The smile disappeared. *"But not if you can't learn to play nice with others."*

She'd understood the point. Afraid she'd be told to drop it, she'd pursued the angle herself. Now that he'd made it clear what procedure to follow, she wouldn't be able to feign ignorance.

In the meantime, she assumed Fisk had brought her in because he was upset about the story. He couldn't do anything about it, of course, so he'd try to find some other way to defuse her.

When she was shown into his office, a meeting seemed to be breaking up, and she had to work her way through a throng of Wall Street types. They were talking excitedly about municipal bonds, which seemed interesting to MJ, but she wasn't sure if she'd get a chance to follow up on it. Especially not after her most recent dressing-down.

A young woman joined them and was introduced as Maya Lopez. She barely spoke, but mostly studied MJ with a nasty stare. She hadn't exactly seemed warm the first time they met, but now MJ felt sure she'd never want to cross her. Fisk glanced in Lopez's direction from time to time.

"Miss Watson," Fisk said. "That was quite a story the *Bugle* ran yesterday. You are keeping the people in my public relations office very busy."

"My job is to report the truth," she said.

"Oh, the truth is an elusive thing," he replied coolly. "Do you believe your story tells the whole truth?"

"A story can never be complete," she said. "The best a reporter can do is relate the facts that are currently available. Once I'd done the research, I contacted your media office and gave them a chance to respond in the piece. No one got back to me."

"Perhaps newspapers view deadlines differently than corporate offices. If you had waited a little longer, you would have received information that cast things in a different light."

"And now you want me to write about this new information?"

"Of course not," Fisk said. "No doubt the story you wrote is an enormous accomplishment for you. You made me look bad. Reporters live for such things, but it is not a matter of great importance to us. Businesses receive cuts and bruises every day. It's the way the game is played, and while this story is a new line on your résumé—something your coworkers may even remember years from now—by tomorrow the public will have already forgotten. I don't concern myself with trivialities."

The fact that she was sitting there seemed to dispute this claim, but MJ chose not to point this out.

"Then what can I do for you?"

"I wonder what your goals are, Miss Watson. I mean your long-term goals. You are a reasonably talented writer, and likely you enjoy working with words, but there are many options other than journalism. There are positions in the corporate sector that would satisfy your need to be creative, but allow you to live a much more… satisfying life."

"Are you offering me a job?" MJ asked. It came out as more of an incredulous burst than she would have intended, but it seemed so ridiculous. One slightly unfavorable story, and Fisk wanted to buy her. It was so heavy-handed. She tried to follow it up with a cheery smile.

He chuckled. It still sounded ominous.

"I'm not offering you a position in my company at this time, no," he said. "I am merely suggesting that a position might open up at a future date, for which you would be very well suited. If you were to ask me to hold such a position for you, I could do so, and even, let us say, advance your salary so that the trifling paycheck you currently receive from the *Bugle* doesn't diminish your options."

MJ's smile felt as though it might fall off and shatter on the floor. This was exactly the sort of thing

Peter had warned her about. She had gotten close to Fisk, and now he wanted to own her. If he couldn't own her, then what?

She'd heard enough stories about his rage to worry. While beating a young reporter to death wouldn't be entirely out of character, it was fairly unlikely. She hadn't just wandered in off the street. Her editor knew where she was. She'd logged in with security downstairs. Then there was the silent woman, Maya Lopez. Judging from the way he kept glancing in her direction, it seemed as if she somehow kept Fisk… contained.

No amount of logic was going to help her deal with this. It wasn't as if she could agree to be Fisk's paid lackey. That meant she had to decline. Of course, there were lots of ways to do that, and the trick would be to appeal to his own sense of ego, rather than anger him.

"I appreciate the offer, Mr. Fisk," she said, "but journalism is my goal—it always has been, I think. I love working at the *Bugle*, and the corporate side of things doesn't hold much of an interest for me right now."

She waited, but Fisk just smiled. "I understand, Miss Watson. I appreciate that you have your own goals. It's worth pointing out, however, that my company has a controlling interest in a number of media outlets."

"I'm sure things would be easier if I had a patron," she said, "and you'd be a powerful ally, but I'd like to see how far I can go on my own before I start asking for help."

"Entirely understandable," he said. "Indeed, it's admirable. I wish more journalists had your integrity."

"I do the best I can," she said. "I suspect most people do the same."

"You may be giving most people far too much credit." He pivoted slightly in his chair, a clear sign that he wanted to change the topic. "I'd like to send you to see one of my senior accounting officers, who will go over some of the numbers you ran in your piece. I'm not saying you had your information wrong, but a lack of context suggests a false interpretation. That could be *very* unfortunate."

Very slowly, MJ let out her breath.

Peter was right. Crossing Fisk was dangerous— but he was an emotional being, like anyone else, and could be managed. She'd stepped into what might have been a dangerous situation, and she'd handled it. She deserved a pat on the back for this one. She also realized she needed to trust herself more. Peter and Fisk had come to blows because Spider-Man came at Fisk with webs shooting and fists swinging. MJ had a different approach, and it produced different results. She had faith in herself.

She wished Peter had more faith in her.

o———————o

MJ thanked Fisk and shook hands with him and Maya Lopez as she left the office. It had been a long, and possibly pointless, meeting. Fisk wanted her to write an article that would largely undermine her previous piece. She didn't want to do that, but agreed to meet with the accountant to see if there were angles she hadn't considered.

Even now, her mind began to churn through feature ideas she could pitch that would allow her to stay on the Fisk story. Throw the man a few crumbs, but still dig deeper. There were angles—covering some of the subcontractors, perhaps, or a piece on how neighborhood planning might be influenced by the new construction projects. Maybe even seeing what the Wall Street types had been up to.

She was so lost in her thoughts that she almost bumped into a trio of men. They wore business suits, but they definitely weren't finance types. They screamed military—or at least ex-military.

"I'm sorry." She looked up at the giant of a man with whom she'd almost collided. "I was lost in thought."

"Not at all, ma'am," he said, looking through her and not at her. Interaction with an unknown female must not have been part of the mission parameters, she thought. Not the friendliest of people, but still, a reporter didn't get far if she didn't at least try.

"I'm sorry if my meeting went on a little long," she said. "I hope I didn't make you wait."

"No, ma'am," he answered expressionlessly.

Okay, no idle chit-chat. She'd try the head-on approach.

"What brings you to Mr. Fisk's office?"

"That's not something Mr. Fisk wishes us to discuss, ma'am," he said.

A swing and a miss, but not entirely a waste of effort. She now knew Fisk was bringing in military types, for something he didn't want to discuss. It might be nothing more than vandalism at a construction site, but somehow she doubted it.

○———————————○

AN hour later, after a tedious and unenlightening meeting with the accounting officer, MJ was on her way out and stopped to say goodbye to the security guard. She was always friendly with the guards on her way in and out.

She was outgoing by nature, which was one of the reasons she wanted to make her living hearing strangers tell their stories. On the other hand, she knew most people hurried past the security desk, treating the workers there as impediments rather than people. A smile and a few kind words garnered no guarantee of anything in return, but it didn't hurt.

"See you next time," she said, peering at his name tag. "Hank." She flashed him a smile. The other one, Therese, was dealing with a visitor.

"You have a good day, Miss Watson."

She started through, then stopped.

What the hell. It was worth a try.

"You know, about an hour ago I almost got run over by these three enormous guys. They looked like ex-marines or something."

He laughed. "Yeah, those gorillas from Roxxon Blackridge. They don't look like they play around.

They're late today, though. Most days they come in by seven-thirty, and they're out the door again fifteen minutes later."

"Well, try not to make them angry." She laughed and waved as she walked off.

So she'd been right. Roxxon Blackridge was a security contractor. She'd have to do a little research, but she was pretty sure they were involved in more demanding work than chasing off teenagers carrying cans of spray paint. MJ smiled as she walked out of the building. Maybe this would go nowhere, but maybe it was a lead.

Either way, finding out was going to be fun.

○———————○

MAYA watched the reporter leave the building, stopping to chat with the security guard on her way out. She'd passed that guard hundreds of times, and never spoken a word that wasn't required by the business at hand.

It must be nice, she thought, *to be so relaxed around other people.* Maya didn't want to be unfriendly, but she didn't really know how to be anything else.

She didn't blame her father. It hadn't been easy for him to be a single parent in New York City. Maya didn't remember anything of her mother, who died when she was very little, but she could recall a few snippets from when they still lived on the reservation in Montana. There were other children there with whom she played, and a pair of kindly women who took care of her. Maya had thought of them as old, but they probably hadn't been more than 40 at the time. One had taught Maya sign language, but then Maya had taught herself to read lips. Even as a little girl, she would not limit herself. She always wanted options, and she never wanted to be in a position of not knowing what people were saying, wherever she was.

"There's nothing you can't do," this woman had told her, her eyes sparkling with wonder. "I've never seen anyone learn like you do. It's like you can echo anything."

It always stuck with her. That she could echo—that she *was* an echo.

There was another powerful memory from those days. A fight involving a man. Someone who came to their house. He'd been drunk, looking to hurt them. The two had fought, and Maya had hidden under her bed, not knowing what was happening, hoping her father would come and tell her it was all over.

Her father didn't come.

The man did. He was hurt, bleeding from his head, and pressing a towel against a wound on his side. He managed to pull her out from under the bed. She wiggled free from his hard grasp, but he grabbed her again. His bloody hand grabbed her by the face, and she screamed. Then the man fell over, and her father stood across the room, wounded and unsteady, bleeding from his own wound in the shoulder—and holding a smoking gun.

She'd looked in the mirror next to her father and seen that the bad man had left a bloody handprint on her face. For years after, she dreamed about herself that way, as though it was a part of her face, like she wasn't herself without that handprint.

They'd left that night. People wouldn't understand, her father had said. The man who had tried to kill them was an important white man from town, friends with policemen and politicians. They would never believe him when he said he'd been attacked.

Years later she'd wondered, but at the time it hadn't occurred to her to question his word. It never occurred to her to complain when he put her in schools where the other kids made fun of her and excluded her, because when she came home he was waiting, and he made her feel like there was a place in the world where she belonged.

There were times when he was gone for hours or days at a time, though, and their neighbors watched out for her. But that was just a part of life, and it didn't diminish the love she felt for her father.

After Spider-Man left her an orphan, Maya's incomplete records, her poor grades, her spotty attendance record, all confused the city's social workers. They treated her as a problem, as a criminal. She could remember that time clearly if she wanted to, but she chose to forget. It was easier to forget. She didn't want to think what would have become of her if Mr. Fisk hadn't taken an interest in the orphaned daughter of a minor business associate.

It wasn't that Maya couldn't be social when the situation called for it. After all, mimicry was her greatest skill. She noted who was successful and who wasn't, and she could make herself emulate their body language. That was easy. Knowing what to say to a near stranger, how to make small talk that didn't feel strained or awkward—that was something else entirely.

It certainly didn't matter for her next appointment, since it was with a man who neither valued nor practiced friendliness. Jameson wanted to meet by the hot-dog vendor again, and when she arrived he was already finishing what she presumed was at least his second dog. She checked her watch to make sure she wasn't late.

"I got here early," he said. "I wanted to talk, and not let you watch my lunch get cold."

"I hope nothing's wrong," she said. "I've heard some of your broadcasts, and I'm told the ratings are strong."

"The numbers look great," he told her. "People want to hear what I have to say. They're sick of what mainstream media types like Robertson are feeding them."

"The incident in Times Square seems to have come at a perfect time for you."

His eyes narrowed. "Maybe a little too perfect."

Maya almost laughed at that. Did he think she would actually coordinate an attack like that, simply to boost his ratings? The attack *had* been coordinated, though. Mr. Fisk had brought Bingham in, and people died. She knew that Mr. Fisk hadn't intended it, and that sometimes, in any great operation, with many wheels turning, accidents happened. She wouldn't condemn him if an accident at a construction site left people dead. A voice told her that this was different, but she didn't want to think about it. Not yet. Not until she knew more.

"Let's not jump to any crazy theories, Mr. Jameson."

"One of my crazy theories was that there was unsavory money supporting my show. You told me I was wrong, but I'm a journalist, young lady. You think all those years behind a desk made me forget how to do a little digging?" He looked straight at her. "The money is coming from Fisk."

"I told you," she said, "that there were business interests in the city that wanted to hear your voice. Mr. Fisk is one of those interests."

"You knew perfectly well I wouldn't have accepted money from the Kingpin of Crime."

"Do *not* call him that," she said. "Those charges were disproved."

"No, they weren't proved," he said, "which isn't the same thing. Still, he's had his day in court, which is more than we can say for Spider-Man."

"No one is doing more to help this city than Mr. Fisk," she said firmly. "He knows the false charges brought against him have biased a number of people, and that's why he wanted to keep his name out of it. But think, Mr. Jameson. You were one of the voices leading the charge against Mr. Fisk before the trial exonerated him. Why would he want you on the air if he had something to hide?"

The truth was, she knew, he wouldn't have wanted

Jameson on the air at all. Fisk's empire was large enough that it might be some time before he realized he had Jameson on the payroll. By then, Maya hoped the show would be profitable enough for Fisk to overlook her part in the project, all without his permission.

For Maya, though, it was something more. This was a way to do something, to push Spider-Man that much closer to exposure. She was playing a part in his eventual downfall, and she wasn't about to stop.

"I don't like it," Jameson said.

"I understand," Maya said casually. What she understood, though, was that having his voice heard all over the city was intoxicating to the man. Being able to voice whatever condemnation came to mind, with no filter, was something Jameson desired very much. She very much doubted he was going to walk away.

He peered at her, uncertain of what to make of her terse reply. He was used to causing people to roll over or flee. He was, she presumed, unused to indifference.

"If I get wind of a story that makes Fisk look bad, I'm not going to ignore it," he said. "I'll say what needs to be said. Honestly, I don't know why I even bother with this radio station. I could have one of those podblasts, and not be answerable to anyone."

"Think of the show as an opportunity to build an audience…" Maya said, "for your future podcast."

"Think you're pretty clever, correcting me, don't you?"

Maya pressed her lips together in an all-business sort of smile. "Mr. Jameson, we only want your candor. No one is asking you to pull your punches. It's why you're vital to this city. Have you reviewed and signed the revised contracts?"

This had been a speed bump. The first contracts had included a critical typo—someone's head had rolled—and they'd had to be redrafted and signed again. Had Jameson really wanted out, it would have been easy for him to sever ties. Still, she wagered he was unwilling to walk away from a growing audience.

He reached into his coat, pulled out a bulky envelope, and handed it to her. She took it, careful to avoid a large mustard stain.

"Signed and notarized," he said. "But that contract allows me to say what I want, and to walk away if you pressure me to do otherwise."

"We want an honest voice," she said. "Nothing more."

"Then that's what you'll get," he said, "whether you like it or not."

○━━━━━━━━━━━━━━○

BINGHAM was too far away to hear what they were saying. He wished he had the deaf girl's ability to read lips. That would be handy. Or mind-reading. He'd like that too—but that wasn't a spider-power, and he could only do spider things, like sneak around without people noticing.

That got him close enough to pick up a word or two, and he'd definitely heard them say something about contracts.

Maybe this time he'd get lucky. After she left the old guy with a thing for hot dogs, she headed east, and Bingham kept after her at a safe distance. He watched as she went into one of the Fisk offices on the east side. She came out twenty minutes later, no longer carrying the envelope.

Contracts. Chances were a copy would go right into the safe. Good thing he'd managed to put a tracker on the envelope before the deaf girl arrived. The old grump had given him an earful for bumping into him, but Bingham had kept on walking. Just another day in the city, right?

He smiled to himself. He was one step closer to his goal.

TWENTY-FOUR

"WHO here wants to play a game of 'guess what the Kingpin is thinking'?"

Spider-Man was in a gambling den under a Hell's Kitchen restaurant. He knew it was owned by Fisk, and it raked in big profits every night. It was supposed to, anyhow. Not tonight. He held a big bag of money that he was going to leave at the nearest F.E.A.S.T. shelter.

Most of the patrons had fled when he came in. Now it was just the boss and the muscle. They weren't going anywhere because they were webbed up in this mess of overturned furniture, scattered cards, strewn chips, and empty beer bottles.

"I'm looking for information," he said. "What's Fisk up to? Why does he have someone impersonating me? What's his favorite brand of protein powder? That dude is huge."

"No one's gonna tell you anything," the boss said. "Just put the money down and walk away. You don't want Mr. Fisk angry with you."

"Yeah, 'cause I can't imagine what that would be like." He held up the bag of money again. "Last chance before I put you on the hook for the missing cash."

No one had anything to say, so he darted out the door, up the stairs, and left. Another evening upending

Fisk operations. Another night that brought him absolutely no closer to finding out what was going on.

○────────────────○

A few hours later, after disrupting another gambling den, a brothel, and a hijacking operation, he was still no closer to getting what he wanted. A call came in from Yuri Watanabe, so he webbed up to a rooftop to talk.

"I hear you're having quite a night," she said. "You stealing from Fisk now?"

"I'm not stealing," he said. "I'm redistributing wealth."

"That's not what the perps are telling us."

"Then I guess it must be true," he said. "Perps wouldn't lie."

"I'm just saying this makes you look bad," she told him. "Check the *Daily Bugle* web page."

After he hung up, he did as she advised. There was the headline.

HAS SPIDER-MAN TURNED SPIDER-THIEF?

Not exactly on the same level as some of the gems from the J. Jonah Jameson days, and not the worst thing imaginable. It was better than SPIDER-MAN CONTINUES TO TERRORIZE CITY, which one of the city's newspapers had run the day before. All part of doing business, he told himself, but he didn't feel all that convinced. How long could he continue to knock over tables and tear up gambling ledgers? None of these guys were ever going to tell him anything. Whatever Kingpin was up to, whatever would make him too big to fail, it wasn't going to be stopped by redistributing his poker earnings.

Every time Spider-Man thought about giving up, he'd see Anika's face and he'd remember what drove him. This was a matter of the purest sort of justice. He'd known Anika, and so she was the face of the twelve people who had died, but elsewhere in the city there were others mourning—parents and children and friends—demanding answers, demanding someone pay. The thought stoked a cold fury in him, a fire he had to channel. He had the power to punish those responsible, and because he had that power, he had the responsibility.

At the hijacking operation he found paperwork leading back to a warehouse supposedly full of goods stolen by Fisk's thugs. He figured he'd go there and see if anyone was feeling chatty. He was on his way when a call came in from MJ.

"Remember me?" she said. "We went to high school together."

"I know," he said with a sigh. "I've been—"

"A little obsessive?" she suggested. "Weird and moody?"

"Exactly. I'm glad you understand."

"For what it's worth, I do understand," she said. "You're not made to sit back and hope something happens. That's why I'm calling. I have a lead that might be of use."

"Really?"

"I was in Fisk Tower today—"

"Again?" It escaped before he could call the word back.

"Peter, my job. Remember? I interview people."

"Not all of those people need to be Wilson Fisk," he said, though he knew it was *exactly* what he shouldn't say.

"Anyhow," she said, speeding over the bumps in their conversational road, "I literally ran into some walking slabs of muscle from Roxxon Blackridge, the military contractors."

"Interesting," he said. "Any idea what they're up to?"

"Couldn't get anything out of them," she said, "but apparently they keep a schedule. They may be getting their marching orders from Fisk on a regular basis." She told Peter everything she'd learned from the security guard.

There was no way to know how it fit into the picture, if it did at all, but it was something—and something was exactly what he needed.

BINGHAM climbed into the window of his apartment, sure no one had seen him. He could never be sure, really, not in New York. Anyone might be looking out their window and see a guy in a spider-suit coming and going. To be sure, he'd have to have some sort of sixth sense. Still, he figured he was in the clear. If not, he'd deal with it later.

Let them try to come for him.

He sat heavily on his bed and pulled off the mask. He liked the feeling when fresh air washed over him, but he also missed the hot, constricted feeling. Something was always lost when something else was gained. He'd learned that one for sure.

It had been an entertaining evening, watching the false Spider-Man messing with Fisk's gambling places. The guy was starting to lose it, and it was fun watching him unravel. A couple of times Bingham had to fight the urge to step in, to take on the impersonator. The true Spider-Man vs. the imposter. That would be something to see—but it wasn't yet the time. It wasn't the mission.

He didn't follow the impersonator every night, but often enough. Bingham couldn't always find him, though there were places he could go to hide and wait, and the impersonator would swing by eventually. He was predictable enough if you knew how to think. Most people didn't, but Bingham did.

Tonight he just watched, but one of these days he'd see an opportunity, a way to make his life miserable. And when he saw it, he'd strike.

o———————o

THE next morning he was there before 7:30, in plenty of time to watch three beefy men in suits enter Fisk Tower. If they came out with assignments—which is what Spider-Man assumed was happening—he could follow them. If he got very lucky, he'd learn something of value.

Perched on the edge of a building, he picked up a cup of coffee he'd bought from a food truck around the block. The owner refused to take his money. At least a few people hadn't given up hope on him.

Lifting the bottom of his mask, he took a sip. The coffee was still steaming.

<hr>

IT was pure chance. She was about to leave her suite and head down for her first meeting of the day when a flash of red and blue struck her from across the street. Though it was distant, she was certain it was a person in a Spider-Man suit.

At first she thought it had to be Bingham, but when she looked through the binoculars, she realized it was him. There were enough minor differences that she could be sure. Maybe a typical person wouldn't notice, but Maya didn't miss those sorts of details.

What was he doing here? It looked like he was watching Fisk Tower, but in broad daylight? She couldn't imagine why. As she watched, he picked up a cup of coffee, folded up the bottom of his mask, and took a sip.

It was jarring. She'd always known there was an actual person under the mask, but she'd ceased to think of him as anything ordinary. That he would sip a cup of coffee and then wipe his mouth with the back of his hand—it was uncanny. On a subconscious level she expected there to be nothing under the mask but a void of evil.

Even if he was a coffee-drinking human being, it didn't make him any less of a monster. He thought he could come here, spy on them, work against everything they hoped to accomplish. What could anyone do about it, after all? It wasn't like anyone would be able to follow him.

He hadn't counted on Maya Lopez. He hadn't counted on a woman who was an echo.

She grabbed her phone and quickly scanned the morning schedule. Nothing that couldn't be rearranged. She sent a quick text to her admin and then prepared to run outside. Then she stopped. A pencil skirt wasn't exactly the right thing to wear when leaping from roof to roof. She needed something that would give her the necessary flexibility. Casting her work clothes onto the floor, she changed into what she'd been wearing when she had chased after Bingham—black pants, a black top, gloves.

Maya looked at her reflection in the mirror. Maybe, she thought, this was the day she would confront him. Mr. Fisk said it wasn't time, but some things weren't about choice. Sometimes destiny chose for you.

Is this, she asked herself, what she wanted to look like when she finally met him in combat? She wanted him to see her true self. She wanted him to look at her and fear her. She thought of that night in Montana, the bloody handprint.

Red wasn't right, though. Something subtle. She

was like a ghost out of her own past. White. It had to be white. She began to search for her old collection of stage makeup from her dance days. It was time for Echo to become more than an idea.

It was time for "Echo" to become a name.

THE contractors came out of the building almost exactly fifteen minutes after they went in. Peter prepared to follow them, but they immediately split up, each taking a different though identical dark SUV. Without much time to consider his options, he picked one at random, and he was off.

Following cars wasn't hard at all when they remained in the city. Bridges and tunnels presented certain problems, though he could usually hitch a ride. The trick there was avoiding getting spotted. Nothing blew a stealthy pursuit like wildly enthusiastic honking.

Fortunately, the car he was following stayed in Manhattan, and this time of the day that meant it couldn't travel too fast. He kept with it as it headed uptown, leaping from roof to roof, wall to wall, careful to stay out of view of anyone on the ground.

The weird thing was the faint tingling from his Spider-Sense. He looked behind him a few times but saw no sign of anyone on his tail. Maybe it was because these guys were dangerous, he told himself. He would need to be careful. He was always careful, but he had to know what they were up to.

The car he was following stopped at Broadway

and 147th Street. Keeping to the rooftops, Spider-Man watched the Roxxon Blackridge contractor get out and linger at a bus stop, all the while keeping his eye on a nearby brownstone. Twenty minutes after he arrived, a woman came out of the brownstone holding a little girl's hand. She began to walk down the street, and the contractor followed her. He had his phone out, and from time to time, he took pictures.

The woman dropped the little girl off at a day-care center. The contractor stepped into a greengrocer, lingering around the entrance. He took a half-dozen photos. She left and he followed her for another four blocks, where he photographed her buying what Spider-Man felt certain had to be heroin.

What did it mean? Who was this woman? Why did the contractor want to get pictures of her buying drugs? The easiest way to find out might be to question her, but she wouldn't likely tell him her life story. When a guy in a costume drops from the sky, you don't immediately volunteer your darkest secrets.

Spider-Man made a note of her address. Maybe he could ask Watanabe to see what she could find out about the woman. Trailing the contractor hadn't turned up the smoking gun he'd been looking for, but it could still turn out to be an important piece of the puzzle.

Following the contractor back to his car, he was careful to duck behind a digital billboard on a rooftop to be sure he wasn't seen. He was watching the contractor drive off when his Spider-Sense went into high gear. He rolled away, trying to get a sense of what exactly was going on.

Then he saw her: a woman all in black, with black hair tied back, and—carrying a spear? She had a white handprint across her face, not exactly a mask but making her difficult to identify. He didn't dwell on it for long, though. He'd been attacked with some improbable things over the years. If he was going to be honest with himself, it could be argued that he was also dressed a little wacky. So who was he to judge? He was more interested in the part where she was trying to kill him.

While the billboard behind him formed itself into a car ad, the woman lashed out with her spear. He dodged to his left, but it turned out the jab was a feint, and he only just twisted out of the way to avoid getting impaled. He dodged and rolled, but she dodged and rolled, as well. He leapt at an angle. She leapt at an angle, mirroring him *exactly*. It seemed as if she could emulate his every move. Meanwhile, the billboard changed again, this time turning into an ad for—of all things—the Fisk Foundation.

Perfect.

The woman with the handprint on her face moved in toward him, her every step seeming to be a copy of his own. For a fleeting moment he wondered if this could be his impersonator, then he discarded the thought. His double had a male voice and physique, and while this woman echoed his every move, she lacked his enhanced abilities. She could leap the way he did, but not as far or as high. She could push herself off walls the way he did, but not cling to them. It was more like parkour. She certainly had no web shooters.

They faced off again, and Peter managed to dodge three fast jabs from the spear. The third one missed him by a mile, slamming into the billboard, sending off a shower of sparks.

"Hold on," he said. "Can we talk about this?"

She came at him with a sideswipe, acting as if she hadn't even heard him. Another miss, and another shower of sparks shot out. He leapt out of the way, wanting to get away from the billboard in case it exploded. He shot out two large webs to catch her, but she rolled away as if she knew exactly what he was going to do, even before he did it.

And *that*, he realized, was how this woman was different. The doppelgänger was like another Spider-Man in his abilities, but not in his style. There were similarities, the way two mixed martial arts fighters or two Tae Kwon Do practitioners would always have certain core moves in common, but their approaches would never be identical. Spider-Man and his imitator were similar because they were working with the same set of abilities, even if they used them differently.

This woman was copying him, and the mimicry was precise. That was the only word for it. Not that she mimicked him as he moved—it was more like she had internalized every move he'd ever made, turning herself into his mirror image.

Yet watching her dodge, leap, attack, feint, and roll, he thought she must have studied hundreds of hours of Spider-Man doing his thing. While she didn't have the gifts he'd received from that radioactive spider, normal abilities were nothing to be sneezed at. He'd been smacked around pretty handily by people who were just regular old human beings.

This one was fast, angry, and she had a spear.

"I like your style," he said. "You seem like a really terrific person, but I've got an impaling phobia, so let's skip the skewering. How about you just tell me what you want?"

Her only response was to try to put a hole in him.

"Well, this is no fun," he said as he leapt out of her way and out of her range. Planting his feet, he turned toward her, hands up in a position of surrender, and walked forward. "Why don't you just tell me what this is all about? We could get lattes."

She feinted twice and he dodged easily. Then she lunged forward, toward a spot where she knew he would be. She was good, and she knew how to anticipate him, but now that he knew what she could do, he was simply too fast for her. By the time the thrust came he was out of the way, if only by inches.

"So you won't talk, and I'm not going to let you slice me open, even if you are the second-best Spider-Man impersonator in the city. So, lady... miss... whatever you are, I'm out of here." He reached out to cast a web, but she'd anticipated that, too.

Her spear came down in a hard swing, knocking his arm. The web shot out to the concrete beneath them and he followed it, hitting the ground hard.

This was an epic fail, and he really hoped no one had caught it on camera. She circled around him with astonishing speed and struck him across the backs of the knees with the shaft of the spear. She was strong.

He rolled out of the way, but she clipped him with the shaft again, propelling him backward into the billboard, sending a halo of sparks into the air. It hurt like hell. She came in for a third swing and he managed to roll away toward the edge of the roof, taking a few photos as he did so. All he had to do was to drop off and he'd be free of her, but the point wasn't really to escape, was it? She'd gotten in some good shots, but he wasn't afraid of her.

Okay, he was a little afraid, but this wasn't like taking a beating from Rhino. There was no chance of getting pounded into goo here. Besides, he was curious. How had this woman learned to move like him? What did she want? Was she connected with the other imitator? Could she tell him anything he needed to know?

Through their entire encounter she hadn't uttered a word, but it was surprising how conversational people became once they were nicely webbed. It was time to stop worrying about hurting the nice lady with the spear and start finding out what she was up to. The next time she came at him, he knew exactly how to play it. She rushed forward, jabbing with the spear. He leapt up, over her head, spun around and kicked.

But she was waiting for him, like she knew exactly what he was going to do. She grabbed his ankle while he was in mid-leap and yanked hard, bringing him down with a painful thud. And then, somehow, she was on him.

His attacker straddled him, a knee on each of his arms, keeping him pinned in place. One hand held the spear as if she was ready to bring it down with a fatal thrust to his throat. The other reached for the seam of his mask. It was like she knew exactly where it was, and she had a solid plan of unmasking him and then killing him.

Throughout the fight Spider-Man had been by turns surprised, confused, curious, and annoyed. Now he was pretty concerned. He had very strong feelings about being unmasked and murdered, and they weren't good feelings. This was definitely something he didn't want to happen. He also wasn't that big on getting his butt handed to him by someone he outweighed by at least thirty pounds of enhanced muscle.

"Getting stuck with a spear is going to ruin my schedule for the week."

Fortunately, he didn't have to. Her knees kept his arms from swinging. Knees were good for that sort of thing, but the thing about knees was that they were narrow and pointy. That left him with a limited range of motion. He shifted his wrist and aimed his web shooter. A jerk of his wrists and he was moving, while she was tumbling off him.

As soon as he was free he spun to face her, crouching and hoping to take advantage of her confusion and pin her in place. The confusion was his, though.

The woman was gone. He'd only had his eyes off

of her for a few seconds, but she'd vanished. Maybe inside the building. Maybe she'd leapt to another rooftop. She could be hiding, or she might have already scrambled down to the street. A person with a hand on their face couldn't exactly blend in, but this was still New York, and she wouldn't stand out either. If he saw someone like that he'd figure she was on her way to a theater or dance company rehearsal. He wouldn't immediately wonder if she'd just been fighting a super-cool hero dude on a roof.

Spider-Man stood and unconsciously scratched the back of his head. He hadn't been stuck like a figurative pig. That was good. He'd managed to get smacked around by a woman who clearly did a lot of strength training, but whose main ability seemed to be watching Spider-Man exercise tapes. That was bad. Also bad was that whatever connection she had to the murderous imitator—assuming there was one—remained unknown.

So, in short, an unimpressive display and nothing to show for himself.

The Roxxon Blackridge contractor was long gone, oblivious to the drama that had played out above his head. Apparently he'd been sent by Fisk to take pictures of an ordinary woman with an extremely troubled life. Another mystery, which was also not a win. It certainly didn't bring him any closer to Anika's murderer.

It was, at least, a clue. And any morning that wasn't a complete disaster was what counted as a victory these days.

TWENTY-FIVE

PETER was supposed to meet MJ for coffee that morning, which was good. He needed someone to talk to. He still didn't know what to make of the woman, who seemed so desperately to want to hurt him, to expose him. There was something about her silence that left him unsettled. Somehow the whole thing had felt personal, yet as far as he could remember, they had never met.

When he talked about it with MJ, she also found the whole thing confounding.

"Maybe she knew someone who died at the sandwich place," he said, keeping his voice quiet so no one could hear them. "Now she blames Spider-Man for it."

"Not likely." MJ shook her head. "From what you're telling me, she'd need months, maybe years, to imitate your moves the way she did. You can't just pick up something like that, even if you're already an athlete."

That made sense. "But how did she know where to find me?" he said. "Even I didn't know where I was going."

"She must have followed you," MJ replied. "It's the only explanation. That means—" she cut herself off. "You said you took a picture of her." Peter nodded and reached for his phone. He'd transferred a photo over from the camera built into his suit.

The picture was somewhat blurry. MJ looked at it and shook her head.

"I've never seen anyone who looks like that. Her outfit is kind of generic—like clothes she bought at a store, rather than a suit that a hero or villain would have custom-made. I can show it around the newsroom, though. Maybe someone there will recognize it."

He nodded. "There's got to be a story to her. And that handprint. It must mean something."

"Hold on," she said. "Let me look again. I'm getting a weird feeling."

"Your MJ-Sense?" he asked.

She laughed. "Exactly. I don't know. It's kind of a déjà vu." She looked at the photo again. "There's something familiar about her. I've seen her somewhere, but I can't—" Her eyes went wide. "Oh my God."

"That sounds like recognition."

She slid the phone back. "That's Maya Lopez, Fisk's creepy assistant. I've met her a couple of times. She sat in on my last meeting with him and never said a thing."

"How many meetings have you had, exactly?"

"Peter, stay focused. I have no idea what she does for Fisk, but she's a top player. It's really odd, because she's clearly pretty young—younger than we are—but he seems to take her seriously. His eyes are on her a lot."

"You think she's his special lady on the side?"

MJ squinted as she thought about it. "I never got

a sense that there was anything romantic or sexual in Fisk's interactions with this woman, and he's famously devoted to his wife. She's out of the country right now, but I don't think it makes a difference to a guy like that. As weird as it sounds, it's like Fisk actually cares about Lopez, or something nearly human like that. He definitely cares what she thinks."

"Huh," Peter said.

"Maybe he's grooming her for something—and when you said she must have followed you, that meant she had to pick you up somewhere. So she either knows where you live, or she spotted you at Fisk Tower and started to follow you from there."

Peter leaned back. "So Fisk has two Spider-Man impersonators working for him. One is assigned the job of making me look bad, and the other one has instructions to turn me into a human pincushion. The two seem kind of at odds."

MJ nodded. "Something's definitely not right."

"The way she came after me was strange," he said, thinking back. "As angry as she was, it felt—I don't know—personal. It was like the hatred was coming off her in waves, even though she never said a word. Hardly even grunted."

"So maybe she's doing this on her own," MJ offered, "which could mean Fisk doesn't know she's trying to kill you. It could be something going on inside Fisk Tower that Kingpin himself might not even know about. I guess for now I'll see what I can find out about her. Also, did you get a clearer picture of the spear?"

"I think so. Why?"

"Just a hunch," she said, "but if it's an antique, maybe it's distinctive. It might tell us something. It might be another lead pointing back to Fisk."

Peter sighed. "MJ, I know you're not going to want to hear this, but maybe that's not such a great idea. You're talking about monkeying around with Fisk's inner circle—his personal life. People have been beaten to death just for *thinking* about insulting his wife. If this woman actually means something to him, then he's not going to play nice."

"Maybe I should pass the story on to someone else then," she said testily.

"That's not what I'm saying."

She folded her arms. "It's not?"

Okay, it was precisely what he was saying, now that he thought about it. "I've seen this before with reporters—people I actually cared about. They think their pursuit of the truth will somehow protect them, and they end up in car accidents or home invasions or the sudden need, without any history, to take their own lives. You're not immune to any of that, just because Fisk pretends to be charmed by you."

"I know all of this," she said. "I also know how to cover my tracks."

"The graveyard is full of reporters who knew how to cover their tracks."

"And our society depends on reporters who know never to back down," she snapped. "Are you saying I should give up and go home?"

"Of course not, but…" He let himself trail off, because he had no idea how he was going to finish the sentence. What he wanted was for her to give up and go home. He didn't want her to give up on reporting, of course. He didn't even want her to give up on reporting about bad people doing bad things. She wanted to investigate, and he respected that. He loved that about her, but Fisk was something different. He was his own level of dangerous. Peter knew she had no illusions about what kind of a person she was challenging, but that wouldn't stop her. MJ's tenacity was admirable and attractive and heroic. It was part of what made her special, but he had a hard time living with it.

"You know my history too well for me to go over it with you," he began.

"Sorry," she snapped. "You don't get to use your uncle as a free pass to tell me what to do. I get it, you want to protect everyone. It's what drives you to do what you do, and that is a big part of what makes you special, but you have to know where to draw the line."

"We're talking about one thing," he said. "Wilson Fisk. I just want to draw a red line around him. Is that so much to ask?"

"What if I start looking into some other crime boss?" she countered. "What if it were about these Blackridge guys? Would *that* be a red line?"

"MJ," he groaned. It was the best he had.

"You go out and face danger every single day," she said, "and I've had to learn to live with it."

"But I—"

"You have abilities. I know you do, but you're fighting people who have abilities, and some of them are more powerful than you. Does that stop you? You think I haven't stayed up nights worrying you were going to be trampled or electrocuted or stung or flung or de-atomized."

"I don't remember any de-atomizing—"

She took his hand, cutting him off. "Peter, I love you, but I don't love having this argument all the time. It's draining me. You are going to have to learn to live with me making my own choices. This is what I've been wanting to talk to you about. I put it off because I know you don't need any more drama, but this is a big deal to me. I can't live the life I want to live if I feel like I've got you hovering over me, asking me to explain every choice I make. You are going to have to trust that I'm responsible enough to weigh risks, just as I've trusted you to do that."

He nodded. "Okay."

"So we're never going to have this fight again, right?"

"That," he agreed, "is the goal."

"And you'll stay out of my business?"

"Except when you ask," he said. *Or if you really need me to interfere.*

○────────────○

A week later, they sat in a restaurant on the Upper East Side. It was their last night with Harry, who was leaving for Europe the next afternoon. Peter had been looking forward to it for days, and he'd been praying that there would be no crisis that would make him late or turn him into a no-show.

Inexplicably, the universe actually did him a solid, and the three of them were enjoying a night of good food, good wine, and good memories. Ideally Peter would have treated his friend, but economic realities being what they were, Harry insisted on picking up the tab.

"Don't fight me on this," Harry said to him before they sat down. "You could be a millionaire a hundred times over if you weren't so committed to doing the right thing. I get to pretend I'm a good guy by spending some money I'll never miss."

Things were still a little tense with MJ. He'd promised to try to do better, to stop being such a worrier, but it wasn't like she was pursuing a new hobby. She was asking for his support as she went down a road that could get her killed. Every time he thought he needed to be more supportive, he remembered what that meant—to look the other way while she crossed Wilson Fisk. How was he supposed to pull that off?

He wanted to put all of it aside for the night, but it wasn't easy. MJ was having a hard time, too.

On top of all that, Peter couldn't shake the feeling that there was something Harry wasn't telling them. The purpose of the trip was still vague—wanting to "find himself," figure out his priorities, discover his passion. It seemed as if he could do that in New York, or with a bunch of quick trips to Europe. He didn't see why Harry needed to relocate there.

Of course, given that his father was Norman Osborn, he might need an ocean between the two of them to feel like he had breathing room. That would have sufficed as an explanation, he supposed, if there hadn't been other hints. Peter had known Harry long enough to tell when his friend was holding something back. He had that feeling now.

There were other ways in which Harry didn't quite seem himself—a little more easily distracted or a little quicker to let his temper flare. Once, Peter thought he saw Harry's hand trembling. It worried him, but he knew when to give Harry space. He just wished he didn't have to give him that much space.

"I'm exhausted," Harry told them as they headed out of the restaurant. "I need to get some sleep before spending an entire day sitting and doing nothing on an airplane. You two should carry on, though."

"I wish I could," MJ said. "I've got a deadline. After this, I'm brewing a pot of coffee and pulling an all-nighter."

They saw her into a cab, and then Peter began to walk Harry to his apartment.

"Try and keep my dad in line while I'm gone," Harry said. "He'll make time to meet with you, so take advantage of that if he starts to do something stupid."

"He seems like he's doing an okay job as mayor," Peter said. "Maybe a little too corporate-friendly, but things seem to be working pretty well."

"We've fought about that," Harry said. "I tried to get him to see things differently, but he's always been a business guy. And once he gets an idea, he won't let it go."

"You can be like that, too."

Harry laughed. "Exactly. And do you have any idea how hard it is to fight yourself?"

The fight on the roof with the woman, Maya Lopez, came back to him. He had a pretty good idea.

"So, any tips?" he asked. "On fighting yourself?"

Harry looked at him like he was crazy, which, under the circumstances, wasn't all that unreasonable.

"Be someone else," he said. "That's the one thing they'll never see coming."

They reached his apartment building and started to shake hands, then turned it into a hug. Harry didn't know his secret, but after MJ and Aunt May, he was the only person who really knew him, who got him. Even though he couldn't tell Harry about everything that was going on with him, having him around helped. Now Peter was going to be one step closer to being alone.

Harry seemed to sense his disquiet. "Things seem kind of strained with you and MJ."

"I worry about her," Peter said, "and she doesn't like that I worry."

"If you hover over her," Harry said, "you'll lose her."

"If she gets herself killed, I'll lose her worse."

"You can't control how she lives her life," Harry

said, "but you can control how much you bug the crap out of her."

It was good advice. After Harry went upstairs, Peter stood on the street, looking up, feeling like one more piece of his life was disappearing.

TWENTY-SIX

MANY blocks downtown, two men stood inside a darkened Fisk warehouse. No one else was there—that had been a condition of the meeting. Just the two of them. No assistants or bodyguards. No witnesses.

"We'll do it at one of my places," Fisk said. "It's harder for you to arrange things without being seen."

"And if someone happens to notice me going in there?" Norman Osborn asked.

"Then it's simply a consultation between the mayor of New York and one of its most prominent citizens. Nothing could be less scandalous."

A table had been placed under a hanging light. On it sat a bottle of wine and two glasses, but neither seemed in the mood to sit, let alone to drink. Fisk watched the shadows dance in the dim light. He was as good as his word. None of his people were present. He had no wish for them to hear what he had to say, and it wasn't as though the mayor was a physical threat. If he needed to, he could break Osborn in half, stuff him in a crate, and drop him into the river—all in less time than Osborn would need to call a cab.

No, the dangers Osborn posed were of a slower and more methodical nature. He was dangerous, but he also presented an opportunity. Fisk didn't trust the mayor to honor a bargain, but he trusted Osborn's greed and ambition. He trusted Osborn's lust for power. Most people saw him as the brilliant entrepreneur who had turned a little tech company into one of the world's most ubiquitous brands. They saw the ambitious man who, having achieved incredible success and wealth, wanted to prove he could govern as well as he could invent and innovate.

The jury was still out on how well Osborn was doing as mayor. The financial sector loved him because they saw him as good for business, but did that translate to being a good leader? He was getting heat from a lot of interests that didn't benefit from Wall Street's success. Guys like Martin Li were on the news every other day, talking about providing services for the homeless and implicitly attacking Osborn in the process.

"Someone has to step up," Li liked to say. *"If the government won't help the people, then the people have to help each other."*

"You have to make Martin Li and his kind work for you," Fisk said. "Make use of the private sector. It's good for business and it's good for the people." He paused, then added, "I'm trying to give you a lifeline, Osborn."

"I don't need a lifeline," the mayor said. "Not from you or anyone else. I'm not drowning."

"You're not exactly thriving, either. People with money love you, but everyone else is calling you the mayor of Wall Street. You can't change who you are—that would be worse. Your base will turn on you, and the people hate a hypocrite. Instead, you have to convince them that your ways will help everyone."

"And embracing Wilson Fisk will do that?" Osborn coughed out a laugh.

"Precisely."

"Sounds like a non-starter to me," Osborn said. "The world hasn't forgotten about your past troubles."

"The state had a chance to make its case against me," Fisk said. "It had no case to make. Am I supposed to be punished for that? That's not justice."

"We're not talking about justice," Osborn told him. "We're talking about public relations."

Fisk smirked. "This isn't some uptight Lutheran town in the Midwest, Norman. It's New York City, and if there's one thing New Yorkers like, it's a comeback. They want to see a man who's been down get back up again. They want to see a villain remake himself as a hero. If you can be part of that, then you become a hero, too."

Osborn kept his face expressionless. "I'll consider your proposal."

"You are doing more than considering it, or we wouldn't be having this conversation," Fisk said. "Tell me what it's going to take to make this work."

Osborn sighed and shook his head. "Fair enough." He handed Fisk an envelope. "There is a list of… requirements in there. Nothing that should be too painful."

Fisk tore it open, took out the paper, and scanned the contents in the dim light.

"I have to hand it to you, Osborn, you've planned

it precisely. If I shave off this much, it will hurt without the wounds being crippling." He looked up and gave the mayor a curt nod. "But if this is what you want, I think we can do business."

"Just trying to do what's best for the city, Wilson," he said. "I have an opportunity to make some real changes. I could be hailed as the most successful mayor in generations, but I need to play hardball if I'm going to succeed."

"Not to mix metaphors," Fisk said, "but are you sure you want to play hardball when you're skating on such thin ice?"

"We're doing business here, Wilson. Is that kind of talk really necessary?"

"I merely remind you of where you stand," Fisk replied. He held up the documents. "As long as we're discussing a carrot, I won't need to show you the stick."

Osborn's eyes narrowed. "You said we're doing business." His mouth became a thin line.

"And I want to *keep* doing business just as amicably," Fisk said. "What you ask for is reasonable for a man in your position. I have no objections when I deal with reasonable men. I only require that you remain reasonable."

"I'm glad to know you're thinking so clearly on this."

"I always think clearly."

"Oh, really?" Osborn laughed. "What about this man who's running around pretending to be Spider-Man? No, I don't have any evidence, but I know how you think. What I want to know is how you found someone who can do exactly what Spider-Man can do."

"If I were behind it," Fisk said, "I certainly wouldn't discuss it with you."

"Still, I'm curious," Osborn continued. "Are there others out there like him? Is there a whole race of Spider-Men waiting to be recruited? Or did you somehow create him? Is there a laboratory in the bowels of Fisk Tower where ordinary men are being—"

"Enough!" Fisk barked, taking a step forward. "Don't speak to me like I'm one of the lackeys you mock with your superior tone. I am Wilson Fisk!"

"And I am the mayor of New York City," Osborn replied, but he did so quietly, and with his eyes lowered.

"If you want to stay that way, you will govern your tongue," Fisk told him. The pounding in his skull began to soothe. His pulse stopped thrumming. He let his fists unclench. "It is human nature to resist the feeling of powerlessness. You can indulge in that fantasy when you play at being a politician. When you speak to me, however, you will remember who and what you are, or I will have you replaced with someone who understands where the city's power truly lies. We have these negotiations because you are an intelligent man who might see things others have missed, not because you have any authority to assert."

Fisk continued to stare at him until Osborn looked away.

"We're done here," Fisk said. He turned and strode out of the warehouse, leaving Osborn to find his own way in the dark.

BINGHAM crouched on a pile of crates watching the exchange, wishing he had popcorn to munch on. Or potato chips. He liked those too. It would be hard to eat in his suit, though. It got hot in there, but he liked feeling like he was cooking, slowly turning into his true self.

He also liked watching these two men talk. It didn't get more entertaining than this. He waited for a signal, a sign that he should jump in. If he needed to take care of business, he would do it, and it would be another high-profile Spider-Man crime. But Bingham knew it was unlikely he'd have to act. Those two were in the same boat, even if they didn't want to admit it. They would stare and threaten and have pissing contests, but it was never going to be more than that because Fisk needed Osborn and Osborn needed Fisk. That's how it was, and it would stay that way until one devoured the other.

The fat man left first, and there was nothing for Bingham to do. Maybe swing around a little, web up some cops for fun, knock over some old ladies, and get his face on the news. He loved swinging, he loved using the web shooters, even though they exacted a heavy toll on his shoulders. He was sore for a long while after flying around the city. The web shooters they'd made for him had a much stronger kick than the ones the imposter used, and they were clunkier, too. It wasn't fair. They'd told him that if his muscles and skeletal structure hadn't been enhanced by the medicine, his shoulder would be dislocated every time he used the web shooters.

The pain was worth it, though.

Any pain was worth it, because he was Spider-Man—and greatness and suffering were part of the same thing, weren't they? He thought so. Or maybe he'd heard it on TV, but either way it was true.

And he loved being himself. He loved swinging through the city, hurting people, scaring them. The other day, while pretending to be the weak Spider-Man imposter, he'd considered pushing a baby stroller in front of a speeding truck. Babies were easily replaced. There'd be no real harm done, and Bingham knew he'd feel no more guilt than if he'd dropped a candy wrapper on the street. He'd held back, though, because he knew the grief he'd get from Fisk was more trouble than it was worth.

The time would come, though, when no one would tell him what to do. Fisk thought he had control, but that was a joke. He controlled Fisk. He pulled Fisk's strings. It was better for now that the fat man didn't know it, though.

Let them think he was stupid. People had always underestimated him. They laughed at him back in Binghamton, and they laughed at him on the streets of New York, but they'd stopped laughing after he met the people from the laboratory.

THE nice lady he met on the street took him to a van where they gave him hot chocolate—the kind with the little marshmallows that melted while you poked them with a plastic stick. They gave him clean clothes to wear and a tuna sandwich that was unlike any tuna sandwich he'd ever had before. It was thick with creamy tuna salad and it had little black olives in it, which surprised him, but he liked them.

"We'd like to take you someplace," the lady told him. She was pretty, and he liked looking at her. "You'll be warm all the time, and you'll have plenty to eat and drink. There will be clean clothes and a bed."

People thought Bingham was stupid, but he wasn't stupid. No one did nice stuff like this without wanting something in return. He understood that.

"What will I have to do?"

She smiled, appreciating how smart he was. She had funny glasses that were very long rectangles with bright green frames. He didn't know how he felt about those.

"We want to test some… medicines," she explained. "They might make you healthier than you are right now, but I'll tell you the truth—they might make you sick. But if you were to get sick, we'd take care of you."

Bingham could picture himself lying in bed, the pretty lady with the funny glasses taking his temperature or bringing him bowls of soup on a tray the way his mother had before she changed. His mother had given him medicine that made him feel better, and let him watch TV as much as he wanted. That didn't seem so bad to him. He would be willing to do that, so he signed the papers that said he agreed to do what they asked, and the pretty lady told the man in front of the van to drive.

It took a long time to get where they were going, and Bingham couldn't tell much about it because the van had no windows. The van stopped, and they climbed out inside a garage that was probably underground. It was cold and his footsteps echoed. The pretty lady with the glasses walked him through some doors and handed him over to a man in a uniform who did not smile at all.

Bingham never saw the pretty lady with the glasses again.

○————————○

HE'D thought they were going to a house, just like the house he grew up in only nicer, with softer beds and prettier furniture, soup bowls that weren't chipped and forks with all the tines pointing in the same direction. It wasn't like that at all. It was more like the hospital where they brought his mother when she became sick. He hadn't thought they were talking about him being sick like his mom, but that was exactly what the pretty lady meant. They meant sick like his mother, and worse.

He didn't even have his own room. He shared it with five other men, but not always the same five, because things kept happening to the others. They would get sick. Sometimes they became feverish and thrashed in their beds. Sometimes they threw up soupy liquid or blood or—one time—what seemed to be the man's own stomach. They grew lumps on their faces and bodies. They screamed and cried for their mothers. They soiled themselves in the night and Bingham found them lying open-eyed and still in the morning. One man clawed his own face off while the others watched. No one brought them soup.

They did have a television, which was nice.

They were supposed to be nice to each other. There were security guards, and it was their job to step in when someone stole another person's pudding cup or hogged the TV or was just mean because they liked being mean.

Zane was mean because he liked being mean. Most of the men were quiet and minded their own business, the way Bingham tried to, but Zane was mean from the beginning. He liked to trip the other patients or yank down their pajama pants just because he thought it was funny to see someone's butt. He stole food and threw it at people and he would take the TV remote and not give it back because he said there was nothing as good on TV as watching the babies cry when they didn't get their way. Zane said Bingham was fat, though he knew he had lost a lot of weight since leaving home, and he was losing more now. They didn't get that much to eat, and he thought the medicine was making him thinner. Sometimes he liked to say, "I'm slim," to people, but not to Zane, because Zane would make fun of him.

Most of the security guards would step in if Zane took things too far. Not at first, because that would mean putting down their phones or their magazines or whatever they were using to pass the time. Eventually, though, they would do something. Not Macgregor. He was kind of old and kind of lazy. He had a shiny bald head with a fringe of gray and a strangely round nose with a big red growth on it. His eyes were weirdly tiny, and he laughed when they hurt themselves.

Macgregor liked Zane. At first he only laughed when Zane was being mean, like he was watching a funny movie, but then he started to help. The two of them would play catch with the TV remote, or Zane would hand Macgregor someone's dinner tray and the guard would dump it in the toilet.

Then there was the business with Reece, who was close to being Bingham's friend. He didn't make a lot of friends, but Reece was really nice to him, and so Bingham tried being nice back. They sometimes talked about things they remembered from the old days, or they would sit quietly and watch TV together. It seemed like they could do that for hours and not get bored.

One day Reece started choking. They hadn't been eating anything, so at first Bingham thought it was a cough, but it kept getting worse. Reece hacked and wheezed and fell over. His face turned red and he clawed at his throat.

There was an emergency call button and Macgregor stood, his finger on the button, but he didn't press it. He just stood and watched, grinning the whole time. Bingham decided he would press the button if Macgregor wouldn't, but Zane wouldn't let him. He held Bingham and Macgregor stood and watched while Reece twitched on the floor for a long, long time. Then the twitching became weaker, and Reece lay still, his mouth open, his eyes glassy, a stain appearing on the floor underneath him.

Macgregor pressed the button.

"Seizure in room seven," he said in a clipped voice. The minute he took his finger off the button, he and Zane broke out in laugher. They high-fived, like they'd just watched their favorite team score.

It was after they took Reece's body away that Bingham came to realize that he was different. He wasn't exactly who he used to be. It wasn't like he was growing. Or like part of the old Bingham was gone, and something else had appeared in its place. He was part old and part new. That's how it seemed to him. His body was changing, but it was still his body. He thought things he'd never thought before, but they were still his thoughts. There was probably a word for when this happened, but he didn't know it.

Later that day, when Zane asked him if he was going to cry for his boyfriend, Bingham took him by the hair and smashed his head into the floor until there really wasn't a whole lot left of Zane's head. It broke, and the stuff that had been inside was everywhere. Macgregor pressed the button really fast that time, but he wasn't breathing either by the time the staff got there.

———o———————o———

THEY took Bingham to the director's office. The director worked for the boss, who was a very important man. No one wanted to upset the director, and they especially didn't want to upset the boss.

Bingham had done both, and while he didn't love living in the facility, he wasn't sure he was ready to go back outside where it was cold and there wasn't enough to eat. Now that Zane and Macgregor were gone, things wouldn't be so bad. It didn't seem right somehow that the very thing that would make his life more bearable would be the thing that got him cast out.

The director was an older man with a long nose and a white beard. He looked very serious, but not exactly angry. There were some questions at first about whether or not Bingham understood what he'd done was wrong, but the man didn't really seem to care very much about the answers. He was much more interested about whether or not Bingham had ever hurt anyone before, if he had intended to hurt Zane and Macgregor, and if he had known he could do the things he did.

The director wrote down everything Bingham said in response to these questions. Being listened to was a strange feeling. Bingham discovered that he liked it.

"Have you been feeling any different lately?" the director wanted to know. "Stronger, maybe?"

"I feel good," Bingham said. "More awake, I guess, like I know everything that's going on. I didn't know that I felt stronger until—until that thing happened."

"But you felt stronger when you attacked those men?"

"Yes," Bingham said. "Am I in trouble?"

"Not in trouble," the director said. "Not if you're willing to help us."

"How can I help you?"

"By taking more medicine," the director said.

"It doesn't make me sick, so okay."

"The boss will be very pleased to hear that," the director said.

It turned out that Bingham wasn't punished for what he had done to those two men. Instead, they gave him his own room. He had a TV that he controlled by himself, and no one tried to take his food away.

TWENTY-SEVEN

IT was strange to be back at the *Bugle*. While he was in high school this place had been like a second home to him, a sort of refuge. He was a kid accepted by adults, and extraordinary adults at that—people who were taking risks and defying the odds to get at the truth.

They did it because it was good and right, and because they were ambitious and driven and addicted to the adrenaline rush of danger and deadlines. They fueled themselves with burnt coffee and stale donuts and street knishes grabbed on the run. Granted, Peter had been doing similar stuff as Spider-Man, but these people were doing it with words and insight and persistence. They didn't have any special powers randomly granted by the universe. They relied on their own grit and determination.

He was happy to say hello to everyone on the way in—Ben Urich, Betty Brant, Robbie Robertson. It was great to see all of them again. At one point he passed a group of reporters gathered around a computer that was playing a live broadcast of Jameson's new radio show. They all seemed to find it hilarious.

Finally he met up with MJ by her cubicle. "I've told everyone I'm helping you with a project for your work," she said, "so keep your voice down. I don't want Mr. Robertson to know I'm doing research that has anything to do with Fisk."

Peter had his own concerns about that, but he had no desire to restart the argument. For now, they were focused on the woman who had been of such interest to the Roxxon operatives. They had a photograph of her and they knew her address, and that was it. Based on that information, however, they were able to establish her identity as Laura Remzi. Nothing else of interest came up about her. She had no discoverable ties to Roxxon or to Fisk or to anyone else either Peter or MJ could identify. Sitting in front of her monitor they dug around for another half an hour, but came up with nothing.

"I don't get it," Peter said. "She seems perfectly ordinary. She's got troubles, but so do a lot of people. There's no reason she'd be of interest to Fisk."

"What if she isn't?" MJ proposed. "What if it's someone she's close to?" She let her fingers dance along her keyboard for a few minutes, and then she slapped her hand down on the desk. "And there it is. Her brother is an assistant district attorney."

Peter thought about this for a minute. "I guess it would be embarrassing for a DA to have a sister with a substance abuse problem, but that's not exactly something you could use to twist this guy around your little finger."

"Maybe," MJ said, "but Fisk has always relied heavily on extortion. It could be that this, combined with something we don't know about, is a powerful enough incentive for this DA to play ball. We know he wants to control people inside law enforcement."

"Okay, this is useful," he said, making note of the assistant DA's information. "Thanks."

"I've also been doing some digging on Fisk's assistant, Maya Lopez. It's all very interesting." She handed Peter a file. "It looks like her father was some kind of operator—first for an organization out west, then for Fisk. Maybe *with* Fisk might be more accurate. They seem to have cooperated on a number of occasions, but they had a falling-out. Police suspected, though they could never prove, that Fisk had Lopez killed after a shipment of guns was seized by ATF. Fisk might have thought Lopez was cooperating with the feds."

"Interesting that he took the guy's daughter in."

"Especially since she's deaf," MJ said. "He isn't exactly known for assisting people out of the goodness of his heart. If he helps someone, it's because he expects to get something out of it. Helping the child of someone who set out to betray him is pretty unexpected."

"Deaf," Peter said, and he snapped his fingers. "That explains why she didn't respond to anything I said."

"Yeah, from what I could see, she can read lips," MJ said. "Your mask is going to be a problem if you run into her again."

Peter began to leaf through the file. "I remember this murder," he said. "I was just starting out, and I showed up at the crime scene thinking—honestly, I don't know what I was thinking, but I was 15 years old and figured I could help the cops or something. It was a disaster. Half of them wanted to arrest me, so I took off, but word of my being there got around. Jameson tried to float the idea that I'd killed the man and had been spotted at the scene, even though I didn't show up until an hour after the cops. That may have been the first time he started going after me. Not that any of that matters."

"I'm not so sure," MJ said. "Lopez worked with Fisk. His daughter works with Fisk. You first encountered the impersonator at a Fisk construction site. Now Jameson is trying to pass off the impersonator as the real thing."

"What does Jameson have to do with it?"

"The company that owns his radio station made some bad investments. Fisk bailed them out, but he got a controlling interest."

Peter shook his head and whistled. "Even so, I don't think Jameson would do this sort of thing for money, let alone dirty money."

"No, but he might not know where the money is coming from," she replied. "Or he may think he's above it all."

"Maybe," Peter said. "Though it wouldn't surprise me if he was planning an exposé of the people who pay him. As much as he can be a pain in the ass, Jonah is a straight-shooter at heart—Spider-Man notwithstanding. In the meantime, none of this points to a larger goal. Fisk is working on something that's supposed to make him too big to prosecute."

"There's one more thing," MJ said. She pulled up a photograph of a spear. Peter knew it only too well, since he'd been looking at the business end of it just recently. "I can't prove for sure that this is the same weapon in your picture," she said, "but it sure looks like it could be. It was stolen from a private collector about fifteen years ago. Lopez's father was implicated, but never charged. There were later pictures of a similar spear in his New York home."

"That doesn't seem like a big deal," Peter said. "Maybe he hid it somewhere, but if it was in his possession, it's not so strange it ended up with his daughter."

"It *gets* strange, though," MJ continued, "because Lopez was stabbed to death with a spear in his own home. It was missing from its display case and never recovered."

"So, Maya Lopez was fighting me with the same weapon that was used to kill her father?" Peter asked.

"That's what it looks like," MJ said. "Either she's cold as ice, or she doesn't know."

Peter found the second option more likely. Maya Lopez had fought with passion, but he hadn't had the sense that she was cruel. She blamed him for her father's death, and that meant the spear was a memento, not a trophy.

"Let's get back to Fisk," he suggested. "I still don't see his endgame in all this."

"Fisk's processes are expansive, not linear," she said. "He isn't chasing a single, shiny object. He thinks in complex patterns. That means whatever we're looking at is only *part* of that pattern. I hate to say it, Peter, but I think you may be giving yourself too much credit. You're asking, '*What does Fisk gain if people hate Spider-Man?*' It's more likely he's asked himself, '*What are the scenarios I need to succeed?*', and just one of them is having a population angry with Spider-Man." She smiled and tilted her head. "I haven't crushed your ego, have I?"

"I may recover… in time," Peter said distractedly. "But keep on crushing, because I like your metaphor. It's like a big spider's web, and if you pull on one thread, you can see what else moves."

"That wasn't really my metaphor at all," she said, "and it may bring us back to the subject of your ego."

"You're brilliant," he said, standing up and giving her a quick kiss. "Your insightful questions have allowed me to solve the case! Okay, not really, but I do think I have a new angle to work. I'll call you later."

"A thread in a carpet works just as well," she called after him. "Just saying."

On his way out, Peter passed a group of reporters who were talking about a story that had just come in. Spider-Man had chased off a mugger and then made off with the victim's wallet.

"Can you believe we used to think that guy was a hero?" one of them asked.

○────────────────○

WHEN he got out to the street, he took out his phone and called Yuri Watanabe.

"Did we ever find out anything about Andy, the victim from the cruise terminal?" he asked her.

She told him to hold on, so she could go somewhere private. She had to be careful when discussing anything that involved Fisk. Peter listened for a few minutes to the distant sounds of a police precinct before she was free to talk.

"Nothing much," she said. "His record is fairly long, but not remarkable. A lot of petty crime—breaking and entering, mainly. Nothing violent."

"It's just a hunch," he said, "but can you maybe dig a little deeper. I have a feeling there's something there. We don't have a whole lot of leads, so I want to make sure we exhaust everything we've got. That night, he said his brother was shady. Maybe look there."

"Okay, I'll give it a shot," she said. "Anything else?"

"Yeah," he said. "I need a home address for someone, and you're not going to like it."

o———————o

HE didn't want to break into the East Side apartment. That seemed like a bad idea for a guy who was supposed to be doing heroic things. On the other hand, he couldn't just ring the bell and hope to get buzzed in. Showing up at the window while the guy was watching TV would be just as bad.

So he picked a compromise. He opened the unlocked window, waited on the outside ledge, but he didn't enter. He was, in a sense, already there, but he hadn't gone inside, so he hoped that would come across as more respectful and less creepy.

After a while the front door opened, the man entered his apartment, put down some groceries, and hung his plastic-wrapped dry cleaning in a closet. He then went into the bathroom and peed with the door open.

Spider-Man grimaced beneath the mask and turned away. This wasn't helping with the creep factor. At least, he thought, it was only peeing. After the man emerged, he entered his living room and turned on his television. Noticing a shadow on the floor he looked up at the window and gasped.

"Hey," Spider-Man said with a friendly wave. "You have a minute?"

Assistant District Attorney Abe Remzi took a step back. He then pointed with the TV remote.

The Web-Slinger held up his hands. "Is this a bad time, Mr. Remzi? I could come back. I have zero problem with making an appointment." Remzi blinked a few times, but then hit the mute button.

"What do you want?"

"First of all, for you not to freak out," Spider-Man replied. "That's definitely at the top of my list… and to talk. I've been waiting here for you, but I didn't want to actually come inside without being invited. I guess that sort of makes me like a vampire. Or a polite person. Hopefully you'll go with the second option."

"Were you watching me pee?"

"No," Peter said quickly, "I turned away, but I may have heard some splashing."

Remzi sighed and then waved him in.

"You seem like the real one."

"So you know the other one is an imposter?" Spider-Man asked as he stepped inside.

"There's no official word," Remzi said, "but it's pretty obvious to me. The other guy is a jerk, he doesn't sound like you, and he doesn't make stupid jokes. Besides, the lines on his suit are too close together."

"Exactly! You're very observant."

Remzi laughed and shook his head. "Honestly, I'm kind of a fan."

"And I'm a fan of hard-working public servants. Guess that makes us a couple of mutual admirers."

Remzi looked at him. "So, there was something you wanted to talk about?" He raised an eyebrow. "One of the cases I'm working on? I'm not sure I can—"

"No, I'm afraid that's not it," Spider-Man replied. "You have a sister named Laura Remzi?"

The DA looked stricken. "Is she… Did something happen?"

"No, no, everything's fine as far as I know," the Web-Slinger said hurriedly. "I don't want to give you too many details, but I was following some guys, and this one took photos of your sister as she went about her business and, um, did things."

"She's using again?" the DA asked, sounding as if he was bracing himself.

He knows. Spider-Man nodded.

"I was afraid of that." Remzi sighed. "Okay, well I can try to get her help. My niece has stayed with me before, so I can make it work."

"Do you have any idea why someone would want this information?"

"Do you know who's behind it?"

Peter grimaced under his mask.

"You don't want to tell me," Remzi said. "I get it. You don't know if I'm compromised or not. So, I'll shoot straight with you." He paused and looked like he was gathering his thoughts. "You want to know if someone came to me and said, 'Do this or we'll expose your sister,' would I roll over?"

"I guess that's the question."

"The answer is no," Remzi said. "My sister has a problem. She's been dealing with it for years, and she's been in rehab once already. Obviously this is all stuff we'd rather keep private, but we're not talking about classified information here. It's not like I'd break the law or risk my career to hide something her friends and our family already know."

"Then why take the photos?" Peter asked. "Again, no specifics, but the guys doing this work don't come cheap." A gentle vibration indicated an incoming call, but he ignored it.

"That's how it's done," Remzi said. "It's like asking a gold prospector why he doesn't just go to where the gold is, instead of working a bunch of bad claims first. You collect everything you can, and see what's of use. My sister got photographed, and that photograph is now raw intel. Someone will go through all that raw intel and decide what's worth using. A little further research will prove it's not worth much, that it can't be used to make me turn. If you hadn't seen it go down, we'd never know it happened. But Wilson Fisk won't get anything he can use on me."

"I never said it was Fisk."

"Come on," Remzi said. "Extortion has always been his go-to plan—and who else would have the means or the desire to spend God knows how much, just to collect heaps of raw data?" He gave a wry grin. "Besides, everyone knows you have a bug up your ass about Fisk."

"Because I'm delicate, I prefer 'bee in my bonnet,'" Spider-Man said, "but both are accurate. Any idea what he's after?"

"Not a clue," Remzi said, "but check this out. I recorded it the other morning, and it's been bothering me ever since." He picked up his TV remote and began searching through his DVR for a clip. After a minute he hit play and unmuted it.

On the screen Norman Osborn came out of City Hall. Reporters shouted questions at him, and he gave off a stream of noncommittal answers until someone asked about the city's "cozy" relationship with business interests. The mayor stopped in his tracks.

"I object to the word 'cozy,'" Osborn said. "It suggests something improper. This city was built on business, and when business does well, people do well. If anything, there is a new wave of civic-minded business in this town we need to encourage—people like Wilson Fisk, who find new ways to make money while helping out workers and families and ordinary people. I don't want to hide that. I want to encourage it."

Remzi paused the feed. "Osborn is going out of his way to praise Fisk. It feels like we're being softened up."

"For what?"

Remzi shook his head. "No idea, but if Fisk is involved, it'll be bad."

TWENTY-EIGHT

REACHING a nearby rooftop, he checked his phone. The message was from Watanabe, and he played it back. It wasn't much, she said, but she had a line on this thief's brother. She gave the name and address, and the message ended.

The location was across Central Park—on the Upper West Side near Columbia. Aiming a web at a nearby water tower, he launched himself into the air. Some quick swinging and a couple of bus rides later—on top of the vehicles, of course—he caught a lucky break.

It was late afternoon and Spider-Man was trying to figure out the best way to get the brother's attention when the guy, Vincent, brought the trash out. He hadn't spent that much time with the victim, but the web-spinner could see the resemblance. This guy was a little older, a little taller. He looked like he spent time in the gym, but they were clearly related.

"Don't be startled," Spider-Man said, and the guy nearly jumped out of his skin. He was upside down and clinging to the wall, which he guessed was maybe a little startling. Still, words counted for something. He hoped.

The man relaxed and faced him. His expression was unreadable.

"You were there," he said. "When Andy died."

Spider-Man nodded and dropped down. "Yeah," he said. "I spoke to him a little while before he was shot."

"Some of the cops think you killed him," Vincent said. "Or that some guy who's impersonating you killed him."

"I think he was killed because he talked to me. He gave me a bad tip, and once he'd done that, my guess is that he had to be silenced so he couldn't be made to talk. That's the best sense I can make of it."

"So, who did it?" the man asked, frowning. "Who killed my brother?"

"That's what I'm hoping to find out," Spider-Man said. "If you have any information, it could really help. He told me you were connected to the Scorpion."

The brother smirked. "Man, he fed you a line. I'm the straight arrow in the family. He was the screwup. 'Til the end, I guess."

"You know anything about who he was in with?"

Vincent shook his head. "Andy had been messing up since he was a kid, but he was trying to get his act together. He really was. He was working on his GED and apprenticing as a riveter. I was so proud of him, you know. It's not easy to turn things around, but he was legit doing it. Then I hear him on the phone, talking about doing a job, you know? I confronted him, and he said he had no choice. He said he had to do this one last thing, and then they'd let him be. I told him I'd go with him, but he lied to me about when and where, so they got him." He wiped at his eye with the back of his hand.

"Why didn't you tell the police about this?"

"Of course I told them. Some dude with a mustache came by and I told him everything. He left his coffee cup in my house for me to clean up, like I was his servant or something."

He'd told the police, but the information wasn't in his file. That was troubling.

"Thanks for talking to me," Spider-Man said. "I'm not sure how, but this will help. I promise I'm going to do everything I can to bring his killer to justice." Andy was a real person, he reminded himself, with a real brother who had to deal with tragedy. That familiar anger sparked again inside.

"I believe you," Vincent said. "It's too bad the police don't care as much as you do."

"There are plenty of good cops."

"I wish I had your faith," the brother said. "Half the cops out there think you're the bad guy, and still you keep on going, doing what you do. I don't know how you keep it up."

Sometimes Spider-Man didn't know either.

<hr />

HE was headed downtown, back in an area where higher buildings made web swinging a lot easier. Trying to organize his thoughts when the call came through. It was Watanabe.

"I'm at a murder scene," she said. "It's Remzi, the assistant DA. He was beaten to death." She let out a sigh that evolved into a growl.

"There's webbing all over his apartment."

"THIS has got to stop," he told her. "Right now. Tonight. I met him. He was one of the good guys. He wanted to help me."

"That's why they killed him," Watanabe said. They stood on a roof adjacent to the building where Remzi's East Side apartment was found.

"No," Spider-Man replied, fighting to control his fury. "I don't buy it. If he had anything to say, if he had any evidence that I could have used, he'd have told me. He was upset that they were messing with his sister. I don't think he'd have held back."

"Then why kill him, if not to silence him?" she countered. "To frame you? People who might think the worst of you already do. It's a lot of trouble to go through if there's no payoff."

There had to be a payoff. They'd killed Andy to keep him quiet, but what about the people in the sandwich shop. What was the payoff there? Why did *they* have to die?

Why did Anika have to die?

Then he saw it.

"We've been thinking about this wrong," he said. "The point wasn't to hide anything. The point wasn't to make the public lose faith in me. The point was to keep me *busy*."

"Keep you busy?" she asked. "But why?"

"Because of what the Kingpin is up to," Spider-Man said. "Whatever it is that's going to make him too big to fail. That's all that really matters to him, and he doesn't want me messing it up."

"So you think Fisk believes you alone can stop it," Watanabe said, shaking her head. "Whatever it is. Again… why? You don't have anything on him. If you were breathing down his neck, if you were one step away from exposing him, then I'd get it—but that's not the case. There's not any reason for him to *think* it's the case."

"And that's why I didn't see it," he said. "I never imagined I could be dangerous to a plan I know nothing about."

"And now you think you are?" she said. "Dangerous?"

"No, but I'm starting to see things in the proper perspective," he told her. "I'm just one thread in the carpet. Fisk knows I have the *potential* to disrupt whatever it is he has planned, and he's trying to neutralize me before I can become a genuine threat. I played a big part in his arrest last time—upended his life and almost had him sent to jail. If there's one person he wants distracted while he's making his move, it would be me."

"So he's got you chasing after the imposter," Watanabe said. "You'd do anything to find the restaurant bomber—in part because you believe it will lead you to Fisk. But while you're looking one way, you don't see what Fisk is doing somewhere else. Meanwhile, the police and the public don't trust you, at least not entirely, which makes your job that much harder."

"All of which gives Fisk plenty of breathing room."

"But even if this is true," Watanabe said,

"how does the knowledge help us? This guy—your double—kills people. We can't just ignore him because he's a distraction."

"He's still a key to nailing Fisk," Spider-Man said. "I don't know that we need to change our approach, but it might be enough to change our mind set."

"I hope that's enough," Watanabe said. "Remzi was one of us, and at least half the force thinks you killed him. If anyone finds out I've been talking to you, I'm toast. We may be on the right track, but until we have the whole picture, Fisk has outsmarted us."

<hr />

KILLING a district attorney. That was going too far, even for a lunatic like Bingham. Had Mr. Fisk authorized this?

No, that was ridiculous. Mr. Fisk didn't kill people. He'd made a mistake when he'd brought in Bingham, and now he would have to undo it. She wished he would ask her to fix it—but she could do nothing without his authorization.

Maya had come as soon as she heard the news reports. Crouching in the deepening shadows, she saw a police officer emerge onto the roof of a nearby building. She looked through her binoculars, and while she couldn't be certain, she thought it might be the woman from Bingham's photo. Was that the cop working with Spider-Man?

It would be best to wait and see what happened next. Before long her patience was rewarded. Less than half an hour later, Spider-Man arrived. The two talked for a while, and while she couldn't tell what he was saying—not with the mask—she knew they were talking about Mr. Fisk. The cop said his name, more than once.

That was bad news.

Mr. Fisk had never intended for anyone to get killed. Bingham was out of control, yes, but that wasn't Mr. Fisk's fault. She needed to make sure this cop didn't create trouble for a man who was working as hard as he could to help the people of this city.

There was one person who would be able to make use of this information, to change the conversation, and quickly. She had to do everything in her power to protect Mr. Fisk, even if it meant protecting him from himself. She wished he would confide in her fully. How could he not trust her?

She picked up her phone and sent the text to Jameson.

**SPIDER-MAN HAS A CONNECTION
INSIDE THE POLICE DEPARTMENT**

**THEY'RE PROTECTING HIM
FROM PROSECUTION**

She hoped that would be enough to buy Mr. Fisk the time he needed—and Maya the time *she* needed. If she was going to remain effective, she had to know more, regardless of the consequences.

TWENTY-NINE

FISK sat across from Mr. Fleisher of Roxxon Blackridge. It was late for a meeting, but he'd been in the building and was trying to set up an appointment while Fisk was still working. He'd waved the man in.

"Does this concern the surveillance subjects?" Fisk asked.

"No," Fleisher said. "The other matter."

Fisk had asked Roxxon Blackridge to perform a security review. Given the sensitivity of some of the material he was keeping in his various safes, he needed to make sure there was no chance of anything going missing or falling into the wrong hands.

"If we're going to discuss that," Fisk said, "perhaps we should reschedule. My assistant Maya Lopez helps me facilitate our security arrangements, and I'd like for her to be included in any meeting."

"I don't know if that's wise."

Fisk raised one eyebrow. "Are you suggesting something?"

"I am prepared to provide you with information," Mr. Fleisher said. "It's up to you to make the inferences." He opened his briefcase and removed a manila envelope. From that he removed a black-and-white photo of Maya walking into his office complex on the Upper East Side. "Miss Lopez entered the building at 9:47 a.m."

Fisk shrugged his massive shoulders. "Her duties require her to visit any number of my properties."

"She proceeded to the executive suite on the 76th floor. Security cameras show her there at 9:53," he said, providing another photograph. It showed Maya in an otherwise empty office. A painting had been swung away from the wall, revealing a safe. Although her back was to the camera, it was clear what she was doing.

"Did she take anything?" Fisk asked in a clipped voice.

"We don't know," Fleisher said. "Moments after we captured this image, the security system experienced an unexpected glitch. It shut down for eleven minutes, and erased all records since the previous backup. We next captured Miss Lopez when she was exiting the building." He provided a third black-and-white photograph of Maya stepping out onto the street.

Fisk steepled his fingers and said nothing.

This was a trick he'd picked up over the years to keep himself calm. It wouldn't do to attack a high-level Roxxon Blackridge executive, but Fisk could envision himself breaking the man's neck. Perhaps something less immediate, though. Punching him in the face, knocking him down, kicking him in the stomach until he vomited blood. Yes, something like that would be more satisfying.

He took in a deep breath and waited.

"We were very lucky," Fleisher said. "Because we

were performing the review, we were piggybacking on your systems. When your network went down, we were blind as well, but some of the records were preserved. Had we not captured these, we would never have known Miss Lopez was in the building." He frowned, then added, "Whoever did it knew how to ensure that the data was unrecoverable."

Still Fisk didn't move. He thought, however, about crushing Fleisher's head with his bare hands.

"There's no way to know what Miss Lopez was doing," Fleisher continued. "Frankly, we can't say that she was doing anything improper. It may simply be a coincidence that you experienced these difficulties while she was present. However, if I were you, I would proceed carefully."

"Thank you," Fisk said, his voice flat and distant. "I appreciate your time."

Fleisher seemed not to understand. "Mr. Fisk, I hope you regard this threat with the seriousness it deserves. If you would like, I could assign a team to—"

"No," Fisk snapped, and the man jumped. "This is an internal matter. I will handle it." He gave a wave of his hand and hoped Fleisher would take the hint. If he didn't…

"Then I'll be on my way," Fleisher said. He stood up and waited a moment to see if Fisk would do the same. He did not, and a look of relief crossed his face. Perhaps he had some sense now of how close he had been walking to the edge of the abyss.

Long after he left, Fisk sat very still. That Maya

might betray him was unimaginable. She had never been anything but loyal, but her loyalty was based on an image he had crafted very carefully. He'd intended, of course, to let her know more about what he did, what he *had* to do, in order to succeed. The time wasn't yet right, though. After the project, he had told himself. Let her get a taste of what it is to succeed, let her see the spoils for which he was fighting. Once she understood what could be achieved, she wouldn't balk at the price.

Had she learned of some of the more unsavory elements of his work? He didn't think so. Nor did he think she would move against him—not without offering him the chance to explain.

Still, he told himself, he would have to be careful. He would not shut her out, but he would watch her with new eyes.

THIRTY

PETER was walking into the lab when MJ called.

"I thought you'd want to hear about this," she said.

A few weeks had gone by since the murder of the assistant district attorney. There had been no major incidents with the false Spider-Man since then, but life was no easier. The media still hotly debated whether the original Spider-Man had gone bad, or if there was an imposter. Morning news shows were full of discussions about why, if the real web-spinner was out there, he didn't speak out. Peter felt like he was aging a year for every week this went on.

Jameson, meanwhile, hammered home his notion that Spider-Man had always been bad.

"What's worse," he shouted from the airwaves, "is that he has help on the inside. I have a source—an eyewitness—who tells me that Spider-Man has regular meetings with a rogue detective within the police department. There's someone working to cover up the evidence, to make sure the wall-crawling menace is never brought to justice. I'm here to tell you, the people of New York won't stand for it."

Watanabe hadn't exactly abandoned her partnership with him, but they were forced to be more careful. It would only take one incident, she said, one hint of exposure to bring it all crashing down. They met less frequently and in more secluded places, always careful to be clear of prying eyes. Peter continued to run missions for her, but more than ever it felt as if they would never nail Fisk.

"You still there, Tiger?" MJ said.

"I'm here," he grunted.

"Well, the last time I went to Fisk Tower—"

"How often do you go there?" he demanded.

"Focus, Peter," she said. "The point is, I keep seeing Wall Street guys there, and some others who seemed to be from the mayor's office. Flunkies, for sure, but they've been there often enough that it can't be a coincidence."

"That may not be such a big deal," Peter replied. "Wall Street types have always been cozy with the Kingpin, and Norman's probably looking to get political mileage out of Fisk's new philanthropic image."

"I don't know," she said. "It feels like something more. It's hard to put my finger on it exactly, but I get the sense that Fisk wants something from the mayor. Either that or the mayor wants something from him. Maybe it goes both ways, and someone in the financial sector is about to make a killing."

"That wouldn't surprise me," he said. "It's always seemed like Norman would work with just about *anyone* if it meant advancing his own agenda."

"That's a safe bet," MJ agreed. "Look, I'm supposed to be shadowing Fisk next week at a fundraiser. It's for the Fisk Foundation, which I've been covering. The amount that goes to charity is pretty hard to nail down. Charitable types tend not to want to give money to a guy who was accused of being the biggest crime lord in history, so most of it comes from foreign sources with ties to places like Russia, Ukraine, and China."

"You're going to this thing with him?"

"Again, you're not focusing on the right facts."

Peter felt pretty sure his focus was where it ought to be. MJ seemed to think hanging out with Fisk was perfectly fine. It wasn't fine. Violence followed him like a storm cloud. If she was digging into the financial shenanigans of his bogus charity, she might as well have a target painted on her back.

"What does your editor think about you digging into the Fisk Foundation?"

"I haven't told her," MJ replied. "Of course. I need to find the story first, and then I'll pitch it."

"MJ, I know you don't want to hear this, but I really think you should back off. Even going to this fundraiser is a bad idea. Things happen to people near Fisk, and they *definitely* happen to people who are trying to uncover his secrets."

"Are we actually having this conversation again?"

"Not if you do what I tell you." He paused for a second. "Okay, that came out wrong. I meant something like '*not if you heed my sound advice*.' I'm not ordering you around, MJ. I'm worried about you."

"I know you are," she said, though there was an edge to her voice. "But your concern is smothering, Peter."

He struggled to think of something to say. He got

it. He understood what she was saying, totally, but he didn't think she understood where he was coming from. He'd faced guys who were bigger and more powerful than he was, but he had advantages of speed and skill and technology. If Fisk came after MJ, what could she do?

"MJ, please just talk to your editor. Talk to Robbie. They know what they're doing, and they'll give you sound advice. Keep you safe."

"If I do that, they'll tell me to stand down," she argued. "I have to take chances if I'm going to succeed. I'd expect you to understand that."

Peter did understand it, but he hated it. There was nothing else he could say without starting another fight, though, so he told her he had to go.

○————————————○

ALL he could do was try to lose himself in his work. At the lab, the boss was developing some new theories about how to speed up the encoding of synthetic neuron electrochemical responses, and he was dumping data on Peter faster than the models could be run. Almost all of the tests resulted in failure, but that didn't seem to bother the boss in the least.

"Experimentation is all about failure," he liked to say. *"You learn as much from what doesn't work as from what does."*

Peter doubted he could be so cheerful if it weren't for the small percentage of tests that succeeded. Those yielded an incredible amount of key data, and they were making strides faster than ever before. If what his employer said was true, they were only months away from creating a working prototype—an artificial limb with the same functionality as an organic equivalent.

THEY'D been going for more than twelve hours, but there was a lull in the work. They had a television in the lab, and though it was muted, Norman Osborn's face filled the screen. Peyton noticed it, and his expression darkened considerably.

"You don't like Osborn?" Peter asked. "He told me you used to work for him."

"*You* know Norman Osborn?" Peyton asked. He looked like a dog had just claimed to be emperor.

"His son is my best friend," Peter explained.

"I hear he has difficulties with his son."

"That's kind of an understatement. It's a pretty chilly relationship." He figured it was a good idea to play up the distance. If Peyton was going to talk about Osborn, he'd probably want to know Peter wasn't going to repeat everything he heard.

Peyton looked grim. "Let's just say I don't like the way he does business." It was as if he had a bad taste in his mouth. "However, as you are friends with the son, I'll say no more."

Peter laughed. "Believe me, if Harry were here, he'd be dying to hear all the dirt you have on Norman."

"Well, you can't be around someone like that and not see how they operate," Peyton told him.

"Osborn's got a brilliant mind—I won't deny that for a second—but it's how he uses it that bothers me. He's unscrupulous, and I worry how that will apply to his being mayor."

"Unscrupulous how?"

"A lot of this is rumor and innuendo," Peyton admitted. "But I've heard things far too many times not to think there's some truth to them. Osborn will work with anyone who can advance his agenda, and if someone has an advantage over him, he'll stop at nothing until he reverses the balance of power. He also has a history of setting honey traps, luring someone in with an offer they can't refuse, but the honey trap will always turn out to be a poison pill."

That seemed like a good opening.

"I keep seeing him on the news with Wilson Fisk," he prodded. "You think he'd get cozy with someone like that?"

Peyton snorted. "He wouldn't hesitate. If he thinks it will bring him greater power, influence, or profit he'll make deals with anyone, including Wilson Fisk. Yet running with a man like that isn't like taking down competitors in the tech industry—and most likely Osborn knows it."

"What do you mean?"

"He never simply does business." Peyton shook his head, as if he was remembering something. "Norman Osborn has a way of turning things around. He wouldn't strike a deal with Wilson Fisk unless he was sure that he could—if he had to—eliminate the person as a rival while simultaneously keeping his own nose clean. If he's dealing with a man who has a history of eating his competitors alive, then he'll be sure he has a way of outsmarting him."

Peter thought about that. He'd always known that Osborn could be ruthless in his pursuit of power. Yet he'd never thought about what it would mean for Osborn and Fisk—two master manipulators—to try to use each other. Norman would certainly be in a position to give Fisk something, political favors or something like that, but could even he somehow make the Kingpin "too big to fail"?

He considered everything they'd uncovered in recent weeks—the extortion, the military contractors, the radio broadcasts, the doppelgängers, the Wall Street connections. They couldn't put a finger on his endgame, but one thing that stood out was the financial element, just as MJ had said. Maybe, he thought, that was the key.

He looked up and saw that Peyton was staring at him.

"Sorry… what?"

"I said, break time is over," the lab administrator said acidly. "Back to work, chop-chop."

"Yeah," Peter replied. "Just give me a minute, okay? I need to make a quick phone call." Before Peyton could respond he rushed outside and pulled out his phone. He was afraid she might not pick up, though.

"Watanabe here."

"What do we know about Fisk's Wall Street connections?"

She snorted. "Which ones? You can't work in New York real estate without having serious ties to the various banking firms. He's totally tangled up with lots of those people."

"Is there anything unusual," Peter said. "Hints that he might be trying to exert pressure on the city's government?"

"Hold on," she replied. "I'll see if anyone in financial crimes has heard something. Can you give me a minute?"

Peter looked back at the building. He didn't want to keep the work waiting long, but this seemed important.

"Yeah, I can wait, if it won't be too long."

Watanabe put him on hold.

○───────────────○

SHE was back after five minutes, though it felt much longer.

"So, there is something," she said. "The NYC commissioner of finance is stepping down. They say it's because of health problems. It was very sudden, and he doesn't look sick at all."

"Maybe he's stepping down so he doesn't develop health problems?"

"Such a possibility has been suggested," she acknowledged. "Anyhow, Fisk is on the advisory board that will name his successor. Osborn has been dropping hints that the next commissioner should be someone with real-world experience, not just another government bureaucrat. He's set to announce the appointment at a gala honoring Fisk for his charitable work."

"What if he just happened to announce that the recipient was Fisk?" Peter said. "What better way to distance Fisk from his sordid past than to make the announcement just as they're celebrating his overwhelming generosity?"

"What will Osborn get out of this?"

"No clue," Peter said, "but let's forget that for a second. He's got his own motives, we can be sure of that, but we're focusing on Fisk. What would he be able to do, what advantage would he gain, if he were appointed to this position?"

"I'd hate to even think about it," she said. "He'd have access to information about the finances of every city employee, every city agency, including the police department. And he'd be in a position to gain from the city's investments. It could be a huge conflict-of-interest issue."

"Provided the people who investigate that sort of thing weren't threatened by him," he countered. "Extortion is his thing, and with the right leverage, he could operate without any real oversight."

"Damn straight," she said.

"And while he'd be in a position to benefit from the city's finances, he'd be able to hurt them too, right?" He suppressed a shudder as the implications sank in. "Like, he could tank the city's investments, causing chaos if he wanted to?"

"I suppose," she said. "It's never come up before.

The commissioner of finance isn't usually someone who'd want to hurt the city—but if it's Fisk, then we're in uncharted waters."

"More like shark-infested," Peter said. "So, if he was appointed to the post, that might make him too big to fail, right? I mean, that's what they say about banking houses, not because they're super-powerful, but because the government can't let them go under because their failure would destroy the economy. If Fisk were to become commissioner of finance, and he went down, he could take the city with him."

"That could be it," Watanabe said in a whisper. "He would be as close to bulletproof as a criminal can get. Cops and DAs would be afraid to touch him. Even journalists might hesitate to bring the city's financial structure tumbling down. No one would want to be responsible for that level of destruction."

"This has to be it," Peter said. "So how do we stop it?"

"Is that a serious question?" she asked. "We may not like it, but by law, the mayor has the right to perform the duties of his office."

"Okay, that was the wrong way to put it," he said. "But we *have* to stop him, or find a way to expose it before Osborn can act. We have to make sure Fisk doesn't get the appointment."

Watanabe groaned. "Usually I have to tell you to simmer down and take things slowly, but in this case I think you're right," she said. "But we can't be sloppy. Let me go over my notes and see if I can come up with a plan. We still have a few weeks, so let's not go crazy."

"You know me."

"I feel better already." She ended the call.

Peter put the phone away and went back inside, where Peyton turned from a computer to glower at him.

"Was I gone a long time?" Peter asked.

"This job isn't a hobby," Peyton said. His round face looked unusually pinched. "Break time is over, and we have important things to do. The director, for whatever reason, is depending on you, and once again you are holding up our progress."

"I know, I'm sorry," Peter said. "It was something important. I'm sorry. Let's get down to business."

Peyton frowned and began opening up programs. Luckily for Peter, he was easily distracted by his research. He was right to be angry, and Peter didn't know how long he could keep getting away with being himself.

THIRTY-ONE

"I need to see you ASAP," Watanabe said. "This is code red." Peter growled inwardly. It was the first time she'd contacted him in days, despite several frustrated messages he'd left on her phone.

He had just walked into his apartment after a twelve-hour shift at the lab. Toward the end of the day, the lab director had made a breakthrough and come up with a new theory about how to increase the simulated synaptic integrity in the prosthetic relays. But Peter's mind had been turning to mush, and he was sent home—told to eat something and shower and be back in two hours.

"What's going on?" he asked Watanabe.

"Just get over here. It's important." She gave him the location, and Peter immediately began to change.

HE showed up twenty minutes later, which was close to a personal best. From the vantage point of the rooftop, he could see Manhattan spread out all around him. Avengers Tower lit up the night in the distance. Car horns honked and people laughed and shouted and cried, and it all echoed through the canyons of buildings. He felt like he was supposed to watch over it all, and it was too much.

Watanabe was waiting for him. "There's a fundraiser at the Manhattan Museum of Contemporary Art tonight," she said.

"Yeah, I know," Spider-Man told her. "Fisk is supposed to be there."

Her eyebrows shot up. Maybe she was impressed that he knew their target's schedule. He wasn't about to tell her that he knew because his girlfriend was following said target around. He'd been worried about it all day, and he'd planned to do some patrolling tonight to keep himself distracted.

"Well, we got a tip that it's going to be hit by Tombstone," she said. "Apparently Fisk has been muscling him out of a lot of business lately, and he's looking for payback. My source tells me he doesn't care if civilians get caught in the crossfire. In fact, he's hoping for it."

Tombstone was bad news. Lonnie Lincoln was an uptown crime boss whose territory had been shrinking since Fisk returned to town. With his pale complexion, superhuman strength, and those crazy sharp teeth, he was also a pretty scary dude. Feuding with Fisk in a public setting was bound to produce a body count.

"What kind of police presence will there be?"

"That's the thing," she said, a sour expression on her face. "There's not going to be anything other than the usual security detail. I tried to kick this up the chain of command, but my boss says there isn't enough evidence to deploy any extra manpower. His sources tell him that Tombstone is lying low, trying to avoid an open conflict with Fisk. I badgered him until he agreed to put the detail on alert, but that won't matter if Tombstone sends an army to shoot up the place."

"Why would your boss ignore this?" he asked. "Could it be that he's in Fisk's pocket?"

"No clue," she said. "Maybe he's right, and maybe the threat actually isn't credible. Maybe Fisk would rather have his own people deal with it. But the last thing I want to see is a shootout with a bunch of civilians in the way."

"You want me to stop it?"

"It's not my first choice," she said, twisting her mouth into a frown. "A lot of cops still think you killed Abe Remzi. Showing your face, so to speak, isn't ideal, but you may be the only option if we're going to keep this from blowing up. If you get over there and see something going on, let me know immediately. If guns come out, maybe you can keep anyone from getting hurt until I can get more units there. Then you scram."

Spider-Man nodded. "On it."

Keeping a bunch of innocent people from getting killed would have been motivation enough, but knowing MJ would be there meant he had no time to lose. Activating the phone in his mask, he gave her a call.

"Mary Jane, you've got to reconsider this fundraiser," he said. "There's going to be trouble."

"What sort of trouble?" She sounded breathless, like she was rushing to get ready.

He gave her the quick version, but MJ didn't seem worried. In fact, it was exactly the opposite.

"I'll keep an eye out, but if anything like that happens, I've got to be there to report on it." She sounded excited at the prospect.

"Do you even hear yourself?" he asked. "You could be killed."

"Look, Tiger, I'll be careful," she said. "And thanks for the heads-up." Before he could respond, she ended the call.

Spider-Man let out a groan of frustration, but it wasn't like he could find MJ and web her up until after the event. Okay, he probably could do that, but it didn't seem like the best approach. His best move was to keep an eye on the event and, if bullets started flying, make sure she was safely out of the way.

He reached the museum and found his way inside through an upper window. The events were scheduled for the main room off the entrance, and there were plenty of shadowed vestibules in which he could hide. Music wafted upward, played by a string quartet. From his safe position he could peer down at the men in their suits, the women in their gowns, the waiters carrying trays of things that looked really delicious to a person who hadn't had a chance to grab dinner.

There was nothing dangerous happening. After a few minutes Fisk entered, with MJ shadowing him. She kept a respectful distance as she listened in on his blather. Each time he finished a conversation she would talk briefly with whomever Fisk had spoken to, then hurry to listen in on the next exchange. He didn't even know why she bothered. It was sure to be a bunch of *blah blah blah*. She could just write that, couldn't she?

No, she probably couldn't.

○————————————○

AS the evening dragged on he checked in with Watanabe, letting her know that a whole lot of nothing was happening. Then he turned his attention back to the riveting scene of people making small talk. Fascinating. And they were eating those delectable bits of food like they were no big deal. That was the privilege of being rich, he supposed. You got to stuff expensive tidbits in your mouth while the ordinary people clung to dark alcoves on the ceiling.

An unexpected movement or a strange flash of color caught his eye. At the same time his Spider-Sense booted up. Off to one side, there were three men in trench coats. They were holding guns. Peter's years of experience suggested that people dressed this way might have questionable activities in mind.

The weapons surprised him though. He would have expected assault rifles, but they had only handguns—unostentatious weapons that looked more like a policeman's service revolver than anything else.

Spider-Man scanned the room again. Watanabe's source said there was going to be a small army coming to attack Fisk, but there were no signs of anyone but these men. Three men could theoretically take down Fisk, and they might do it with a lot less collateral damage. While the pistols weren't exactly sniper-grade weaponry, the chances of a bystander getting hurt were unacceptably high.

He was going to have to intervene.

I'd better get a thank you from Fisk, he mused. *At least a fruit basket.*

He called Watanabe to update the situation.

"Maybe you should hang back unless they make a move," she suggested.

Not an option. MJ was down there.

"Making a move isn't going to take them long," he said, "and it's going to involve pieces of lead moving at high velocity."

"Okay, I'm calling it in," she replied. "Hold off for as long as you can without risking anyone getting hurt. Backup will be there soon, and if you can get out of there without being seen, it'll make everyone's life easier."

As soon as he ended the call, he saw that the three men were moving out of the shadows and approaching the crowd. No one had noticed them yet.

He shot out a web so he could swing down, but as soon as he leapt off his perch, he saw three more men in trench coats emerging from the other side of the room. That meant he couldn't take all of the invaders at once. Worse yet, once the commotion started, people would panic. In the confusion the gunmen would have a harder time finding their target, but the risk to innocents would be much greater.

He turned back to the original trio—and realized that he had made a huge mistake.

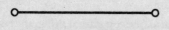

IN the instant he'd been distracted, the attackers had removed their coats, which were lying behind them on the ground. Underneath, the gunmen were dressed as police officers.

"Officer under attack!" one of them shouted, and he began firing his gun.

Spider-Man flipped in the air, convulsing to twist away from the bullets. He could feel them zipping past him, missing him by inches. The other three men lost their coats as well, and raced in, their own weapons at the ready. Worse, there were real cops in the room, and they thought their fellow officers were in danger. That would make them far more likely to shoot first and take stock later.

Everything unfolded as if it were being choreographed. People shouted and ran. As the real policemen rushed forward, the imposters melted back into the crowd. They grabbed their coats, which they would use to get away. The real police, in the meantime, drew their guns, aiming them at the deranged lunatic in a costume who was—as far as they could tell—assaulting the gathering.

Someone was going to get hurt—most likely him.

He launched himself into the shadows to get out the way he'd come in. Someone discharged their gun, and plaster shattered into dust on the ceiling. His Spider-Sense exploded, and he webbed across the room, hardly aware he was changing direction. Another blast of gunfire, and he changed direction again.

As soon as one cop started firing, the rest followed suit, and he was vaguely aware of a discordant popping as he dodged back and forth, webbed up and dropped down to avoid gunfire. There was dust in the air. More screams. It was a mess.

He saw his chance to make it to the skylight and shot out a web, hurling himself forward. Risking a quick glance over his shoulder, he saw MJ looking up at him as though he'd failed her utterly.

○━━━━━━━━━○

WHILE he waited on the roof, Peyton called from the lab to find out where he was.

"I'm totally sorry," he said. "I got caught up in some personal business."

"Personal business," Peyton repeated.

"Yeah, I know it sounds lame, but—"

"We had an important experiment to run," Peyton said. "The integrity of the synaptic firing is key to the project's success, and I needed you here. As it is, I had to handle the operations by myself. Do you know how difficult that was?"

"I know," he replied. "I'm sorry." He wanted to say it wouldn't happen again, but couldn't bring himself to say something that was so obviously a lie.

"Your mind is not second-rate," Peyton said, "but I'm afraid I've concluded we would be better off with someone a little less intelligent and a little more reliable."

There was a long pause.

"I'm saying you're fired, Peter," Peyton snapped.

Peter felt his mouth hanging open. He'd worked at the lab since college. He loved working there. He *couldn't* be fired, but while he tried to figure out how to say all of that, Peyton hung up.

○────────────────○

EVERYTHING was falling apart. He already felt horrible, so he decided to go for broke. He tuned his suit's receiver to Jameson's radio station, where there was a special broadcast in the wake of the museum incident.

"Even his defenders," Jameson said, "of which there are far too many in this city, wonder tonight why Spider-Man would attack police officers performing their duty. No one knows. Well, I know. I've got breaking news, and you'll be the first to hear it.

"There are foreign agents operating inside our police force, acting on behalf of the webbed menace. Whether he's pulling the strings, or there's someone above him, there's no way to know. Most cops are good people, hard-working men and women who risk their lives every day. But there are always a few bad apples. We all know that, and I'm here to tell you those bad apples are working with this web-slinging terrorist.

"What these crooked cops hope to gain is anyone's guess, but we'll be exploring that question in the days and weeks to come."

He cut the signal and slumped down while he waited.

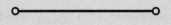

WHEN Watanabe arrived, she looked miserable.

"That was all my fault," she said breathlessly as she came through the door. It looked as if she'd just run up the stairs. "It seemed like a good tip, but Fisk must have gotten to my C.I. It was a setup."

"Just to make me look bad?"

"Someone found out you were working with a cop, and he wanted that to stop. Unfortunately, that's a win for Fisk, because we're going to have to take a break for a while."

"You can't be serious."

"The heat is on," she said. "We're all being watched, and my work is going to be scrutinized even more closely. I've got to make sure nothing I'm doing can be linked to you—at least for now."

Something clenched in his gut. "But we're running out of time. If Fisk gets the appointment, we'll never be able to stop him."

"I know," she said, "and I'm going to do everything I can to keep that from happening, but I'm going to have to do it alone. At least for now. That means you have to stay away from Fisk, too. If it looks like you're still working with the police department, it's going to make my life a whole lot harder."

"I can't just ignore all this," he said.

"Look, this is a setback," she admitted. "We got played, and we lost. Now there are consequences. Maybe you can work on exposing the imposter, but stay away from Fisk and his properties. I'm asking you as a favor, and as a professional. If you don't, you'll only be helping him. Right now, you're toxic."

He shook his head, but in the end he agreed.

There was nothing else he could do.

"WHAT are you doing here?" MJ asked him when he crawled in through her apartment window. Her place was a mess, just like his, with magazines and books and clothes and takeout containers scattered everywhere. It was better lit, though, which he supposed made it less depressing.

"I just needed to talk to you."

She folded her arms and shook her head. "You're the last person I want to talk to right now. I can't believe what happened tonight. Did you really attack those police officers?"

"No, of course not," he said. "How can you even ask me that? It was a setup. We got played. I shouldn't have rushed in the way I did. I made a mistake." It seemed like the right thing to say, but Peter wasn't actually sure. People who looked a whole lot like they had badness on their minds had taken out guns. He couldn't just wait and see what happened next, on the off chance they weren't really planning on hurting anyone. He didn't have the strength to explain all that, though.

It seemed easier to admit guilt.

"Let me ask you something," MJ said. "If I hadn't been there, would you have made the same mistake?"

Peter sighed. He didn't know the answer. Maybe

he would have been a little more cautious, but how could he know for sure? He'd done what he thought he had to do to keep people safe.

She took his silence as an answer.

"That's what I thought."

"Are you saying that I shouldn't act if I think you're in danger?"

"That's not it," she insisted, "but sometimes you see danger where there isn't any. You're so determined to keep me safe that you stop thinking and start acting. You could have been killed. You could have gotten other people killed."

"I know," he said, "but the alternative was to do nothing, and you know that isn't an option for me."

She took a deep breath. "Peter, I love you, but I can't keep living like this. You're smothering me. I'm afraid to tell you what I'm doing, afraid when I *do* tell you that you'll show up. You aren't letting me live my life."

"I know you feel that way, but—"

"But you have to be who you are," she said. "I get that, but maybe it's time for you to be who you are with a little distance from me." She took a step toward him, but then reversed herself.

The silence lasted for only a second or two, but felt impossibly drawn out. It seemed as if gravity had increased. Peter's body felt heavier. The air was thick in his lungs.

"Are you breaking up with me?"

"I just think it's better," she said. "For now. For us to, you know, be apart…"

He didn't want to hear more. He couldn't. He was out the window and swinging through the night before he was even aware of it—flying through the dark, unaware of which direction he was headed. He didn't hear or see anything or anyone. The noise and the sights of the city were a blur, a fog, no more intelligible than static.

○━━━━━━━━━○

HE wasn't sure how long he'd been going, but he knew he must have gone in circles. He stopped without thinking, landing on a rooftop. The expanse of city lights loomed behind him.

Everything had been ruined. He'd lost his job. Yuri didn't want his help. She didn't even want him going after Fisk. His best friend was gone, and not likely to come back any time soon, and now his girlfriend had broken up with him because he'd made a mess of things.

He wanted to list all the reasons why she was wrong, but he knew she wasn't. He knew that he had blown everything. Being Spider-Man had made his life a mess, and he didn't see any way it was going to get better. He'd shattered nearly all of his relationships, and was utterly alone.

THIRTY-TWO

BINGHAM had no way of knowing how long he had been in the lab. There were no newspapers or television broadcasts. The TV didn't work like the one in the other room, where he could just turn it on and there would be shows. Here there was nothing on at all unless he chose something.

At first he was glad not to have to argue with anyone about what he watched. He could sit in his room and watch what he wanted for as long as he wanted, or even watch the same thing over and over again. After the fun of that wore off, however, he began to get lonely. The doctors and techs and guards didn't make conversation with him. When he asked if he could go back into his old room, he was told there was no one left there.

They were all gone.

That meant they had died. He knew that, but he didn't want to say it out loud. That sounded bad, and it took away from what was really good. They had died, yes, but Bingham had survived. He could do what none of the others could do. He could live.

His mind was working differently. He knew that. They gave him tests where he had to answer questions or write things down or pick shapes or talk about pictures. He didn't always understand the tests, but he could tell he impressed them. He'd never done well on tests before, and he liked the feeling.

His body was changing, too. He had grown lean and muscular, even though he hadn't worked hard to get it that way. He hadn't changed how he ate, and he never lifted weights except when the lab techs asked him to. It happened from the medicine.

He could jump now—crazy distances that made no sense. And he could climb walls, even smooth ones. Sometimes they made him fight the guards, and at first he hated it. Bingham had always hated fighting, because he would get hurt. He wasn't getting hurt anymore, and he discovered he liked being good at fighting. These guys would come in with their shirts off, trying to look tough with their big muscles, but Bingham was stronger. He was faster. He somehow knew what they were going to do before they did it. His body reacted without him telling it what to do.

"When can I fight again?" he would ask the director, and the director would smile like he had a secret. One time he attacked the director. He didn't remember it well—it was like there had been a fog in his mind. The guards must have stopped him, though, because the director kept coming. Each time he entered with guards already pointing their guns.

Bingham understood things that people said, but he also understood what they meant when they said nothing. That was new, too. He was smarter now. It was like the medicine had cleared the fog away. He could see things in a way he had never seen them before—and he would make connections. They would serve him a hamburger, and instead of just eating it, he would understand things about hamburgers, like where it had come from and how someone had to cook it. He would suddenly realize that all the hamburgers he'd ever eaten had become part of him. That he was part hamburger. Not all of him, but a part. He couldn't come into contact with something without it changing him, and without him changing it. Understanding this gave him a kind of power, but he didn't want to use this power yet.

Not yet. He was waiting for the right time.

One day the director came into his room. There were four guards with him, and they all had guns pointed at Bingham. He didn't mind the guards and the guns. They wouldn't shoot him unless he did something, though now he looked at them and wondered if he could get the guns away from them without being hurt. In his head he saw how he could do it. How they wouldn't be able to stop him, but Bingham didn't do it because he was afraid the director might get mad at him. What if they stopped giving him his medicine? That frightened him the most.

"The boss is very disappointed with you," the director said.

This upset Bingham. He felt panic, and couldn't figure out what he had done wrong. Maybe he *should* take the guns away from the guards, before they did something to him. But Bingham decided he would listen a little more to what the director was saying. It was the sort of thing he could understand now that he had never understood before.

"What did I do?"

"It's not your fault, Michael," the director said, "but the medicine doesn't work on you the way the boss wanted it to. He wanted it to cure a disease."

"Do I have a disease?" This was alarming news. Bingham had never felt healthier.

"No, you don't, but from the way your body responds to the medicine, we can tell if it would cure this disease. The boss had hoped your body would react one way, but it reacted another way instead."

"It made me able to do things," Bingham said.

"Yes, it did," the director agreed. "Let me ask you a question, Michael. Do you know who Spider-Man is?"

Bingham thought about that night on the street. He'd needed help, but Spider-Man had ignored him. He'd wondered about that for a long time, and he'd decided that Spider-Man wasn't real. He was like one of those stories about old gods and heroes—but now Bingham could do so many of the things that Spider-Man was supposed to be able to do. There was really only one conclusion he could draw.

He hadn't seen a real person that night.

He'd seen his own future.

"I'm Spider-Man," Bingham said.

The director said nothing for a very long time. He looked at Bingham and blinked a great deal, a sure sign he was trying to figure something out.

Bingham noticed that sort of thing now.

"I think the boss will be happy to hear that," he said at last.

After that, they began giving him a lot more of the medicine, and they began his training in a very different way.

THIRTY-THREE

THERE was a segment on the news about Fisk, and Peter picked up the remote to turn it off, but he couldn't will his thumb to do the work.

Every day seemed like the one before it. The weeks since the events at the museum—since Watanabe ended their partnership, since MJ broke up with him—had passed in a fog. Peter still went out as Spider-Man. He even faced both the Scorpion and Electro again, this time sending them to the Raft. The city still needed protecting, after all, even if many of the people he saved were afraid of him. He stayed away from Fisk because Watanabe asked him to. It would make things worse, she said, but he didn't know how they could be any worse.

Through it all he remembered Anika. Anger flared up, but now it was mixed with despair and a sense of helplessness. Her death would remain pointless. Nothing could change that.

He watched as a reporter hovered outside Fisk Tower.

"Mayor Osborn will announce the new commissioner of finance at the gala," the reporter said, "and there's been a great deal of speculation that his choice will be Wilson Fisk. Once a controversial figure, the real estate giant has reinvented himself as a new kind of businessman, beloved by both the wealthy and ordinary citizens. A recent surge in municipal bonds serves to suggest that Wall Street favors the appointment."

As the reporter talked, Fisk emerged behind him, shadowed by Maya Lopez. Reporters pushed forward and shouted questions as the two made their way to a limousine.

"I'm not looking to become commissioner of finance," Fisk said, "and I have no expectation that Mayor Osborn will ask. However, I stand ready to serve this city which I love, if and when I am called upon."

The segment ended, and Peter managed to turn off the TV. There was a knock at the door, which he assumed was his pizza, but when he opened it he found MJ standing there. She wore faded jeans and a white T-shirt under her brown leather jacket. Her hair was a little windblown.

She looked fantastic.

Peter didn't say anything because he didn't know what to say. It had been weeks since he'd seen her. He thought about her every day, thought about visiting her every time he was returning from a patrol. She was the one person with whom he could discuss his dual life, but he didn't want to impose on her. She'd asked for her space, and he was going to give it to her.

"Hello," MJ said. "I think that's the traditional greeting."

"Uh, sorry," he said, moving aside to let her in.

"Hello. I was just expecting a pizza."

"I get that a lot." She edged past him and surveyed his apartment, which looked as if the authorities had come in and ransacked his usual mess. "You were never much good at housekeeping, but this is a new low."

"Saturday was a new low," he said. "I've cleaned up since then. This is a new medium." She looked up, and they locked eyes. "MJ, what are you doing here?"

"I came to see you because you're depressed." She lifted a tower of dirty dishes from a chair, setting them gently on the floor. She examined the seat, and then sat.

"How would you know that?"

"Because I know you," she said. "Peter, we've been friends a lot longer than we were a couple, and I'm the only person you can talk to about the different parts of your life. Just because we're not going out doesn't mean we can't talk."

He folded his arms. "You said you wanted space."

"I'm pretty sure I never—"

There was another knock at the door. MJ beat him to it. She paid for the pizza, and then searched for a reasonable place to put it down. Finally she cleared some real estate on the kitchen counter.

"Look, if you don't want to talk to me, I'll go," she said. "Just as soon as I finish my share of the pizza. Are there any clean plates?"

"I've got some paper towels."

"I guess that's something."

There was no point fighting it. Besides, he was glad to see her. MJ really did understand him better than anyone else, and she was right that he needed someone with whom he could talk. Once they both had paper towels and pizza, Peter quickly ate a slice, which gave him the energy to start a conversation.

"How are things at the lab?" MJ asked.

"Wouldn't know," Peter said. "I got fired."

"Oh, Peter…" she began.

He realized he was being unfair, playing for sympathy. "You know I never got along with Peyton. I'm going to talk to our boss about getting the job back, but I don't have the energy for that right now."

"Because you're busy sitting around a messy apartment?"

He shook his head. "I just don't know what to do. Maybe I don't have any options, and have to accept doing nothing. If Osborn offers Fisk that position, then he really will be impossible to stop. He'll have power and leverage and access, and the police won't be able to go anywhere near him.

"There doesn't seem to be any way to stop it from happening," he continued. "I could go to the gala and create some chaos, but we all saw how well that worked at the museum. At best I could prevent the announcement from happening that night. In the long run, it really wouldn't make a difference."

"So you're giving up?"

"You have a better idea?"

"I've got no ideas at all," she said, "but this pity party you're throwing yourself isn't doing anyone any good."

"Why shouldn't I feel bad?" he protested. "I've been trying to stop Fisk for years. He kills people. He's killed someone I *knew*, and not only have I failed, I've played into his hands. Now I'm out of options. I can't web this problem away."

"You're not out of options," she said, taking a bite. "Just ideas—so get some new ones. The Peter Parker I know wouldn't give up. You can't solve this with webs, then solve it with brains. Use your compassion. Peter, sometimes you care too much about other people. It can be a problem. It became a problem for us, but it's also one of the things that makes you great. Somewhere out there is an answer that will lead you to a third way. Maybe it's a person, maybe it isn't. You just have to figure it out, and follow your heart."

"That's easy for you to say," he snapped.

MJ wiped her fingers on the paper towel, and then set it down on the pizza box.

"That's right," she said calmly. "It's easy for me to say, and it's hard for you to do, so maybe you should get started." She stood up. "Right now you're busy telling yourself why you can't stop him. When you decide to turn that around, let me know." She left without waiting for an answer.

Peter sat there with a slice of pizza drooping in his hand. He considered kicking over some furniture, but he decided that would be unseemly. Instead, he thought maybe he should clean up his apartment, and began by moving some dirty dishes to the sink. The actual washing was a project better left for another day. Then he dropped down onto his sofa and decided he was angry.

Being angry wasn't proof that she was wrong, and that bugged the hell out of him. Annoyingly, it might be proof that she was right. He *was* giving up. But he didn't see how his compassion was going to stop a monster like Fisk. It had been a pep talk, but she was right. He couldn't allow Fisk to win.

He had to try, to *really* try. He needed a way to get to Fisk—to stop him—that didn't involve a direct confrontation. That might mean going through someone else, but who? Watanabe was out…

Damn it, she's right, he thought. For the first time in weeks he felt himself smiling. MJ had just outsmarted him, and when Mary Jane did her thing it was a delight to behold. He was also smiling because he had an inkling of an idea.

o———o

THE next morning he showed up unannounced at the *Daily Bugle*. To make up for the intrusion, and for being a jerk the night before, he brought her a latte and a muffin, which he set down on her desk.

"Maya Lopez." He pulled up a chair .

MJ smiled. "Go on."

"She hates me. She loves Fisk, but he has to be lying to her. She thinks I killed her father. If I can convince her that she's wrong, maybe I can get her to help me."

"Let me get my file," MJ said.

WHEN she saw it, Maya thought her heart might simply stop.

She emerged from her bathroom after showering, and found the note attached to her wall. No, webbed to her wall.

We have unfinished business. Meet me on the roof. Bring an open mind. But you can leave the spear at home. Please.

Spider-Man. Why was he doing this? Did he want to fight her? Did he fear what she knew? Did he think she was a threat to him, that she might attack him again when he wasn't ready? Perhaps he wanted to confront her at the time and place of his own choosing.

No, that made no sense. Spider-Man was a coward, a bully who hid behind a mask and pretended to be a hero. If he wanted to stop her, he would attack unannounced. He would strike her down the way he had struck down her father.

It had to be a trap of some kind. She ought to ignore the note. There was no reason why she should play by his rules. Just walk away, go about her business. Let him wait for her and understand that she wasn't a puppet for him to manipulate.

But she couldn't let it go. She couldn't ignore him. He had challenged her, and she had to answer.

Maya reached for her makeup.

ECHO stepped out onto the roof, prepared for him to swing down and attempt to catch her in his webs. She was prepared for him to be hiding, waiting to ambush her from some carefully chosen spot. She was even prepared for him not to be there. It might be a mind game, and when she came out onto the roof, she might find nothing but the wind and her own rage.

She hadn't left her spear at home.

Maya had always imagined that her final confrontation with him would take place somewhere dark, maybe with fog, certainly with jittery, uncertain lighting. Here he was, though, in the bright light of a cloudless morning. As she strode out in her stage makeup, holding her spear, she saw him on the other side of the roof, sitting cross-legged, leafing through a file.

"You dare to mock me?" she asked. "Are you amusing yourself with my anger?" She hoped it sounded as imposing to him as it did in her head.

He looked up and folded the bottom of his mask up, so she could see his lips.

He knows…

"This is not mockery. This is me trying to look non-threatening. I swear, Maya."

"Call me Echo," she said.

He knew she was deaf, and he'd exposed part of his face. It meant nothing. Even with her perfect memory, she doubted she could identify him from just a mouth, but that wasn't the point. Masks and costumes and the handprint—these were all forms of armor. He was exposing himself, making himself weak. His suit was part of his power, just as much as his webs and his abilities. If he wished to weaken himself, she would show him strength.

She charged.

Seeming to take his time, as if he was unafraid, he rose slowly. He placed the file on the ground and shot a small strand of web to keep it in place. He then turned to face her.

"I do not want to fight you," he said. "I want to talk."

Maya thrust her spear at him, but he sidestepped it easily. She began to feel a current of doubt course through her. She knew how to fight him when he was behaving like himself, when he was fighting back, but he was behaving strangely. Echo didn't know how to counter that.

Yet she needed to try. She ran toward him and jabbed again. This time she anticipated his dodge. She'd seen it once, and she knew it was coming. Maya raised the spear, and his legs collided with the shaft, throwing him off balance.

Spider-Man tumbled and landed on the roof, but he bounced back quickly and faced her. She braced herself, but he didn't charge. He didn't shoot his webs. Twenty feet away, he stood with his hands up.

"This is the part where we talk."

"You killed my father," she said. "Stop playing games and fight me."

"I am not playing a game," he said. "Please just listen."

It had to be a ploy. A trap. If she knew what he intended, she could beat him. In her mind she reviewed everything since she'd set foot on the roof. Where had he started? Where had he moved? Was he trying to maneuver her into a specific position? Nothing added up. He was acting like… like he really did want to talk to her. If that's what he wanted, though, it was the last thing he would get.

She charged forward again, moving as though she planned to jab at him, but this time she tossed the spear, a bullet to his chest.

His mouth fell open in surprise. He dropped down to his back as the spear sailed over his head and then shot out a web, catching it before it could go over the side of the roof. While leaping to his feet, moving himself out of her way, he yanked the spear back to him. He caught it by the shaft, set it down gently, and stepped away from it.

"You can have it back," he said, "if you promise to play nice."

He took a few steps back.

"You think you can belittle me," she snarled. It made her furious that he would toy with her this way. Yet he stood with his hands up, palms forward. He shifted slightly, so she'd be able to read his lips.

"I am not belittling you or playing games. I am trying to talk to you. I understand your rage. I know what it is to lose people, but I didn't kill your father,

Maya. You have been told that I did, but it is not true."

"You're a liar," she said, and she swung at him, but he was already gone, already in the air. He landed and faced her again.

"Not lying. I did not kill him, but I know who did. I have proof—in the file."

"You're trying to trick me." She scooped up the spear and jabbed at him. "To put me off my guard."

"Why would I do that?"

Why *would* he do that? It was a good question. What did he have to gain by lying? She wished she could see his eyes. She could often tell lying from what people did with their eyes, but he wore that mask. Seeing his mouth wasn't enough. She thrust the spear forward again.

"If I wanted to hurt you," he said, stepping out of the way, "why would I come up here to talk to you. I know where you live. I can follow just about anyone, without any difficulty. Ambushing someone is easy. Trying to talk to them while they try to impale you is a little harder."

She took a step back and braced herself, raised her spear as if to ward off an attack. It never came.

"Did you ever review the police file?" He took a step back. His shoulders looked relaxed, as if he knew she was softening. "Did you ever look at the evidence?"

"Of course I did." She jabbed at him again, pointlessly. He was making a fool of her, and she was letting him pull her strings. So she stopped and placed the butt of the spear on the ground, watching him, ready to let him say what he had come to say. She would wait for her moment, though. She would be ready to strike.

"If you had reviewed the file, then you would know that I could not have killed him."

"The file says no one else could have killed him."

His mouth twisted. "Fisk got you the file, I suppose."

She said nothing.

"You must have seen a fake," he said. "I have a copy of the real police file, right here." He pointed at the file on the ground. "Look at it. I read it, and do you know what it looks like? Whoever gave you that spear is the person who murdered your father."

She took a step back. "You're trying to throw me off my game." He took a step forward, his hands up, as if he was surrendering. She turned the spear toward him.

"I want you to hear the truth," he said. "I am making myself vulnerable because I want you to see how serious I am. Just look at the file."

"Whoever surrenders his power is a fool," she told him.

"Maybe so," he responded, "but I would rather be a weak fool than an evil crime lord. A really fat evil crime lord. With giant fists. They're like—" he lowered his hands and held them in front of him, making a shape like a ball "—they're like crazy big. How does he, I don't know, unwrap a piece of gum with those things? They're like bowling balls made out of ham."

Something strange happened. Something Maya hadn't expected.

She laughed.

Spider-Man had made her laugh, and she didn't know what to do with that fact—because she could see he wasn't a monster.

Just because a person is charming doesn't mean they can't be evil, she told herself, but even as she thought it she knew it was wrong. It wasn't that Spider-Man was charming. He was sincere. Yet, if what he had to say was true, then it meant—

She couldn't even think to herself what it meant.

The spear dropped from her hand. The words didn't feel as though they came from her own mouth, but she knew they were hers.

"Let me see the file."

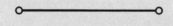

"HOW do I know it's real?" She closed the file.

"You're the victim's daughter," Spider-Man told her. "You can go to the police and request a copy for yourself. You'll find what's in here, not what Fisk has shown you."

She blinked several times rapidly. "I've been living with the man who killed my father. He lied to me about everything."

"Yes."

"The other things they say about him," Maya said. "The Kingpin of Crime. Is that true?"

She really didn't know. He thought it was amazing that she could work with him, live with him, and have no clue. Maybe she'd needed to hide it all from herself.

"Yeah," he said. "I've seen it. I can get you police files on that too, if you need to be convinced. But he's a bad guy, Maya. He fooled a lot of people. I guess he fooled you."

He thought she was going to cry. Her face seemed to soften, but then, at once, it was all hard lines.

"We have to stop him," she said. "He has to pay for what he's done."

Peter had to work not to smile. "I was hoping you would say that."

THIRTY-FOUR

"HIS tool is extortion," she said. "He has something on anyone who can help or hurt him. He has something on Mayor Osborn, though I don't know what. He keeps those files on thumb drives, one in each of his safes."

They had moved to her private apartment in the Fisk Tower suites. Maya had gone down to her office, opened the window, and waited for Spider-Man to crawl in. He had seen her watching him, as if eight years of hatred were at war with a new understanding of how the universe worked. She wanted to welcome him, but she also kind of wanted to bash him over the head with the first heavy object she could grab.

He'd have to keep an eye on her, too.

They sat at her dining room table. She was still wearing her Echo clothing, and he had again rolled up the bottom of his mask. This was among the strangest meetings he'd ever had, though probably not the strangest. His mind wandered back to his chat with Scorpion and Herman Schultz in the Bar with No Name.

Yeah, definitely not the strangest. Still, a couple of people in costumes just hanging out and chatting.

"How many copies does he have of his blackmail file?"

"At least half a dozen." She raised a hand to her face as if to rub it, but then stopped when she remembered her stage makeup. She looked tired. Exhausted and lost and scared. Her whole world had been turned upside down, and yet she was trying to forge ahead.

"Maybe you need a little time to sort through all this," he suggested. "We can meet up again—"

"No," she snapped. "What am I going to do until then? Keep pretending? Forget it. You showed me the lie, and now you have to deal with it—with me, right now, because I can't go back."

Spider-Man nodded. "I just wanted to make sure you don't need some space."

"I don't," she said. "I don't need space or distance or time or anything else to distract me from what needs doing. A problem exists, so it must be confronted. Now and without hesitation or regret."

That was impressive. He couldn't choose a brand of breakfast cereal without hesitation or regret. He admired Echo's confidence. On the other hand, he wasn't sure this situation was as straightforward as she wanted it to be, but he understood about the need to do something, to solve a problem rather than let it sit.

"Then let's figure things out."

"Good," she said. "Now, there may be more copies of the file that I don't know about. We have the best network security you can imagine, but he's of an older generation that doesn't trust the cloud, so he's gone for redundancy."

"So, physically destroying all the data probably isn't an option," Spider-Man said, "but could we get our hands on one of those drives? If we knew what we were dealing with, we might figure out our next steps."

"I have access to some of the safes. I've been within inches of those drives more times than I can count, and it's never even occurred to me to take a peek." She smirked. "Okay, it's occurred to me. I'd even have done it, if I thought I could get away with it."

"And now?" Peter prodded.

"I can do it, but it's an endgame. He'll know it's gone immediately. That means there will be no turning back for me, no pretending to still be loyal. I'll be cut off."

"You've made it pretty clear that pretending isn't an option."

"I know," she said, closing her eyes while she considered something. "Still, it would be an advantage, and I hate to surrender an advantage—*any* advantage—but I won't go back. So, yes, I can get one, but he'll have the rest, and he'll know he's been compromised."

She couldn't even bring herself to say Fisk's name, Spider-Man noticed.

"It's easy to believe that Osborn would have secrets," he said. "No one, no matter how squeaky clean, could run a company like Oscorp and be mayor of a major city without racking up some things he'd rather keep hidden—and Osborn is a take-no-prisoners kind of leader. He'll have skeletons in his closet for sure. But that means he would never just roll over. He must have something planned."

"I had the same thought," she said. "He seemed too cooperative, but I assumed that meant the blackmail material was so damning that it cut the legs out from under him. It doesn't matter, though. If we don't have sole control of the information, then knowing about it doesn't do us any good."

"I'm not so sure," Spider-Man replied. "I mean, if what Osborn is hiding is that bad, then maybe the public *should* know. And if the public knows, then Fisk can't use it to get what he wants."

"You're talking about exposing Osborn."

Spider-Man nodded. "Fisk can't manipulate the mayor if everyone already knows the secret."

"But what if the mayor is hiding something that's not the public's business?" Maya asked. "An embarrassing relationship, or a health problem, or something like that? Do we expose a secret if it's not illegal or corrupt?"

He shrugged. "I wish I'd taken that Ethics of Blackmail elective back in college. I don't think we can say what the right thing is until we know what Fisk has, so I guess we'll have to cross that bridge when we come to it. Besides, we might not have to go public with what we find. It may be enough to let the mayor know someone besides Fisk—someone working *against* Fisk—also has control of the file. What's the point of caving if someone else could expose you? Fisk loses his grip as soon as Osborn knows we have the data."

"All of this is theoretical," she said. "For it to be

anything more, we have to get hold of one of those thumb drives. There are two days before the event, so what is your plan?"

"You're the trusted employee," he said. "I was kind of hoping you'd have one."

Maya went silent and scrunched up her face. It looked as if she was thinking hard. She also looked totally miserable.

"I'm sorry I dragged you into this," Spider-Man said. "You were living a lie, but it was one you believed in. I pulled the rug out from under everything you thought was true."

She studied him, as if he was a strange specimen under glass. "Do you always apologize for doing what you have to do?"

"Not always. Let's say about half the time." Then he leaned forward and grew deadly serious. "New subject: You need to tell me everything you know about the Spider-Man impersonator."

o———————o

AFTER all these weeks of sitting on his hands, he was finally taking action—and that action involved breaking into one of Fisk's buildings. Then into one of his safes.

The only one for which Maya knew the combination was in the Upper East Side offices. She wanted to do it herself, but Spider-Man insisted on going with her. He wanted to be on hand in case she ran into any trouble, and he wanted to keep an eye on her. The decision to turn on Fisk appeared real enough, but he had to be certain.

Unfortunately, they had to wait until the night before the event. Fisk would be in that very building, hosting a real estate conference, and security would be especially tight. It was safer to wait until he returned to Fisk Tower.

It was late when the opportunity presented itself. Maya could dress in a skirt suit and walk through the front door. Spider-Man found a way in through the roof, and made his way to the office through a combination of climbing, crawling, and dodging the security cameras. By the time he slipped inside, Maya was already there.

She had her laptop set up and a cable was run between it and a port on the safe. The sun had gone down, and the building was quiet. They used only dim lighting, not wanting to draw attention to themselves.

"The safe has an internal sensor log," she explained as she worked the laptop's keyboard. "All activity is recorded, and anything suspicious is flagged. That includes any time the safe is opened, especially when Fisk isn't in the building. I'm uploading a program that should mask the activity."

"Why bother?" Spider-Man asked. "He's going to know it's been stolen soon enough."

"It should still be after we're out of the building," she said. "It's preferable to make your exit without security guards shooting at you."

"Can't argue with that," he said. "Hopefully, we

can stay a step or two ahead of him."

"People say that," Maya grunted as her fingers danced over the keyboard, "but few actually do it. He sees the world as a chess match, and he always likes to say that there's no countermove to checkmate. Now stop talking to me. I can't read your lips and run this program at the same time."

He held up his hand in apology and let her do her thing, remaining alert for any sign that they'd been detected. All seemed quiet in the building. His Spider-Sense didn't even twinge. After a few moments Maya's laptop emitted a little chime, and she looked up, smiling.

"That should do it. We can open the safe now, and he won't know until the next time he looks in and notices the missing drive." She stared at him. "You've got the combination, right?"

"Are you *kidding* me?"

She grinned. "Yes, I am kidding you. I'm used to dealing with Fisk and his associates all day. Do you have any idea how long it's been since I've had the opportunity to make a joke? You seem like you might have a sense of humor."

"I can't believe I'm saying this," he growled, "but sometimes humor is not appropriate."

Maya shined her flashlight on the complicated series of dials. Opening the safe required a lot more effort than Peter's old school locker, but Maya moved through the series of turns and reversals as if it was second nature.

There was a click and what sounded like a magnetic release. The safe door swung gently outward. Maya pulled on it and opened it all the way. She pointed her flashlight inside to reveal emptiness.

She ran her hand through the safe, as though she didn't believe her eyes, as though the thumb drive might have become invisible.

"It was in here," she said breathlessly. "The thumb drive, files, contracts, even jewelry and artwork. It's all gone."

"Could he have moved the contents somewhere else?" Spider-Man suggested. "Maybe for the duration of the conference?"

"You don't move things out of a safe to keep them safe," Maya shot back. "That's why they call it a safe."

"Can't argue with that." Spider-Man raised his hands in surrender. "What does this mean, then?" And that's when his Spider-Sense lit up. Without pausing to think about it, he pulled his mask all the way down while he leapt into the air, spun, and gripped the ceiling.

Fisk stood at the entrance to the office.

THIRTY-FIVE

HIS face was hacked into lines and angles of rage. He was on to them, which meant they wouldn't get another chance to steal the files. They had blown the one opportunity they'd had to stop Osborn from making him untouchable.

If he tried to stop them from leaving—and that seemed a certainty—Spider-Man could beat him…he hoped. He and the Kingpin had squared off before, and it was a mistake to underestimate the big man. He was large, yes, but shockingly fast and devastatingly strong. There were few opponents in the world, even people with enhanced abilities, who could stay upright after one of his best punches.

Even so, Spider-Man's smaller size and greater speed gave him advantages. If evasion was the goal, then the Web-Slinger had the advantage. Still, just one mistake would exact a heavy price.

, Maya was also fast, Spider-Man thought, and elusive. She could get away, but he worried she wouldn't try. She was smart as hell, no doubt about that, but she was also driven by rage—the newfound knowledge that the man who had pretended to care for her had killed her father. He hoped the strategic side of her would be in full command here. If so, there was no reason the two of them couldn't get out, regroup, and live to fight another day.

No reason except for the imposter.

The doppelgänger came in from the hall, blazingly fast, and leapt up to the ceiling. While it was impossible to read his expression under the mask, Spider-Man felt certain he was smirking at them. Once again, the fire began to burn in his core.

Time slowed down. Spider-Man's emotions went still. This man—Bingham—had dressed like him and killed innocent people. He'd killed Anika, and Remzi. And there, next to him, as though holding his leash, stood Fisk. These people were pure evil, and he was going to stop them.

He was going to make them pay. In his mind, he could feel what it would be like to hit that madman, to bring him down, to make him suffer the way he'd made others suffer. He wasn't going to just web him up and let the police come, only to release him. He was going to—

He didn't know what he was going to do.

But it would hurt. That much he knew.

"It's true," Fisk said to Maya, his voice resonant with sadness. "When they told me you'd betrayed me to this… this nuisance, I didn't believe it. Yet here we are."

"Is it any less than you deserve?" Maya spat. "You killed my father. You raised me to believe a lie." She dropped into a defensive stance.

"After all I've done for you," Fisk said, "you believe his deceptions. Think, Maya. Think of what your life would have been without me. Think before you decide whom to trust."

"Without you, my father would still be alive."

"Without me," he countered, "he'd have been killed long before he left Montana. Has that never occurred to you? Once I saved his life, it belonged to me, and it was mine to do with as I pleased."

He was vaguely aware of this conversation, as if it was happening at the distant end of a winding tunnel, but then he snapped back into the moment. He *would* have justice. He would, but he had to be smart. He had to keep his head in the game. They weren't going to win anything in the next few minutes. No amount of punching or webbing was going to put this matter to rest, because whatever happened, Fisk would still have his leverage over Osborn.

I worried about Maya being emotional, he told himself. *I need to worry about myself, too. I need to play this smart.*

"So, that sounds like a confession," Spider-Man said, though it occurred to him that Maya wouldn't hear anything he said.

"You know what?" the doppelgänger said. "I'm bored. Let's get to the part where we kill them." Suddenly he put his hands to his cheeks. "Oh, no! The deaf girl doesn't know what I'm talking about." He began to wave his hands around in a mockery of sign language. "We-are-going-to-kill-you," he said in a sing-song voice. "You-and-the-fake-Spider-Man."

"Wait. *I'm* the fake?" the Web-Slinger said.

"That's actually your position? Are you also Alexander the Great?"

"You *are* the fake!" the imposter snapped. "I'm the original. They made me. I'm not a false Spider-Man, afraid to act, afraid to do what's necessary. My hands are covered in blood, and I'm the Blood Spider. Yes, that is my true name! Blood Spider!"

"And it's super cool," Spider-Man responded. "You're an amazing big boy for sure." He paused. "So where's the thumb drive again?"

"Safe," the imposter said. "It's safe, but it's not in the safe. It's *safe*."

"Enough," Fisk shouted. "Kill him!" He gestured toward Spider-Man. "But be warned, I want Maya unharmed."

"You won't have me at all," she said. Maya ran at Fisk, picking up her laptop and whisking it at him like it was a throwing star. It spun, end over end, and looked as deadly as any weapon as it hurled toward its target. Fisk barely dodged out of the way before she leapt into the air and slammed her heels into his chest.

We're not supposed to be fighting, Spider-Man thought. *We're supposed to be skedaddling*, yet there was no way to tell Maya that without lifting his mask. And though fighting was the wrong move here, Spider-Man would have loved to watch Willy get pounded by someone a tenth of his weight.

Unfortunately, he had problems of his own. The imposter—Blood Spider, as he called himself—was coming at him. He was scatter-shooting his webs, so

Spider-Man had no choice but to go on the defensive.

"Where'd you get the webs?" he asked as he dodged out of the way.

"They made them for me," Blood Spider bellowed, "because I'm Spider-Man!"

The Web-Slinger had learned a thing or two from Echo about fighting someone who mimicked his style, but this was different. She moved like Spider-Man did, but the Blood Spider had a style all his own.

Spider-Man liked to think of his fighting style as employing surgical precision. He fought larger, stronger, tougher enemies, but he won—or at least kept himself from losing—by being careful and deliberative. His moves might look spontaneous—and they often were when playing defense—but he carefully chose the moments to go on the offense. A guy who was smaller and, yes, sometimes weaker than the people he fought had to choose his moments.

If he was a scalpel, Blood Spider was a hammer. There was no nuance in his attack. He filled the space with webs. He wound up for roundhouse punches and tried to move in for powerful jabs.

He wouldn't stand a chance against me in the open city, Spider-Man thought, but in the tight confines of Fisk's office, it would be easy to get jammed up. He didn't have room to set up attacks and defenses. All he could do was avoid getting hit and try to hit back. This was going to turn into a brawl, and that meant they'd be playing by Blood Spider's rules.

He needed Maya's attention, but she was locked

in a deadly face-off of her own with Fisk, who had the upper hand. He'd managed to get one of his massive hands around her throat, and was slamming her against the wall.

"You know nothing about gratitude," he said in a disturbingly quiet voice.

For a gratitude seminar, head-pounding seemed like the wrong pedagogical tool. Spider-Man turned to lend Maya a hand. In that moment of distraction, Blood Spider shot out a web that pinned his right wrist to the wall. Bingham then released another that hit his left arm near the elbow.

The Web-Slinger yanked hard. Blood Spider's webs were impressive, but—he noted with some satisfaction—they were an inferior product. They weren't as strong. He doubted an ordinary person could break free, but he could. He was loose and ducking as Blood Spider tried to land a rapid punch to his head. Spider-Man hit back hard, a blow to his stomach, his ribs, and when he turned slightly, to his kidneys.

Blood Spider was momentarily stunned. Spider-Man unleashed his own wave of webbing, pinning his opponent to the floor. He then spun and sent a web around Fisk's ankles. He yanked hard, using all of his strength, and toppled the huge man. Another web to keep him pinned to the ground, at least for a while. Hopefully as long as he needed.

He ran to Maya, lifting up the bottom of his mask as he did so.

"Are you hurt?"

She shook her head. "Nothing serious."

"Time for the escape plan," he said.

"But the thumb drive!"

"It's not here," he said. "And getting killed won't help us."

She nodded, took out the device—a modified car fob—and hit the red button. The window burst open. Peter grabbed her, found a target for his webs, and leapt into the air.

It took a lot of trust for her to put herself in his hands this way, he guessed. She didn't look frightened, though, and she didn't wriggle out of his grasp. As they soared into the night at speeds that would terrify any rational person, she didn't even squeeze her eyes shut.

o——————o

BINGHAM broke free of the false Spider-Man's webs. They were stronger than his, he hated to admit, but not beyond his ability. Fisk struggled though, which was funny. He pulled out a device designed to dissolve his own webbing. It didn't affect the imposter's strands, but it did help clear out the room a little.

He went over to Fisk to help yank him free. Once mobile, the big man rose like a monster in an old horror movie, waving his arms and stumbling forward. His fists opened and closed in a repetitive, almost soothing, rhythm.

"This," Bingham observed, "is where the big baby has his temper tantrum."

"*Goddamn* it!" Fisk screamed. He slammed a fist into a desk. It cracked in at least three places and collapsed.

"Called it," Bingham said. Fisk strode over to the safe and peered inside.

"It's empty," he shouted. "They took everything. They took the thumb drive! Do you know what this means? The entire operation is compromised!" Fisk drove his fist into the wall, sending chips of wood paneling flying like shrapnel.

Bingham hopped onto one of the remaining desks. He made a show of examining his fingernails, which was silly because he wore gloves. He liked the effect though. He liked showing Fisk that he had nothing but contempt for the fat man.

"This is one of those good news/bad news type situations," he said. "The good news is that they didn't get the thumb drive."

Fisk slowly turned to him. There was a light in his eyes as his rage zeroed in on a new target.

"What have you done?"

"The bad news," Bingham continued, "is that your safe is made by First Line. Yes, it's earned its reputation as being the manufacturer of some of the most secure safes on the planet. The thing is, it's a privately held company, which is why they didn't make a big deal out of being bought by Oscorp last month."

Fisk took a step toward him. His face was a mask of rage.

"So this safe, the other safes, the ones at all your buildings, all your hideouts..." Bingham waved his arms around theatrically. "Not so safe, these safes. We thought we knew about all of them, but that's where owning the company came in handy. There were a couple we'd missed, but once we had company records, we were able to track them down. I mean, if you have any safes by another company, then the plan is shot, but if not…" He shrugged. "Then I win."

"Osborn," Fisk growled. "He put you up to this."

"I'm not going to say I could have done it without him," Bingham replied. "We've all got our skills. Outwitting fat people is one of his—but, there are some things Norm doesn't know, that he doesn't control. He thinks I'll be eternally grateful to him for helping me find my true self, for allowing me to go from being the Spider-Man in my mind to the Spider-Man in the world. And I am, but that doesn't mean I'm his puppet. I'm no one's puppet."

Fisk gritted his teeth and stared at Bingham. His nostrils flared, and his breath came out in short, hard bursts. He planted a foot hard on the ground as if he was ready to charge, but he did not move. Not yet. Anger might course through his veins, but he wasn't ready to let go of rational thought.

"What do you want?" he demanded. "Where are all the thumb drives?"

"There is no *all*, Lardo," Bingham said. "There's only one. I destroyed all the rest. Osborn said to bring it to him, but I'm not going to do that. And do you know why? Would you like to know? I'll tell you. It's because this one is *mine*."

"What do you want for it?" Fisk asked. "I can make you rich. I can give you power. Soon I'll be in a position to pull the strings of this city."

"Not if I hand the drive over to Osborn, you won't," Bingham corrected. "So, it's not a question of what you can do for me, but what I can do for you. You see, there's been a change in the organizational chart. You still control Osborn, but I control you. That means I'm not just Spider-Man anymore. I'm also the Kingpin of Crime. I'm the Kingpin of Blood."

Fisk charged forward, fists raised, head down. His will to think, to plan, to strategize was gone. He wanted only to crush the enemy. Bingham was expecting it, but he wasn't expecting the speed the big man could muster. Fisk landed a massive punch to Bingham's head before he could dodge.

The world went dark and weird. Ringing filled his ears and lights danced on the periphery of his vision. He was sliding across the floor. He would have been finished if he'd been an ordinary man, but he wasn't ordinary anymore. He hadn't been ordinary since the experiments in Osborn's lab.

Osborn hadn't found the cure he was looking for, but he'd found something else. A way to make Spider-Man. It killed everyone else they'd tried it on, which just proved that there could only be one Spider-Man in the world. That was why the imposter had to die. Every moment he breathed, he weakened Bingham. Anyone could see that.

Bingham had other problems at the moment,

such as the giant who was barreling toward him again. This time he was ready. He knew what Fisk could do, how fast he could move, and that made it all the easier. He leapt up and over, landing behind his attacker. He yanked on Fisk's pants, hoping to pull them down. Nothing would throw a guy like Fisk more than a good humiliation. Those pants seemed to be glued on, though, and Bingham leapt back to get out of Fisk's range.

"I will kill you," Fisk growled.

"You need to accept the new order," Bingham said, leaping up to the ceiling. "You thought you owned Osborn. Now I do. I can still make him do what you want, so long as you understand that you work for me."

He let the webs fly—four, five, six—seven blasts to his face. Seven was a lucky number, but not for Fisk, who couldn't breathe. Bingham knew better than to punch him in the stomach. His fist would get lost in there. The face would be satisfying, but it might dislodge some of those webs. So he went for the knees to topple him, and then kicks to the ribs. Fisk grunted and writhed. The pain, the suffocation, the humiliation. It must have been terrible for a man who thought himself so powerful. Now he was just another stupid kid in a stupid town whose mother ignored him and who got laughed at by everyone.

Bingham thought back to another time, another fat person, another suffocation. The pain. The terror. The absolute and abject terror. When you did something, it was no longer something that could be done to you. Bingham realized this with startling clarity. He was setting himself free, liberating himself from his past. He was taking the final steps toward becoming Blood Spider, the only true Spider-Man.

He activated the device and dissolved the webs. Fisk gasped as his lungs filled with air.

"So this is how it is," Bingham said. "You can be my friend, or you can be my victim. Which do you choose?"

Fisk stood there, opening and closing his fists, breathing deeply until it slowed. Then he peered at Bingham, and his face became unreadable.

"Friend," he said.

"Good," Bingham said. "You'll like being my friend."

He didn't trust Fisk, of course. The man would betray him the first chance he got. And Osborn—when he found out he'd been outsmarted, that was going to be quite the blow. But they would learn. They would all learn. Blood Spider couldn't be outsmarted. Once a person named Michael Bingham could be used and toyed with and tossed away.

Those days were over.

THIRTY-SIX

HE would have liked to have time to put together a smart plan. Unfortunately, there was only time for a stupid one, so Spider-Man figured it was best to go all the way and make it a *really* stupid one.

Everything was against them. The event would take place in a Fisk hotel. There were Roxxon Blackridge security guards everywhere. Norman Osborn was on the scene, which meant there was a heavy police presence. If that didn't make things bad enough, the crowd was full of people Spider-Man cared about.

Peering from their hideout in a janitorial station— one with a vent that overlooked the ballroom—he saw MJ trying to interview the most prominent and wealthy people in attendance, ostensibly for an article in the *Bugle*'s style section. There was Aunt May, accompanied by her boss, Martin Li. Yuri Watanabe was present as part of the police detail, and J. Jonah Jameson. While there were times Spider-Man would have been happy to shove JJJ onto a manned mission to Uranus, he wouldn't actually wish harm on his old employer.

Maybe just some mild public humiliation.

If it came down to a fight, the people he treasured most in the world were going to be in danger. That was a problem, because the plan involved it coming down to a fight.

The ballroom, at least, was huge, with high ceilings and balconies that overlooked the gaudy furniture and bordello-red carpet. On the other hand, there were glittering chandeliers that could come crashing down, so not an ideal location for a public showdown. But still—spacious.

Spider-Man was depending on Maya, because she had way more experience with this nut Bingham.

"He's insane," she'd explained, "but he's predictably insane. He's exhibited some of the same behaviors in each of my encounters with him. He's a braggart, and seems to think he is the *real* Spider-Man. He's aggressive and cruel. What gives us hope is that he has rampant hoarding tendencies. He keeps things, and the things that are most important to him he keeps close."

"So you think he has the thumb drive?" he asked.

"I know he does. You told me what he said. 'It's safe, but it's not in the safe.' He has it, and he'll have it with him—I know he will," she said. "Or I'm reasonably certain he will. Like 90 percent certain."

"What if it's the 10 percent?"

"Then we've risked everything," Maya said, "for absolutely nothing."

"On the other hand, we have no alternative."

"Then you understand the realities of our situation."

If they were going to succeed, they would have

to rely on the consistency of Bingham's madness. This seemed to Spider-Man its own sort of madness. On the other hand, they had no choice but to try.

"It's not like a king granting Fisk a title, though," he said. "Osborn can *say* that Fisk will be the new commissioner of finance, but if tomorrow we get the thumb drive, and let Osborn know, then all bets will be off. It will be an embarrassment for the mayor's office, but he'll deal with it."

"Agreed, but after tonight there's no guarantee we'll be able to get the thumb drive—tomorrow or ever again. Tonight at least we know the lunatic will be nearby. We know he'll have the thumb drive on him. He won't be able to resist proving that he is the real Spider-Man. But Bingham is powerful, not clever.

"No, if we're going to succeed, it has to be tonight," she concluded. "This time tomorrow Fisk might have figured out a way to get the thumb drive away from him, and then we'll never be able to stop him."

o———————o

HE couldn't help but think of what Watanabe had told him, though. A public attack on Fisk was going to make it harder for her to advance her own investigations. Even if they prevented Fisk from becoming the commissioner, they might be making it harder, even impossible, for the lieutenant to nail him legally.

He could second-guess himself forever, though, and that wasn't an option. If Osborn placed Fisk in that position, bad things would result. He couldn't let that happen. He had to deal with the crisis in front of him. He'd deal with the fallout later.

That was why Spider-Man had stopped arguing with Maya. He was never going to convince himself that this was a great plan, but he knew he had to go ahead with it.

She was dressed as Echo, perhaps to conceal her identity, perhaps because she felt freer to fight dressed like that. There was something else, too, he suspected. Fisk had played a role in shaping Maya over the past eight years. Echo was a role she had created for herself. Even before she knew about Fisk's betrayal, being Echo had been an act of rebellion. He understood what it was to put on a costume and feel liberated from your ordinary life. She probably needed that even more than he did.

The party had been going for more than an hour when Echo tapped him on his shoulder.

"What are you waiting for?" she asked.

"I don't know," he said. "Some kind of a sign that the time is right. An indication that Bingham is here. If I go out there, and he's not even watching, it's going to be a disaster."

"He's here," she said. "I'm sure of it. He loves to spy on people, and he won't be able to resist watching how things play out. But even if he's not, your appearance will make the news, so you'll just have to wait for him."

"Basically, keep from getting shot by cops for—

what? —twenty, thirty minutes until he can get here?"

"If he's close," she said. "You'd better hope he's not out in Brooklyn."

"You know, I think you were easier to deal with before you discovered humor."

"I'm telling you he'll show," she said. "This is the gamble. We're betting on it, but a bet is never a sure thing. We have to put everything on the line, and hope for the best."

That was probably the best pep talk he was going to get. So he pulled down the bottom half of his mask, but then he turned back to her and rolled it back up to expose his mouth again.

"What?" she asked.

"Before we get started," he said, "I should probably pee."

"LADIES and gentlemen, may I have your attention for a moment?"

The room went silent as all conversations came to a halt. The piano quartet stopped playing. He winced at the sound of MJ doing a facepalm. She had to think this was the most idiotic stunt of his career, and he wasn't entirely sure she was wrong. Definitely top ten.

Someone should really do a supercut.

"I just want to offer a few words about my friend, Wilson Fisk," Spider-Man said loudly, standing with his feet on the ceiling. "Businessman, philanthropist, kingpin, super gigantic dude. You all know him. You all hate him, but you have to pretend to like him because you don't want to wake up with a horse's head between the sheets."

"It's the Web-Head!" Jameson shouted to a group of police officers. "Shoot him."

The cops looked unsure, confused. Watanabe was talking to some of them, trying to keep them from drawing their guns. She had no idea what was going on, and must have thought he'd lost his mind. He'd have given her a heads-up, but she'd have tried to talk him out of this, and she might even have taken steps to prevent him from going ahead.

"I understand the mayor—hey there, Norman! —is thinking about naming Fisk the commissioner of finance. That may not be the smartest idea." He scanned the room for Bingham, but still didn't see him. "That's really all I wanted to say, so I'll stop disturbing your evening… except to ask that anyone here who might be the Spider-Man impersonator, please step forward. If you're the one going around trying to smear my name by hurting people, committing murder, and generally being a jerk, come on. Show yourself. Don't be shy."

"You're the imposter!"

And there he was, rolling in from an upper balcony, flipping to land on an overhanging ledge.

"I'm the real Spider-Man!" Bingham shouted as he thumped his chest. "The Spider-Man whose hands are dipped in blood!"

"One of us has spent the last eight years trying to

help this city!" Spider-Man announced. "The other one is dipped in blood. So let's see a show of hands. Which one is the imposter?"

"I told you that jerk was a fake," he heard a cop say.

"It's *not* an imposter," Jameson shouted back. "There's more than one of them. They're breeding!"

As people started to talk and the volume rose, Spider-Man had to tune them out. Here was the man who had killed all those innocent people, had killed his friend. Anika was dead because of him. It hurt less with the passing of time, but the anger hadn't gone away—not entirely. And that was a good thing.

Bingham was insane, yes—dangerously so—and it would be up to a court of law to decide what a fit punishment was. It would be up to Spider-Man to hand him over to the authorities, and that wasn't likely to be easy. He needed to keep a clear head.

Bingham made his move, swinging toward his perch on the ceiling. As he did people started to panic, and there was a rush for the doors. That made it harder for the cops to react.

Spider-Man's impulse was to dodge out of the way, but he couldn't do that. He had to get in close and—as unsavory as it sounded—search for the thumb drive. He was going to get hurt, and there was no way to avoid it. He was going to have to deal with the pain.

It was a good thing he had a lot of experience.

STANDING next to Fisk, Norman Osborn permitted himself a smile. "On second thought, Wilson, I don't think I'll be offering you that position."

"It was you all along, wasn't it?" Fisk sought to control his expression. "You sent him to me as a spy."

"I just put him in your way, and you snapped him up," the mayor replied. "But I knew what you would be dealing with. I knew he was unstable. It was a calculated move. Either he'd do what I told him to do, or if not, he would destroy you from the inside. I don't know how this will end with him, but your hold over me is done."

"He still has a copy of the files," Fisk told him. "You'd better pray I don't regain control of it."

"I don't pray," Osborn said. "Praying is for people who leave things to chance." He glanced around the room, taking in the chaos. People ran for cover. They knocked each other down as they tried to force their way to the exits. Police officers drew their guns, but had no idea what to do next. There was Jameson, screaming at anyone who would listen. Cameras flashed as reporters took pictures. TV reporters stood in front of their cameramen and tried to remain still as they were jostled out of their frames.

"You imagine yourself as someone who sees every move in advance," Osborn said, "but I'm afraid you've been outclassed. If you'd wanted to do business, Fisk, we could have done business, but you had to try to force my hand. That was a mistake."

"No matter what you think," Fisk told him, "we

are not finished. You've crossed a line from which there will be no retreating."

Osborn gazed at the pandemonium around him and remained as placid as if he were gazing at sculptures in a museum.

"Nice party," he added.

THEY met mid air, and Spider-Man was ready. At least he *thought* he was ready.

He had some ideas about general readiness, and it was all great inside his head, but to be honest with himself, he had no clue what he was doing. The first hint he had was when—as they hurtled toward each other—Blood Spider punched him in the face.

Spider-Man rolled with it, minimizing the impact, but it still—what was the word?—*hurt*. Yes, that was it. It hurt. A lot.

This is still the best plan we've got, he reminded himself as pain exploded inside his head.

He'd learned a lot from fighting Echo. He'd learned about his own style, how he relied on moves and patterns he hadn't even known were in his lexicon. Then he'd learned how to force himself to think differently, not like himself. It was shadow boxing, so he'd had to find a way to trick his shadow.

Bingham wasn't Echo, though. He could do what Spider-Man did, but he'd never studied his moves. He wanted to be Spider-Man, but he hadn't taken the time to learn *how* to be Spider-Man.

It was time for a lesson.

Even as they plummeted toward the ballroom floor, Bingham squared his shoulders, readied his fists. He wanted not simply to fight, but to *brawl*. He wanted to punch his enemy in the head, in the torso. He wanted the two of them to square off.

Spider-Man decided to give him what he wanted.

They landed on their feet, facing each other. The Web-Slinger's jaw already felt swollen, but he ignored the pain. He raised his fists, like a boxer.

Blood Spider's head snapped to attention, fully alert, maybe for the first time. His webs shot out and snagged the real Spider-Man's shoulders. A quick yank pulled the Web-Slinger forward, off balance. Blood Spider aimed another web toward the ceiling and shot upward, taking his enemy—the man whose existence was an insult—with him.

Spider-Man felt a lurch in his stomach, the sudden ripple of being out of control, and calmed his mind to search for an anchor. An instant before he fired off his own webs, Blood Spider released him. He began to plummet downwards. Again he aimed, but before he could fire, Blood Spider barreled into him like a mid air football tackle, driving his shoulder into his opponent's stomach.

The breath shot out of him and then he hit the ground, hard. His lungs were already on the exhale, and Spider-Man found himself struggling for air. He coughed and almost vomited in his mask—never a good idea—as he tried to breathe again.

All around, people gasped. Some fled, others moved closer. Cameras flashed while TV news crews turned their lights on the two masked men.

"They'll love watching you be destroyed!" Blood Spider cried as he struck Spider-Man in the face with a balled fist. Then again, and a third time.

"You talk and you joke and pretend to be a hero," Bingham railed, "but you haven't got the guts to follow through. You knock your enemies down, and they get back up again. You want the world to play by your rules, but there *are* no rules. When the Blood Spider knocks you down, you'll stay down."

Spider-Man was able to suck air into his lungs, but then pain blinded him as blow after blow landed on him. He reached out to the ground, trying to push himself up, but took another punch—this time to his temple—and stars erupted in his vision.

He felt his arms start to go limp.

No!

This guy had stolen his name, but much more importantly he killed people, killed Anika, and now Blood Spider was going to beat him to death—in public. In front of MJ. In front of his aunt. They would take the mask off his body, and Aunt May would learn his secret.

The plan—his ridiculous, impossible plan—was all but forgotten as he struggled to remain conscious. As he struggled to strike back harder.

Yes!

He'd hardly been aware of it, but he was standing

again. He'd hit back, and hard, too. His mind had drifted, but his body had taken over, and that gave him just enough to land a blow. Then another. Then it felt like someone had turned the lights on. Spider-Man hit Bingham again, and then *again*, and Bingham was staggering backward.

He unleashed two strands of webbing into Blood Spider's face and then pulled down, *hard*, slamming the man's head into the floor. Bingham struggled. Spider-Man released the slack and slammed again.

For Anika.

For all the victims.

He released a third time and then he saw MJ, across the ballroom, staring, open-mouthed. Was she worried that he was hurt, or that he was going to kill Bingham?

Her face, what she saw in him, it was enough to make him stop. But he wasn't there to kill Bingham.

No, the Web-Slinger had a plan—a plan to save people, to protect the city, and to do it the *right* way. Spider-Man would outfight his enemies if he had to, but he would out-*think* them when he could. And he would use his powers responsibly, always using them to save lives, never taking them. *That* was the difference between the two of them.

That was what it meant to be Spider-Man.

He dropped his webs, and let Bingham get to his feet.

"Ready to call it quits?" he asked.

"Oh, we're just getting started," Blood Spider spat back.

"No, we're finishing up," Spider-Man told him. "You took me by surprise before, but that's the only way you could ever hope to beat me. A fair fight? You'll go down every time."

"No," Bingham hissed. "I am the Blood Spider."

"More like Bloody-Nose Spider, right now, I'm guessing."

With a roar of rage Bingham rushed toward him, but Spider-Man leapt easily out of the way. It was time to close the deal. The guy wanted a fight. Spider-Man would give it to him. Just not the way he wanted. He kept his distance, moving clockwise, careful to keep Bingham engaged.

"If you think you can take me fairly," the Web-Slinger said, "then let's go. One-on-one, no tricks. We can decide, once and for all, who the real Spider-Man is."

"Yes," Bingham said, his voice rising. "Yes, let's see who's stronger. Let's see which of us is *real*."

"But it's called prize fighting for a reason," Spider-Man said as he circled his opponent. "There has to be a prize, right?"

"What do you want?" Bingham responded. He sounded confused. "What could I give you, other than an end to your miserable life?"

"Tempting, but I think we need something a little more interesting," Spider-Man said. "Oh, I know—the thumb drive. If you've got it on you, we could fight for that. It seems like a pretty good prize. How's that sound?"

Bingham put a hand to his hip. Most likely he had an inner pocket there, but it was still kind of cringey. A second later he pulled out the drive and clutched it in his fist.

"I'm glad I don't have to touch that without gloves," Spider-Man said.

"We fight," Blood Spider announced. "The winner takes it. The *winner*, which means you'll never have it. *Never.* You can't beat me."

"Dude, I've already beaten you. I just won. That's not your thumb drive. I switched them while we were fighting."

Blood Spider paused and looked at the thing in his hand. Somewhere under the mask, Spider-Man was sure Bingham had to be squinting, trying to decide if he remembered what the drive looked like, and attempting to decide if it looked just like this.

Could he be sure?

Then it was gone.

Echo leapt down from one of the balconies. She snatched the drive from Bingham's hand, landed, rolled, and came back up again. Bingham turned to watch, frozen in place.

"She forgot to say 'yoink,'" Spider-Man observed. "So can I say it? Can I say 'yoink'? I love a good 'yoink' moment."

Blood Spider spun and charged him.

THERE *are cameras in the room,* Echo told herself. *People are watching. These images will be all over the news, so don't grin like an idiot.* She was a hero now, an ally of Spider-Man. That was something to take seriously. But she couldn't stop herself. She did not want to.

She grinned.

Echo stepped forward, and came face-to-face with Fisk.

His eyes were red and dark and hooded. He didn't even seem to see the drive in her hand. He saw only a betrayal. Her first reaction was shame, but it was quickly followed by indignation, then anger. This was the man who killed her father. Who caused her to build her entire life on a lie.

Echo was fast, but she wasn't fast enough to dodge an attack she couldn't see coming. His fist shot forward with an impossible ferocity. He was still, and then he was striking her in the face.

She couldn't avoid it, so she leaned back and away, avoiding the worst of it. That didn't stop the pain. Being grazed by a speeding truck was better than a full-on hit, but it still hurt. She stumbled backward and the drive fell from her hand.

That seemed to shock Fisk out of his fury.

He looked at Echo. He looked at the drive.

Pain shot from her face in electric sparks, but she put it away, compartmentalized it. It was just pain. Maybe a broken jaw, but mostly pain. Right now she had a second to react. People were watching them. They were likely shouting things, but she couldn't take her attention away from Fisk. If he got hold of the drive, he would be in control again.

He would never let himself be vulnerable again, either.

Echo couldn't let him have it, but to grab it, she would have to take her eye off her enemy, and Fisk knew it. She would be vulnerable, and if any man alive knew how to exploit a vulnerability, it was Wilson Fisk. If she tried to take it, she would lose it. She knew that with absolute certainty.

The look in his eyes said that he knew it, too.

"Checkmate," he said. "You betrayed me and you lost."

Information was power. She knew that Spider-Man wanted desperately to know what Fisk had on Osborn. Whatever was on that drive was so explosive that Osborn had been willing to risk control of the city, rather than let it get out. Spider-Man would try to find another way.

She wasn't Spider-Man.

Lunging forward, she drove her heel into the drive. She could feel the plastic crack under her shoe. *Better it be lost*, she thought, *than in Fisk's hands*.

"Upending the board," she said with a grin. That sent a new wave of agony rippling across her jaw, but it was worth it. "That's the countermove for a checkmate."

He lunged for her again, but this time the police were there, holding him back. Fully a half-dozen or more. He tried to shake them off, like they were little children, but there were too many. Enough that they could also turn their attention to her.

Echo pivoted, saw a ledge, and leapt.

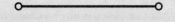

SPIDER-MAN circled Bingham, his fists raised.

Bingham took an exploratory jab. Then another.

"We're not done," he said between punches. "We have to fight to see who's stronger. I don't care about the thumb drive. I only care about beating you, about showing the world who is better."

"Yeah, but that's *your* problem," Spider-Man said. "I don't go around trying to prove I'm better than anyone else. The only one I need to convince is myself." He moved left, then right, keeping clear of Bingham's powerful jabs. He needed to end this. A few carefully placed webs might stop this creep, but Bingham was fast. There was a good chance they'd miss and hit a bystander.

Spider-Man shot off some strands toward his sparring partner's feet but, as he feared, the Blood Spider was just too nimble.

"You think we're the same," Blood Spider snapped.

"It's like you read my mind," Spider-Man said, thinking *not*. "Do another one." Keep the guy talking.

"We're *not* the same. You're not like me," Bingham spat back, hardly seeming to hear his opponent's words. "You can't beat me in a fight, you're not fast enough to use your webs, you're not smart enough to figure out what I'm going to do next. So, what's your plan, huh? Run away? Call it a draw? Then the next time I come back, put a few people in the ground, you'll shrug and say you did what you could."

Spider-Man crouched and propelled himself into the air, aiming a devastating kick at Bingham's chest, but the man had already moved. He reached out and tried to grab Spider-Man by the ankle, but thanks to his Spider-Sense, he was already twisting out of the way.

"Maybe I'll blow up another restaurant," Bingham said, "just for fun."

He's trying to mess with my head, Spider-Man thought, *make me lose focus*. And it was working. He felt the fury pumping through him, and it mixed with a heavy dose of frustration. This guy was cruel and violent and arbitrary. He hurt people because it made him feel powerful—and it had to stop.

Easier said than done. Bingham was fast, he was strong, and he was agile. All of the things he boasted were true. Except the part about him being smarter. That definitely *wasn't* true.

And it was how he was going to end this.

Spider-Man moved in for another punch, faking left and jabbing right. Bingham dodged it, just as he would have. Just like he'd predicted. Instead of putting his energy and focus on the jab, Spider-Man instead concentrated on the sweeping kick that hooked around from behind, knocking Blood Spider to his knees.

That's how it's done, Spider-Man thought. He shot out another barrage of webs, trying to keep Bingham on the ground—but even off his balance, Blood Spider was too fast. He crabbed backward and side to side, eluding blast after blast. Then he was on his feet and charging forward.

Bingham was furious. Spider-Man might be struggling to control his emotions, but Bingham didn't even bother to try. He *was* all rage, and he was moving like a freight train.

Spider-Man held his ground, and then spiraled out of the way at the last moment. As he did, he unleashed another barrage of webs at Bingham's feet. One caught the man by the ankle and Bingham went down, hard. He face-planted, and a voice in the back of Spider-Man's head chimed in with the hope that someone had caught it on video for later.

If he survived—because that wasn't a guarantee.

Bingham pushed himself up like an acrobat and yanked free of the webbing.

"All those people are dead because of you!" he shouted.

He's just talking, Spider-Man told himself. *There's no logic to it. He's just trying to get under my skin.*

Bingham swung and missed. The Web-Slinger saw an opportunity but didn't take it. He'd likely miss if he made another attempt to connect. He wasn't going to play by Bingham's rules. He was going to make the rules for the both of them—and then Spider-Man would find his moment.

"They laughed at me because of you," Blood Spider snapped. He came in hard with another punch. Spider-Man ducked under it, just barely, and a good thing too. It was strong enough to take his head off his neck.

"My mother ignored me because of you,"

Bingham cried out, and he tried to connect again.

"That one's true," Spider-Man countered as he danced backwards. "She didn't have as much time for you once she started coming over my house and baking cookies for me." It wasn't the most dignified thing he'd ever done, but he had to use what was available. Blood Spider was nuts, so he hit him where it seemed like it would hurt.

It must have succeeded. Bingham screamed and came at him again, but this time more sloppily. He was nothing but fury now. Spider-Man ducked under his blow and then came up hard, landing a sledgehammer of a punch into Bingham's chin.

Blood Spider staggered back, but he looked to be steadying himself. Spider-Man moved in again and struck him in the jaw. Bingham stayed on his feet. He bunched his fists, readying to strike back, so Spider-Man hit him again. This time he didn't wait.

He hit again, and then again, and then—

And then he stopped.

This man had killed Anika and Remzi and Andy and so many others, but he wasn't a monster—not like Fisk, who plotted his schemes and cared no more for the dead than he did for fallen pieces on a chess board. Bingham was damaged. Anyone could see that. He needed to be locked up, not beaten to a pulp.

Now was the time for the webs. A barrage aimed at Bingham's calves set him off balance. As he lurched in place Spider-Man circled him, wrapping him in a cocoon even his advanced strength couldn't break.

Bingham continued to waver, half-conscious. His eyes rolled in his head.

"You're right," Spider-Man told him between panting breaths. "We're not the same. We're completely different."

Bingham began to topple. The kind thing would have been to step in and ease his fall. Forget that. Spider-Man wasn't like Bingham, but he never claimed to be a saint.

Blood Spider hit the floor.

The Web-Slinger stood there, trying to figure out what to feel. There were so many people around him. He'd been vaguely aware before, but now he felt all those eyes. He felt the lights of the TV cameras. It was time to run, but not yet.

He needed to be still, just for a moment.

He'd caught Anika's murderer. He hadn't killed him, destroyed him, or made him beg for mercy. He'd caught him. He'd taken on that responsibility, and he'd seen it through. Breathing hard, he looked up to face all those eyes. Then he felt the pain from the beating he'd taken.

Best not to say "ow," he thought. *Might tarnish the image.* Many of the guests had fled, but there were still plenty around, pressed to the sides of the ballroom, watching the excitement. Reporters were there, including MJ—who was grinning at him. Even Aunt May seemed pleased. It was nice that, over the years, she'd become a Spider-Man defender.

Reporters snapped photos. Video cameras

followed his every move. He watched as Yuri Watanabe talked down some of the police who still wanted to move in for an arrest.

"Here's the fake Spider-Man," he told them. "This is the restaurant bomber. He should have some pretty interesting stories to tell you."

"Arrest him!" Jameson shouted, pointing at Spider-Man. Then he was pointing to where the Web-Slinger had been.

Spider-Man was gone.

THIRTY-SEVEN

STILL in his Spider-Man suit, he used his phone to watch video footage of the police leading Wilson Fisk out of the ballroom. Nothing was going to stick, of course, but everyone had seen him punch Maya. There would be questions, and the media was sure to find out that Maya was his foster child.

Still, she was dressed in a costume, and it would be easy for Fisk to argue that he hadn't recognized her, that he'd felt threated by someone who could have been as dangerous as one of the Spider-Men or any other powerful criminal. It was a safe bet that Fisk's lawyer would have him out on the street in an hour.

Whatever the Kingpin had on Norman Osborn was lost forever. Spider-Man wasn't sure how he felt about that. No one should be able to blackmail the mayor of New York, of course. On the other hand, it would be better if the mayor wasn't doing things that left him susceptible to blackmail. The world, however, was a complicated place, and he'd have to hope that Norman Osborn would seek power through being an effective leader, rather than abusing his authority.

Wilson Fisk was never going to be commissioner of finance, though, and that was a huge win. It wasn't a win like seeing Fisk tried for murder, but it gave

Spider-Man time to dig in further. It gave him room to breathe. And Bingham, the false Spider-Man, was in custody. On the news they said he was being sent for psychiatric evaluation. It was likely he'd end up in Ravencroft, rather than a prison. That was fine as far as Spider-Man was concerned. Clearly the guy was nuts. As long as he was kept off the streets forever, it didn't much matter what flavor the confinement came in.

"Don't expect Bingham to talk," Echo said when they met again in the janitor's closet. "Guys like that never do, so there's not much chance he'll turn on Fisk. Besides, it's pretty clear that he is insane, which means anything he says will need to come with hard evidence. That won't be the way to destroy Fisk."

"The goal isn't to destroy him," Spider-Man said. "It's to see he goes to jail."

"That's one opinion," she responded.

"Look," he began, "I know you were raised not to believe in subtlety, but we have to let the police handle this. Even better, we have to *help* the police to handle it."

"Do you have any idea how many people Fisk controls inside the police department?"

"So, you want to take justice into your own hands?" he asked. "That never works out well."

"I don't know what I want to do," she admitted. "I need time. Before he found out I'd turned on him, I raided some files and found out that I still have cousins in Montana. The first thing I will do is head out there, talk to them, see if maybe they can help me learn more about who my father really was. Maybe I'll stay out there."

"Echo, I could always use your help here," Spider-Man told her. "We could do things the right way and make a huge difference."

"Maybe," she said, "but you've got pretty good instincts. I have a feeling that you'll figure out what needs to be done—and when that happens, you'll see things through."

Spider-Man nodded. "Family's important, so I understand, but if you ever decide you want to come back, I'll be happy to have your help."

"Might be fun." She smiled. "In the meantime, I have something for you." She held out a thick file bound together with straining rubber bands. "Think of this as a going-away present."

○————————○

HE turned when he heard the stairwell door opening. Yuri Watanabe came out onto the roof, and much to Peter's surprise, she looked happy.

"I've only got a few minutes," she said. "People will start to wonder where I am."

"Look, Lieutenant, I'm sorry," he began. "I know you told me to stay away, but the situation was critical. I had to act."

"Yes, you did," she said. "And I'm not angry. You don't work for me, and you do what you have to do. I would be angry with you if it hadn't worked out, but you stopped a bad guy. And when it comes to Fisk, you've bought us some time. That's what's important."

"So, I haven't blown the investigation?"

She laughed. "People aren't worried that Spider-Man is a criminal—cops on the force were wasting too much time looking for you. That takes a lot of pressure off anyone who might be seen talking to you, too. It doesn't mean we can have lunch together, but it *does* mean maybe we can get back to work."

"That's good," he said, "because I have a present for you." He handed her the file that Maya had given him. "It's from an insider. Lots of details about Fisk's operation. It may make a difference."

Watanabe took out her phone and used its light to scan through the documents.

"I'll need time to digest this, but it looks huge." She gave a low whistle. "Really huge. There are lots of avenues to pursue. It could take months to run it all down, but if even some of what's in here checks out, it could make the difference."

She turned and walked back into the building, still reading. He sat down on the edge of the roof, letting his legs dangle. It had been a long time—a very long time—since there had been any sort of win. Fisk would likely remain a free man, but he was tainted now. Done were the days he could sell himself as the savior of New York. Anika's killer was in police custody. There was justice for all of the victims of the restaurant bombing. For Abe Remzi.

He'd spent so much time wondering if he could

really make a difference. Now he was starting to think that maybe the world was better off with Spider-Man after all.

At least for now.

EPILOGUE

IT was the police scanner that woke him up.

"All units: level four mobilization. Location: Fisk Tower."

Peter sat straight up in bed.

It had been months since the fight at the hotel, and he'd been dreaming about MJ, but he hadn't spoken to her for a long time. He'd wanted to give her space—that was definitely part of it—but he'd also worried that he could never be the boyfriend she needed. He couldn't stop worrying, and he cared enough to give her the freedom she wanted, rather than hinder her career.

As he'd predicted, Fisk had walked away from the incident with no charges, but that wasn't to say he was untarnished. Footage of him punching Maya Lopez—a woman who had been his legal ward—was all over the national news. A man who was acquitted of criminal charges could remake himself as a scoundrel, but a man who punched his foster daughter on national television was bound to get a *lot* of negative publicity.

It cost him a lot of business.

Thanks to Yuri Watanabe—who'd received a promotion to captain shortly after the incident—links leaked to the press, connecting Fisk to the murder of Maya's father. Various reporters, like Ben Urich, had written scathing pieces that made it seem as if evidence had been buried by crooked cops at the time. The district attorney was talking about reopening the case. Even J. Jonah Jameson had become interested. He'd switched his show over to a podcast, cutting his ties with Fisk, and he seemed to have more listeners than ever.

Fisk remained a free man, but he'd been wounded. They hadn't stopped him that night, not the way they wanted to, but they'd done damage, and that felt pretty good.

Now Peter struggled to get his Spider-Man suit on.

"SWAT is 10-84 at Fisk Tower," the police scanner squawked. *"All units stand by. Warrant is en route."*

A warrant! Could this really be it? All the work they'd done, and the files provided by Maya Lopez were making a difference. Watanabe kept telling him that. Was it possible that something major had shifted, and they were actually going to take down Fisk?

His heart raced as he sped out the window.

More importantly, how could Watanabe not tell him? Now that she was a captain, had she forgotten the little people? While swinging toward Hell's Kitchen, the Web-Slinger used his new in-suit phone to call her.

"I thought you were going to tell me before taking down the big guy," he said as soon as she picked up.

She didn't have to ask who was calling.

"We think he got wind of it a couple of hours ago,"

she explained, "so we're moving fast. Still waiting on the warrant. Just need to secure one last piece of evidence."

"What can I do to help?"

"Nothing," she said. "This needs to go by the book. You know his lawyers."

That didn't slow him down. No way was she going to box him out. Not now. She knew it, too. He figured she was just putting up a fight out of procedural instinct.

"Come on, Yuri," Spider-Man said. "I've been working the last eight years on this. Taking down Fisk is kind of a big deal to me."

"Hold on a sec," she said. It sounded as if she was dealing with a crowd of people over there. Launching an assault against a major figure like Fisk had to be a logistical nightmare, especially when he was unlikely to go quietly.

"Okay," she said when she got back on the phone. "Now's your chance. Get to Times Square. Fisk's men are trying to keep my guys from getting to the scene."

"You got it," he answered quickly, before she could change her mind. "Thanks, Yuri."

Yes! He was going to be a part of it.

Somewhere in the back of his mind he couldn't help but think he was already supposed to be at the lab. It turned out that Peyton hadn't had permission to get rid of Peter, so the boss had hired him back and fired Peyton instead. For a while Peter had actually been pretty good about showing up on time and being where he was supposed to be.

He hated to fall into the old habits, but this was Fisk, and some things couldn't wait. The boss was going to be furious with him, but he could live with that. To get Fisk, he could live with almost anything.

There was an incoming call from the lab. He hated having these conversations. He hated letting anyone down. Being Spider-Man could be a burden. There were a lot of days when he wanted to set that burden aside.

This wasn't one of them. He was going to see Fisk behind bars, and after that—well, he'd deal with it when it happened.

He let the phone take his boss's call. Spider-Man flicked his wrist and shot out a web, loving the feeling of hurling himself, not away from anything, but *toward* something—toward something important.

He felt alive and electric, full of the joy of movement and action. He wanted to act, *needed* to act, to be part of making the city a better and more just place.

Soon, he thought, when Fisk was finally behind bars, his life would finally calm down. It couldn't get any crazier, right?

ABOUT THE AUTHOR

DAVID LISS is the author of eleven novels, including *A Conspiracy of Paper* and *The Whiskey Rebels*, both currently being developed for television. He is also the author of the Randoms space opera trilogy, as well as numerous comics, including *Black Panther: The Man Without Fear*, *Mystery Men*, and *Angelica Tomorrow*.

ACKNOWLEDGEMENTS

MANY thanks to all who helped make *Marvel's Spider-Man: Hostile Takeover* possible. I could not have put this book together without the hard work of my partners at Marvel: Becka McIntosh, Eric Monacelli, Caitlin O'Connell, Jeff Reingold, Jeff Youngquist, and especially Bill Rosemann. Thanks to Christos Gage, and Bryan Intihar and Jon Paquette at Insomniac. I am also deeply grateful for the guidance and advice provided by my crack editor, Steve Saffel. My agent, Howard Morhaim, helped keep me in line. And I am grateful, as always, to my family.